"How *boss*! Good girl Bebe Bennett dons her best Jackie Kennedy suit as she tracks down a murderer—just a little detour as the naive Virginia darling moves to Manhattan. Think 60s! Think bangs and a flip! Think *That Girl!* meets Miss Marple and you'll have a ball."
                    —Jerrilyn Farmer, author of *Mumbo Gumbo*

"Add a dab of Dippity-do, a pinch of *That Girl!* and a dash of Miss Marple, and you've got the makings for a groovy new series that cozy mystery lovers will fall head over heels for. *It's a Mod, Mod, Mod, Mod Murder* and ingénue sleuth Bebe Bennett are a blast from the past!"
                    —Susan McBride, author of *Blue Blood*

"Groovy, baby! Rad, cool, far-out, and, oh yes—deadly."
                    —Kasey Michaels, author of *Maggie Without a Clue*

A swinging suspect

My heart was pounding in my chest. Darlene should not be leaving New York City. "But the police told Darlene and me not to leave town," I said to Stu.

Darlene waved a hand. "The Hamptons are still New York. They don't count. Stu, you're a dreamboat." She hurried from the room.

Stu grinned at me and began packing up pizza remains ⌐ his tablecloth, humming Elvis's "You're the Devil ⌐ Disguise."

I walked ⌐ up one of the candy ciga⌐ considered the matter of ⌐ were way too ready to p⌐ r solution was to frolic i⌐ decided right then, there⌐ s going to be able to get ⌐ ⌐ ⌐ of this murder investigation.

Me.

I inhaled too hard and choked when the candy hit the back of my throat. . . .

It's a Mod, Mod, Mod, Mod Murder

A MURDER A-GO-GO MYSTERY

Rosemary Martin

A SIGNET BOOK

SIGNET
Published by New American Library, a division of
Penguin Group (USA) Inc., 375 Hudson Street,
New York, New York 10014, USA
Penguin Group (Canada), 10 Alcorn Avenue, Toronto,
Ontario M4V 3B2, Canada (a division of Pearson Penguin Canada Inc.)
Penguin Books Ltd., 80 Strand, London WC2R 0RL, England
Penguin Ireland, 25 St. Stephen's Green, Dublin 2,
Ireland (a division of Penguin Books Ltd.)
Penguin Group (Australia), 250 Camberwell Road, Camberwell, Victoria 3124,
Australia (a division of Pearson Australia Group Pty. Ltd.)
Penguin Books India Pvt. Ltd., 11 Community Centre, Panchsheel Park,
New Delhi - 110 017, India
Penguin Group (NZ), cnr Airborne and Rosedale Roads, Albany,
Auckland 1310, New Zealand (a division of Pearson New Zealand Ltd.)
Penguin Books (South Africa) (Pty.) Ltd., 24 Sturdee Avenue,
Rosebank, Johannesburg 2196, South Africa

Penguin Books Ltd., Registered Offices:
80 Strand, London WC2R 0RL, England

First published by Signet, an imprint of New American Library,
a division of Penguin Group (USA) Inc.

First Printing, April 2005
10 9 8 7 6 5 4 3 2 1

This book is dedicated to Alana Zoe Stevens,
born February 11, 2004.
May you find peace and happiness in this world, princess!

Acknowledgments

This book would not have been possible without the creative vision of my editor, Ellen Edwards. Ellen, I am forever grateful for the day at Malice Domestic when we talked and the idea for this series was conceived. You then went a step further, helping me form the fun world of Bebe and Darlene. Thank you! I'm so glad to finally be working with you.

To my agent, Harvey Klinger (also known as Harvey the Wonder Agent), all I can say is, you're the greatest!

To my friend, Donna Andrews, award-winning author of the Meg Langslow mystery series and the Turing Hopper mystery series, I owe a great debt. Brainstorming with you made the process of creating this story hilarious. I've learned so much from you. Thank you.

I also want to thank Barbara Metzger, Melissa Lynn Jones, and Cynthia Holt-Johnson for reading over the final manuscript. I promise I'll try harder with the commas.

To Chakkri, the best cat ever, for sitting on my lap while I wrote this book. I miss you since you passed away from cancer on March 16, 2004, and I think I always will.

Finally, I appreciate the love and kindness of my family: Tommy (even though he said "Get out of My Way" sounded like a bad Kelly Osbourne song!), I love you so much. And Rachel, who brought me such joy this year, I love you and Alana. I am a very blessed woman.

Chapter One

New York City
April, 1964

I never dreamed when I met Darlene, a stewardess on my flight to New York City, that her showing me around town would include our finding a dead body. Although it was hardly Darlene's fault, no matter what the police suspect. It just doesn't make sense. Why would Darlene want to kill pop star Philip Royal? After all, on a flight over from London, she and Philip had joined the Mile-high Club.

"You mean you got together with a group of people who'd all been to Denver, the Mile-high City?" I had asked.

Darlene looked at me funny, then whispered in my ear. My eyes grew wide. Frankly, I was shocked. Then skeptical. To tell the truth, I still don't believe Darlene would do *that*. I think she's exaggerating. In the month I've been her roommate, she's often tried to amaze me with the details of a stewardess's fast life. But I'm not buying it. I'm sure Darlene's a nice girl, like me. Besides, some of her stories just don't ring true. Really, how could two people fit into an airplane lavatory?

We stood in the groovy plush gold-and-brown lobby of the Legends Hotel on Sixty-eighth Street near the park. I was thrilled to be there. To tell the truth, I'd been in a perpetual state of excitement and optimism since I'd arrived last month in the city of my dreams.

Looking around eagerly, I remembered that the hotel boasted a clientele that included political bigwigs, pop stars, and even movie stars. I'd read once in a movie magazine that Burton and Taylor had trysted at the Legends!

The snobby desk clerk kept glancing our way and turning up his nose, as if he knew we couldn't afford the hotel's prices. I turned my back on him. Nothing was going to spoil my fun.

"Bebe, you look so *boss* in that Jackie Kennedy suit."

"Do I, Darlene? I mean, this is my first date since moving to New York. I'm worried that I look like a fuddy-duddy in this lavender outfit, especially when I'm supposed to be going out with the *lead guitarist* of Philip Royal and the Beefeaters!" I almost squealed, I was so excited.

"You're putting me on, Bebe. You look like you could be Marlo Thomas's cousin. Keith will take one look at those big brown eyes and fall at your feet. Believe me, I *know* men."

"That's what you're always telling me," I said.

Darlene pulled out a compact. She patted her short, teased red curls and examined her face. Darlene had freckles, but she carefully covered them up with foundation and Erace. She said men liked a flawless complexion on a woman. Frankly, I didn't see why any man would object to Darlene's freckles when she had the most fabulous figure, all curves, not like me with my flat chest and narrow hips.

The first night I moved into her apartment on East Sixty-fifth Street, we talked late into the night about the beauty tips Darlene learned in stew school. I picked up a lot from her, especially how to keep false eyelashes from crawling down into your eye. And how women who favored the beehive could wrap their hair in toilet paper at night to protect their coif. Darlene claimed to be an expert with Dippity-Do. She showed me how to use the gel to keep the ends of my hair flipped up.

We chattered away until we both fell asleep, exhausted, around three in the morning. I was so happy to have met someone with such a cheerful, friendly personality who needed a roommate.

Luckily Darlene had a late flight out the next day. She kept an odd schedule with the airline. And my job as secretary at Rip-City Records didn't make it cool for me to stay up until the wee hours.

"Bebe, put on a little more lip gloss. Philip and Keith will be down here any minute. In fact," she said, tapping one red pump impatiently on the floor, "they are late."

I pulled out my own compact and a black daisy pot of pearlescent pale pink Mary Quant lip gloss. Darlene had brought one for each of us on her last flight to London— the trip where she met Philip. I touched up my lips and checked that my thick black eyeliner wasn't crooked. My false eyelashes were glued in place, just the way Darlene taught me. My bangs were straight; my dark hair was teased back and fell to my shoulders, where the ends flipped up. I was ready for Keith. My heart took a tumble at the thought of going out with an English guy. Of course, he wouldn't be John, my favorite Beatle, but he'd be the same clean-cut type with a cute accent.

"Listen, Bebe," Darlene said, looking at her watch, "I'm going down the hall to the house phone and calling Philip's room to see what's taking so long."

"How do you know what room he's in?"

"You don't have to know the room number. You just ask for the person's room. Anyway, I told you. We're a couple. I saw him to the hotel this morning when we flew in." She winked at me. "I stayed long enough to see him settled in."

"Whatever you say, Darlene."

Darlene giggled and patted my hand. "Stay here, and I'll be right back."

"Do you think I have time to go to the coffee shop

and get a Tang? I'm thirsty." Looking around, I encountered the nasty glare of the desk clerk. I noticed he had a large brown mole on his right earlobe. I held back a snicker. The mole looked like an earring. The thought of a man wearing an earring made me want to laugh out loud.

Darlene said, "Better not go for a drink. With any luck we'll be on our way to the Peppermint Lounge within five minutes. We'll have a great time there doing the twist and having cocktails with the guys."

I chewed my bottom lip. I wasn't much of a drinker. Okay, back home in Richmond, Virginia, I'd had wine occasionally, but cocktails were a different story. I'd had a couple of highballs at the Christmas party for Philip Morris, where I worked in a boring job at the time. They made me feel all fuzzy.

I straightened my shoulders. This was in New York! Everything would be different here. People in New York didn't behave like they did in Richmond. Not that I didn't like my hometown, but the idea of being a single woman in the big city was ten times more exciting.

I walked with Darlene as far as the elevators, then watched her go down the long hall, past the coffee shop, and around a corner. A man coughing next to me caught my attention. He was an older gentleman dressed in the uniform of an elevator operator. I dug in my lavender purse once again.

"Here, sir, would you like a Smith Brothers cough drop? I keep them in my purse because my work requires me to answer the phone. If my voice gets scratchy, I use one of these."

The man looked at me suspiciously. "You're not from around here, are you?"

I smiled. "I'm always surprised by the number of people who say that to me. My boss, Br—I mean, Mr. Williams, says it's because I have a slight Southern accent. If you don't want the cough drop, I have a roll of those new Fancy Fruit Life Savers in here somewhere."

"No, the cough drop will do me fine. Thank you, miss." He accepted the lozenge and popped it into his mouth. "You want me to take you upstairs?"

"No, I'm waiting for a friend."

"I see."

"We're meeting dates for the evening, and they're late, so my friend went to call and find out where they are."

"Stood up, huh?"

"Oh, no! I'm sure it's nothing like that. The guys are probably adjusting to the time change. They're from England." I chatted with the elevator operator, who turned out to be a Mr. Duncan, about his family (wife, three children, and seven grandchildren) until finally Darlene came back around the corner. She looked flustered but gorgeous in her red A-line dress.

"There was a lady ahead of me at the house phone. She wouldn't stop talking. I had to wait forever. Then Philip didn't answer his phone. Let's go up there."

"Darlene!" I put a restraining gloved hand on her arm. "We can't just go up to a man's hotel room. It wouldn't be proper."

"Bebe, you're being prudish, living up to your real name," Darlene said, just like an older sister. She was twenty-five to my twenty-two.

You see, my mother, a true Jane Austen fan, had taken advantage of marrying a man with the last name of Bennett and had named me Elizabeth after the main character in *Pride and Prejudice*. Being a thoroughly modern woman, I had gone by Bebe since I turned twelve.

"There is nothing wrong with what we're doing," Darlene went on, "Besides, I'm from Texas. Where I come from we don't put up with men not doing what they say they're gonna do. We take action!"

"I don't know. . . ."

Darlene sneezed. Oh, no. Darlene always sneezed when she got nervous or upset. In another minute her mascara would run. Maybe one of her false eyelashes would droop despite the glue. I gave in. "You're right. I'm sure this is the way they do things in New York." I hesitated. "As long as we stand outside the door and don't go into the room, I'm game for anything."

"Sure, Bebe, sure," Darlene said.

With Mr. Duncan frowning, we stepped into the elevator car. Darlene said, "Fifteenth floor."

We stopped on the fifth floor.

Puzzled, Darlene and I turned as one to the elderly man. He said, "Aren't you getting out?"

Realizing he had a hearing problem in addition to his cold, I raised my voice loud enough for him to hear, but not enough for him to think I was shouting at him, and said, "I'm afraid there was a misunderstanding, Mr. Duncan. We wanted the *fifteenth* floor."

He closed the doors and punched the number fifteen. I exchanged a look with Darlene, one that pleaded for her not to say anything. She was quiet, and a few seconds later we reached our destination.

"Take care of that cough now," I said as we exited the elevator.

"Come on, Bebe!"

I followed Darlene down the hall, where the faint sounds of Betty Everett telling us "It's in His Kiss" seeped out from one of the rooms, until we came to stand in front of room 1514.

"Darlene, the door is open a crack," I whispered.

Darlene's hand hung suspended alongside the door where she was about to knock. Slowly she lowered it to the knob. "Well, so it is."

Before I could protest, she swung the door wide open and marched inside. "Philip Royal, you'd better tell me right this minute why you've been keeping us waiting!"

I had just crossed the threshold behind her when Darlene screamed.

Chapter Two

Darlene raced back and plowed into me.

"My goodness, Darlene! What is it?" I said when I was steady on my feet again.

"Philip." Darlene sneezed violently.

"He's not with another woman, is he?" I asked. Then I blushed at having such a thought. But didn't all pop stars lead wild lives?

Darlene sneezed again. She took me by the arm and led me to the open bathroom door. In the full bathtub lay a man with an electric guitar across his chest and a towel over his face.

I turned away quickly. "He's naked!"

"He's dead!"

I raised my hands in the air as if to ward off a blow. "What?" We both turned away to escape the sight, and bumped into each other in the bathroom doorway.

"He must have been electrocuted." Sneeze. Sneeze.

"Are you sure it's Philip? He has a towel over his face."

"Grits and damnation, it's got to be him."

"You mean you can't tell by his . . . his . . ."

Darlene frowned. Then sneezed. "I'm not sure. The lavatory was dark when we . . . you know . . . on the airplane, and I didn't really look at *it*."

I thought about this for a second, feeling it was more proof that Darlene had made up the whole story of her and Philip doing *that*. "We'd better take the towel off his face and be sure, Darlene."

"I guess so."

"You do it. He was your boyfriend."

"What a crummy thing to have to do. I've only known him a day." Darlene hesitated. Then, "All right, Bebe."

Darlene inched across the bathroom tile and reached in gingerly with thumb and forefinger extended to the very tip of the washcloth covering the dead man's face. With the flash of a magician, she whipped it off and let out a shriek. "It's him." She began to cry. "What a horrible accident."

Standing in the bathroom, I held her while she sobbed, trembling myself. I had never seen a dead body before, except for my great aunt. And she'd been dressed in her casket, not naked in a tub full of water with a guitar in her hands.

Since I was averting my eyes from the naked dead man in the tub, I finally noticed the bathroom wall. We'd been so shaken up with the horror of finding Philip, we hadn't taken in our surroundings.

On the wall, written in something black, were the words:

> *Starvin' for the good life, baby, with-out any*
> *   ooofff you*
> *Starvin' for the real thing, on my own, be-in' true*
> *Here it is on my plate, if only I could reach it*
> *Oh, it's so sweet, I can almost taste it——man*
> *Get out of my waaaayyyy*
> *Get out of my waaaayyyy*

I said, "Look, Darlene, someone's written lyrics to a song on the wall."

"Why would Philip write lyrics to a song on the wall in"—Darlene picked up a black eyeliner pencil from the white-tiled floor—"black eyeliner, then get in the tub and play his guitar?" Darlene gasped. "You don't think he deliberately killed himself, do you?"

"No, Darlene, I don't think Philip did this to himself. Surely there are easier ways to kill yourself. It's worse than that."

Darlene's blue eyes rounded. "What are you saying, Bebe?"

"If Philip plugged his guitar into the electrical outlet and then stepped into the tub of water, he would have been electrocuted immediately and fallen in the tub. Instead he's lying down with a towel over his face."

"Bebe! Clue me in here."

"Someone did this."

Darlene's eyes almost popped out of her head. "Are you saying Philip was murdered?"

"It looks that way. Maybe he was in the bath, playing his guitar without plugging the amplifier in. Someone came in meaning to kill him, saw the opportunity with the guitar, and took it. Then whoever did it wrote those song lyrics on the wall. Why, I don't know." I paused for a thoughtful moment. "I didn't know pop stars wore eyeliner. Do you think John Lennon does?"

"Bebe, you're way off base, and you've got quite an imagination. Who would want to kill Philip? He just came to the United States for the first time. We got in this morning. Hardly anyone here even knows him. It must have been an accident."

"We'd better call the police, Darlene." I moved away from her out of the bathroom, into the bedroom, past empty pizza boxes and beer bottles, and picked up the phone next to the rumpled bed.

Somehow I managed to speak calmly into the receiver and give my name and location. The dispatcher on the other end of the line instructed me to stay where I was, and not to let anyone into the room under any circumstances until the police arrived. I agreed and hung up.

Almost immediately there was a knock on the door.

"Come on, Philip, we're late meeting up with those

American birds," a voice with a thick English accent called from the other side of the door.

Keith.

And we hadn't closed the door all the way.

Darlene rushed from where she'd plunked down in a chair and slammed the door in the lead guitarist's face. "Ouch!" she cried, grabbing her right foot.

"Blimey, Darlene, was that you?" came a muffled voice through the door. "Why'd you slam the door in my face?"

Darlene looked wildly at me, her body guarding the door, hands splayed against it, injured foot forgotten for the moment.

"Tell him there's been an accident and you can't let him in until the police get here. It's the truth," I stage-whispered.

Darlene shook her red curls in the negative. Instead, she looked through the peephole and said, "Philip and I can't be disturbed right now, Keith. Come back in an hour."

"Got the other bird in there with you?" was the response.

I felt the heat rise to my cheeks, my mouth open in shock.

"Yes," Darlene said unforgivably.

I stood to my five feet, seven inches (I do have decent long legs, God's way of making up for my lack of chest) and placed both hands on my hips, glaring at petite Darlene.

She put a finger to her lips in a shushing motion.

The sounds of fading laughter came from the hall. "Philip and the birds. Always has a flock."

Darlene checked the peephole again and turned back to where I was sitting. "He split."

"How *could* you tell him that about me?"

"Bebe, we've got a dead body in the bathroom. Keith's thinking we're doing a threesome is the least of our problems."

"But my reputation!"

"Bebe, you've got nothing to worry about."

"I'd better not. Mama always says a girl's reputation is priceless. What's wrong with your foot?"

Darlene balanced on one high heel and looked at the bottom of her right foot. "I stepped on something sharp. It looks like a tack or something."

A brisk knock on the door halted the conversation.

Darlene pocketed the tack.

"Police! Open up!"

The room suddenly filled with men wearing blue NYPD uniforms and a plainclothes detective who took Darlene aside and questioned her while a police officer stood guard over me. Another officer was busy talking to the hotel detective, who showed up demanding to know what was going on. More officers were doing God only knows what in the bathroom where Philip lay. An ambulance crew arrived, and a man I think was the coroner. Flashbulbs went off, over and over. All of a sudden I realized I was shaking.

"Miss Bennett?"

I looked up from where I was sitting at a small round table near the window. The plainclothes man loomed over me, notebook in hand. He wore a gray suit, white shirt, and navy tie. His hair was dark and styled in a crew cut. I figured him for about thirty. As he sat down in a chair opposite, a feeling that I had done something terribly wrong came over me. His brown eyes were condemning. I had been the one to electrocute Philip Royal, those eyes said. I had wanted to see Philip dead. Never mind that I'd never met him. I swallowed with an effort.

"Yes, I'm Miss Bennett."

"I'm Detective Finelli, in charge of this case."

"Pleased to meet you."

His face didn't change. If anything it grew more stern. "You live with Miss Darlene Roland at 138–140 East Sixty-fifth Street, apartment three-B?"

"Yes. It's a walk-up, but very comfortable. Well, we

don't have much furniture now because Darlene's ex-roommate took it all, but I plan to surprise Darlene with some new things because she's not charging me much rent."

Detective Finelli remained blank-faced at all this information. "And where do you work?"

I sat up taller. "I'm secretary to Bradley Williams. He's vice president of talent at Rip-City Records, and very good at his job. He's the one who discovered Philip Royal and the Beefeaters in London and brought them over here to launch their first album in a few weeks. Mr. Williams is a well-known man-about-town."

Detective Finelli began to look strained. "I'll take your word for it. Now, Miss Bennett, why don't you tell me how it came to be that you are at the Legends Hotel today."

I began twisting my fingers together under the table, where I hoped the detective wouldn't see, but somehow I felt he could. "I'm here because my friend Darlene set me up on a double date."

"With who?"

"With Keith."

"Keith who?"

"Gee, I don't know his last name. He's the lead guitarist for Philip Royal and the Beefeaters." Then it struck me that there was no longer any such band. "I mean he was until—"

"Until what, Miss Bennett?"

"You know," I said, nodding toward the bathroom.

Detective Finelli took notes. "So you came here expecting a date. How did you end up in Philip Royal's room?"

"What do you mean?"

"Was that the plan all along? Were you two girls just coming up to the guys' rooms?"

"No! We were supposed to meet them in the lobby and then all go to the Peppermint Lounge, but the guys hadn't shown up yet and Darlene went to call, and Philip didn't answer, so the nice elevator man, who had a cough and is hard of hearing, brought us up here, and the door was open, and that's when we found Philip!"

I took a deep breath.

Detective Finelli blinked and jotted down a few words. I didn't think I liked him even though he wore a wedding ring and was probably a nice family man with several young children.

"Were you with Miss Roland when she went to call Philip Royal?"

"No, the house phone was down the hall. I stayed behind and helped the elevator operator, Mr. Duncan, with his cough."

"With his cough?"

"Yes. It's only right to be helpful. You know that, being a policeman."

"I'm a detective. Now, how long was Miss Roland gone?"

"I don't know. A few minutes."

"Ten minutes? Twenty?"

I tilted my head and stared at the ceiling. Finally I looked back at him. "Maybe fifteen minutes."

"Then the two of you came up here and discovered the body?"

"Yes. Darlene thought it was an accident, but I didn't think so."

"Why did Miss Roland think it was an accident?"

"I don't know. Didn't you ask her?"

Detective Finelli removed his handkerchief from his breast pocket and wiped his brow. "You thought it was a murder?"

"Yes, and before you ask me how I knew, I'll tell you. Because if he'd tried to do away with himself, he wouldn't have been lying down with a towel over his head after he'd plugged in his guitar."

"Very astute of you, Miss Bennett."

"Thank you. Is that all?"

"For now. We're taking fingerprints and doing our job

here. There will be an autopsy to determine the time of death. I must tell you that you cannot leave town until this matter has been investigated and resolved."

"Then it really was a murder!"

"Don't leave town, Miss Bennett."

He got up, but one of his underlings brought over Mr. Duncan. I gave a tiny wave at the elevator operator, and he twisted his lips in a weak smile. He obviously didn't want to be involved in any of this.

"This is Mr. Duncan, sir. He brought the girls up."

Detective Finelli introduced himself while I sat there shaking. I felt out of breath, like I had back in gym class when the teacher made us run around the football field.

Darlene was being questioned between sneezes by yet another police officer. I could just hear the conversation between Detective Finelli and Mr. Duncan.

"So Miss Roland was gone from the lobby of the hotel for at least fifteen minutes, maybe longer?"

"Yes, sir, that's right. I hope I won't get into any trouble. All I did was give those two girls a ride up to this floor. I don't know anything about any murder. I've been with the hotel goin' on eighteen years now—"

Detective Finelli interrupted him. "You'll need to come down to the station and sign a statement saying what you just told me, that's all. You may have to testify in court. But I don't see where your job would be in jeopardy."

Mr. Duncan was allowed to leave the room. He did so with a glum look on his face. Detective Finelli walked over to Darlene and the police officer, and words were exchanged. Darlene started to cry. I fought the urge to go to her.

Finally she was free from questioning, and she ran straight into my arms. We stood there shivering.

"Let's get out of here," I said.

Tears streamed down Darlene's face. "Bebe, they say I can't leave town. They think I did it because I admitted Philip and I were, er, close on the plane."

"*You* did it? That's ridiculous! Don't worry. They told me not to leave town, either."

"But don't you see, I can't account for that fifteen minutes."

"What fifteen minutes?"

"The ones Detective Finelli told me both you and the elevator operator said I was gone. No one saw me at the house phone except the lady who was ahead of me, and we'll never track her down."

"Oh, no, Darlene, I feel responsible." Guilt curled in my stomach.

"It's not just you; it's Mr. Duncan, too."

"I'm so sorry. Truly."

"Not only am I under suspicion for murder, Bebe, but if I can't leave town, I can't fly! Don't you see what this means? How can I be a stewardess if I'm grounded?"

Chapter Three

We got off the bus at Lexington and East Sixty-fourth Street. Yellow Cabs raced past us while we waited to cross the street to Joe's Market. There we stocked up on cakes and candies, forsaking our ongoing diets. Darlene bought a bottle of wine. This was a crisis, after all. Once we finished loading up on goodies, we were walking home when, as we were passing Donohues Steakhouse, with its pink-and-black awning, a wino appeared out of the shadows.

"Can you shpare some shange?" he slurred.

I hesitated. The poor man smelled as if he hadn't showered in at least a month. A thick growth of gray beard covered the lower half of his face. His eyes were red-rimmed and watery. Rags that passed as clothes hung on his thin body.

"Bebe, come on," Darlene whispered, shifting the bag of groceries from one arm to the other. "He's been out here before, and he'll never sober up."

"But Darlene, he looks hungry."

"Don't give him anything. He'll only spend the money on booze."

But I couldn't help myself. I pulled two quarters from my Lady Buxton wallet and handed them to him. "Please get something to eat."

"Harry thanks you, ma'am. Sheen you 'round. Have a sweet face."

"Bebe, come on!"

Without any further exchange, we turned right onto East Sixty-fifth Street. St. Vincent Ferrer Catholic High School stood on the left side of the street. The side and back of the school faced our apartment building. All was quiet for the evening. It was about nine o'clock. We reached our building—brick with dark green trim— Darlene lecturing me the whole way on how foolish it was to give Harry any money. We climbed the two sets of stairs to 3B, sagging with relief as we made our way inside.

"Pajamas, cake, candy, and some wine," Darlene said.

"Sounds perfect. What kind of wine did you get?"

"Mateus. It's choice."

While Darlene went to open the wine, I admired our bachelorette pad. The apartment opened to an average-sized living room, one wall of which was all white brick with a fireplace. If you went immediately right when you came in the door, you entered what passed for the kitchen, with its green linoleum floor. There was room for a tiny table for two in there, but otherwise barely enough space for Darlene and me to move around together. Then, to the left of the living room, there were two bedrooms, both small, with a bathroom in between that we shared. The shower barely trickled out enough water for a good washing, which was hard when you were trying to get a day's worth of Aqua Net out of your hair. Worse, sometimes the water turned freezing cold without warning. It was just an inconvenience, though. I loved it here, no matter what! The pulse of the city drove itself into me the first day I arrived on New York soil— or pavement, I should say.

I went to my room. When I moved to New York, I brought all my new clothes. Daddy had been extremely generous with me before I left Richmond. He sorta dotes on me, since I'm an only child. He himself took me to LaVogue, Clothes for Ladies and Their Daughters, a very fashionable shop in downtown Richmond.

Daddy said I could have whatever I wanted, that if I was going to "do this darn fool thing," I should look fabulous. He wouldn't have any New Yorker thinking I was a hick from the South. Mama didn't say anything. What Daddy says in the house rules. Plus, Mama is . . . well, delicate, and stays home mostly and looks after Daddy. Her only hobby is gardening.

Anyway, now I had so many pretty suits and dresses, they didn't all fit in my minuscule closet. I'd had to go out and buy a clothes rack.

I'd also brought my record player, my albums, and my 45s. And, of course, pictures of The Beatles. So the dingy, off-white walls were covered with shots of John, Paul, George, and Ringo.

The single bed—there really wasn't room for a double—was secondhand, with a black-painted head-board and footboard. Who knew what kind of wood it had been initially. I had bought a new mattress and box spring, and at a secondhand store I found an almost-new-looking bedspread with big black-and-white-and-yellow daisies on it.

Then one day I had found The Banana, a long, bright yellow vinyl chair that reminded me of a banana. I was walking the streets near my apartment, exploring the neighborhood, when I saw a couple moving the chair out of their building and taking it to the street for the trash.

Reminding myself I was a mature, modern woman, and a lot of "curbside shopping" was done in New York, I raised my voice and said, "Excuse me, but are you trying to get rid of that chair?"

"Yes," the middle-aged woman replied, glaring at the man next to her. I assumed he was her husband. "It doesn't go with the rest of our décor."

"May I have it?"

"Do you like the shape?" the man asked with a leer.

"Shut up, Rob," the woman snapped. She turned back to me. "If you can haul it away, you can have it."

I had hurried back to the apartment, tipped the super

heavily to help me move it, and now The Banana was mine. The chair was in great condition and remarkably comfortable, though it did take up the last bit of space in my room. Still, I loved to curl up in it and read or listen to music.

Sometimes I'd lie on it with my feet dangling off the side and take out my list of things I wanted to accomplish in New York. I had jotted notes during the last days before I left Richmond. Written in an old steno pad, one side was serious things and the other, fun things. I took it out from under the cushion of The Banana. It was private, and I didn't want Darlene or one of her stewardess friends reading it.

I opened it up now and glanced over it.

So far the serious side read:

1. Find a job I love. (This one was scratched off.)
2. Get married to the man of my dreams by age twenty-five. (That gave me three years to reel in a certain person I knew with gorgeous blue eyes.)
3. By twenty-six, move into a house that my husband and I love. With a big bedroom.
4. Have a healthy, beautiful baby—a boy for the first—by my twenty-eighth birthday. A girl within the two years following.
5. Live with my husband for the rest of our lives.

Now for the fun side:

1. Have breakfast at Tiffany's. (My favorite movie! When I saw it almost three years ago, my plan to move to New York began. Plus, I could shop for my engagement ring there.)
2. Eat an oyster at the Oyster Bar in Grand Central Terminal.
3. Float a sailboat in Central Park.

4. Visit the world's biggest bookstore, the Strand, on Broadway and Twelfth Street.
5. Go to the top of the Empire State Building!
6. Take the ferry to see the Statue of Liberty.
7. Go to the Macy's Thanksgiving Day Parade.
8. Attend Mass at Saint Patrick's Cathedral.
9. Stroll down Fifth Avenue and window-shop.
10. Kiss one certain guy next to the clock in the lobby of the Waldorf-Astoria. (This was a recent entry.)

Oh, I knew the list was only a fraction of all the wonderful places to go and things to see in New York. But it was a start, and it grew all the time. Most of all, I wanted to have fun and enjoy life. But first there was that murder. . . .

I took off my lavender suit and hung it carefully on my suit rack. After grabbing a pair of embroidered blue pajamas out of the only other piece of furniture in the room, an "antique" wooden dresser with mirror I'd found at a junk store, I changed clothes and joined Darlene in the nearly empty living room. One pole lamp with three black shades lit the room, and a small black-and-white TV squatted on the floor in the corner. On the wall opposite the white brick, Darlene had hung three framed op-art posters. The disks of black going into white played tricks with the viewer's eyes. I liked to stare at them.

Darlene was sitting on the wooden floor cross-legged in a pair of Japanese silk pajamas. In front of her was the bag of goodies, the bottle of Mateus, and two wineglasses. The black-and-white TV in the corner played *The Adventures of Ozzie and Harriet* without the sound.

"The fuzz are going to arrest me for murder," Darlene said unhappily, her fingers hovering over a Sugar Daddy, then a pack of Chuckles, before finally deciding on a packet of Jujubes. She popped two into her mouth and poured us each a glass of wine.

I sat down across from her. "No, Darlene, you mustn't think that way." I picked up a Hostess cupcake. "The police don't have any evidence that you did it, because you didn't do it."

"I still can't believe it all happened. I feel numb with shock." She put the rest of the Jujubes aside and moved on to a Twinkie.

"I know. I feel like I've been run over by Grandpa's tractor. And I feel so responsible." I took a big bite of the cupcake so I could reach the white cream.

"What do you mean?" Darlene asked, licking a crumb from the side of her mouth, then washing it down with wine.

I swallowed. "If it hadn't been for me, the police wouldn't know about your being away for those fifteen minutes. They wouldn't think that's when you went upstairs and killed Philip."

"That's not true, Bebe. Mr. Duncan, that elevator guy, would have told them. I don't hold you responsible. Try one of those candy cigarettes."

"You're sweet, Darlene, but I still feel like a rat, even though I was just being honest with the police." I drank some wine and pulled one of the cigarettes out of the pack. "What are you going to tell the airline?"

"That I'm sick. Bronchitis should do. That can linger on for weeks. Though I hope all this will be cleared up faster than that. How am I going to keep from going crazy, stuck on the ground for who knows how long? I've gotta have my wings, gotta fly."

Reaching out with the hand not holding the candy cigarette, I touched her arm. "Somehow it's going to be okay. The police don't arrest innocent people. You'll be all right. But I do wish we had someone to help us with this."

Darlene's eyes widened. A big smile lit her face. "Stu!"

"You're hungry for stew?" I said, puzzled.

"No, Stu. He's a stew-bum. His first name is really Bert, but everybody calls him Stu."

"Huh?"

"There's a type of guy who dates only stewardesses. He hangs around airports, looking for them, asking them out. Some people call them airport johnnies, but Stu isn't like that. He's a cut above. I've known him over a year now, and he's always been the perfect gentleman with me, taking me to supper clubs and plays. And he's super rich! He's the son and sole heir to the Minty-Mouth Breath Mints fortune. I'm going to call him right now."

"You think he's home?"

Darlene jumped to her feet. "He keeps all hours. If anything, he may be out with another stewardess—or in Paris or the Caribbean."

This last was said with a slight pout. But almost immediately Darlene was in the kitchen, dialing the wall phone. Soon her excited voice could be heard.

"Stu, honey, I need you. I'm in trouble. Can you come over?"

Pause.

"Yes. Okay. Pepperoni sounds great. 'Bye."

She hung up the phone and came back into the living room, a triumphant gleam in her eyes. "He's bringing pizza. I'm going to change. You might want to throw a bathrobe over your pajamas."

"Shouldn't I change too?"

"No," Darlene said over her shoulder. "I told you, he dates only stewardesses. Oh," she said, pausing and taking something out of the pocket of her pajamas. "This is what was stabbing me in the foot in Philip's room. I stepped on a tie tack, and it pierced the sole of my shoe. Luckily it didn't ruin my red heels."

She handed me the small metal object. Orange, blue, and white, it looked like some sort of sports team insignia. I guessed it would have to be returned with Philip's things to whatever family he had back in England. I put it on the kitchen counter, tucked near the wall so it wouldn't fall off and get lost, then went to get my bathrobe.

About thirty minutes later, there was a knock on the door.

Darlene appeared from her room in a lounge outfit of black slacks and a green tunic. She looked pretty in a playful way. I had thrown on my pink chenille robe—the one with big coffee cups on it—and had cleaned up the evidence of the candies and cakes.

"Stu, honey, I'm so glad to see you," Darlene said, flinging the door wide and reaching up to kiss a tall man.

"Bet you're glad to see the pizza too, doll. Here, who is this? No, wait. This must be Miss Bennett, your new roommate."

I smiled. "You're right, but please call me Bebe."

Balancing the pizza box with one hand, Stu held out his other hand. "Stu, here, and I'm always pleased to meet a beautiful woman. Have you ever thought about becoming a stewardess, Bebe?"

"Nice to meet you, Stu." I shook his hand. "And no, I'm very happy being a secretary for now." He was a nice-looking man of around forty with silver threads running through his dark hair. His brown eyes fit that often-heard description of laughing eyes. He had a strong jaw and a wide smile, and seemed like the type who was always ready for a good adventure. All in all, a charming person.

With a flourish, he spread on the floor a white table-cloth he had brought and placed the pizza box in the middle. Darlene and I laughed.

"Stu, you're such a card. I'll get plates and a wineglass for you," Darlene said.

Soon we were settled and eating pizza.

"So, doll, tell me what's got my favorite gal upset."

"The fuzz are going to arrest me for murder!" Darlene declared.

Stu laughed. Hard.

"You terrible man. I don't know why I called you," Darlene said with a sexy pout.

"I'm sorry, doll. It was the image of you in a striped jail outfit that got me."

Darlene acted like she was mad at him, so he had to tease her out of it. Then the whole story came spilling out. I had to interrupt her several times to insert what I thought were critical points. Like the lyrics written in black eyeliner on the wall.

"You've memorized them?" Darlene asked me.

"Yes, and I wrote them down in a little notebook I keep in my purse. I have trouble remembering numbers, you see. They get all mixed up in my head. So I carry this notebook to write them down. It comes in handy for other things too."

"What a smart girl," Stu said. "I may have to call you Scarlett. You are a Southern beauty."

Perhaps jealous of the attention being taken from her, Darlene said, "And this big ol' detective just wouldn't leave me alone, Stu. He kept at me until I thought I'd tell him I killed Philip, just to get him to stop badgering me."

"That's the way they operate, doll. Now, listen. It seems to me that whoever killed this Philip must have been someone who came over on that flight with him. No one in the U.S. knew him, right?"

"Except my boss at the record company," I said. "He's the one who discovered the band, and I remember him saying he was the first Yank the band had ever actually spoken to."

"Okay. But your boss wouldn't have any motive to kill the golden goose, so to speak."

"Oh, absolutely not," I said, shocked. "And Br—I mean Mr. Williams—would never, ever kill anyone. He's a very honest and respectable gentleman."

"Gentleman?" Darlene smiled at me.

I put my hands on my hips. "Yes!"

"Okay, we believe you, don't we, Stu?"

"Sure. Now, there would have been Philip's bandmates, his manager, and his girlfriend, if he had one," Stu said, ticking suspects off on his fingers.

Darlene shot me a warning glance when Stu said *girl-friend*. and said, "I think he had an ex-girlfriend, but she's been hanging out with the drummer of the band."

"Excellent possibility there. The police will have their hands full."

"Not if they think Darlene did it," I inserted.

Silence fell.

Then Stu said, "But Darlene had no motive."

Stu didn't know about the "close" relationship Darlene had with Philip.

Suddenly rising to his feet, Stu said, "Come on; I know exactly what you need, doll. Pack your things."

"What?" Darlene said, jumping up in excitement. "Where are we going?"

"My place in the Hamptons. Some sea air will do you good. Make you forget all this."

"But what if the airline calls, Darlene? You're supposed to be sick," I reminded her.

"You can cover for me, Bebe. It will only be a day or two." Turning to Stu, she said, "Sounds like a blast, honey."

"Pack your bikini," he said, and winked.

Darlene threw him a flirtatious look. "Stu, it's April. I'll freeze."

"I'll keep you warm, doll."

My heart was pounding in my chest. Darlene should not be leaving New York City. "But the police told Darlene and me not to leave town," I told Stu.

Darlene waved a hand. "The Hamptons are still New York. They don't count. Stu, you're a dreamboat." She hurried from the room.

Stu grinned at me and began packing up the pizza remains and his tablecloth, humming Elvis's "You're the Devil in Disguise."

I walked into the kitchen and picked up one of the candy cigarettes. Pretending to smoke it, I considered the matter of Philip Royal's death. The police were way too ready to pin the crime on Darlene, and her solution was to frolic in the Hamptons with Stu. Yes, I decided right then, there was only one person who get to the bottom of this murder investigation.

Me.

I inhaled too hard and choked when the candy hit the back of my throat.

Chapter Four

At Charlotte Marie's Secretarial School for Young Ladies in Richmond, Virginia, we had learned typing, shorthand, filing, and dictation; telephone etiquette, grooming,
and coffeemaking; how to remind your boss to eat lunch
if he got too involved in his work, the importance of
volunteering to stay at the office if he was working late,
and, last but not least, how to marry him.

We didn't learn how to solve a murder. But I wasn't
going to let that stop me.

I wanted to meet Keith, the band member I was supposed to go out with. Actually I wanted to meet all the
band members, but Keith was the one I had an excuse
to see. First, since it was a weekday, I had to go to my
job as Bradley Williams's secretary at Rip-City Records,
something I looked forward to every day.

Dressed in a navy suit, with matching heels and purse,
pearls, and white gloves, I arrived at the office to find
everyone talking about Philip Royal's death, the news
having made page two of the *New York Times*. And
Darlene's and my names were in the article!

The doorman: "Terrible thing for a nice girl like you
to see, Miss Bennett. Was he all blackened from the
electrocution?" The receptionist at the front desk: "Is it
true your roommate murdered that pop star? You can
stay with me for a while if you need to. Did they take
her to jail?"

Iris in the typing pool: "I saw Philip's picture." Sob. "He was so cute. I wanted to meet him and get his autograph." More sobbing.

Janet, secretary to Mr. Purvis, the company president: "I'm sure Mr. Purvis will keep in mind that Bradley Williams could not have known Philip Royal would be murdered and cost the company so much money."

This last comment was something I hadn't thought of yet. Would Bradley—that's what I always called him in my head, and I worried one day it would slip out in front of him—be in trouble because of Philip's murder? Would Mr. Purvis frown on him for jeopardizing the success of the Beefeaters' first U.S. record album?

I reached my desk, uncovered my typewriter, and quickly removed my gloves. I placed my gloves and my purse in my desk drawer and looked anxiously toward Bradley's closed door. Normally his door was open during the workday unless he was in a confidential meeting.

Did he already have his coffee? I supposed he would buzz me if he needed something. I put on a fresh pot. I couldn't wait to see him.

I had fallen hard for Bradley Williams the first time I met him. And I wanted him for keeps. He was the one on my "serious list" whom I wanted to marry. Of course I tried very hard to conceal this fact from him. So far I thought I'd done a good job. Men liked to think they were the ones chasing. Besides, he thought of me as an unsophisticated girl from a small town in the South. Not his usual type. Which actually gave me an advantage, I thought. Anyway, he was quite the ladies' man, and I couldn't bear to be just one more conquest. Oh, no. I heard he loved 'em and left 'em. That was what had happened with all his other secretaries. At least, that was what I finally figured out the employment agency meant the day they told me about the interview for the job.

"Mr. Williams, who reports only to Mr. Purvis, president of the company, has had six secretaries in the past year, Miss Bennett. We do not want you to go to the job interview ignorant of the facts," Mrs. Fitzwalter, a stern matron with black glasses, had said.

"Is he so very hard to please?" I'd asked.

Mrs. Fitzwalter had cleared her throat. Twice. "There's no sense in keeping things from you. Mr. Williams is an attractive man. The young ladies employed by him have not behaved professionally, shall we say, in their position as his secretary."

"You mean they didn't perform well?"

"They performed all *too* well, Miss Bennett, and were subsequently asked to leave by Mr. Purvis," Mrs. Fitzwalter said briskly.

Thoroughly confused, I sat there, saying nothing. Was this what Mama meant when she said men didn't like it when women appeared smarter than them? Were the girls fired because they acted too intelligently? Or was it . . . Something Else?

"Now here is the address, and your interview is for ten o'clock on Friday. Please be prompt. I know the Charlotte Marie girls are just as well trained as the Katherine Gibbs girls, so I needn't worry," Mrs. Fitzwalter said with a forced smile. "Just be the honorable person I know you are, and all will be fine."

"Yes, Mrs. Fitzwalter."

On that Friday, I had been nervous as I discarded one outfit after another. One was too frumpy for a record company, another too frivolous for a job interview. I finally decided on a pale blue suit with navy piping, navy shoes, purse, hat, and, of course, white gloves.

I had been ushered into the office by a woman perhaps in her early sixties. She was plump, with soft gray hair, and wore a shirtwaist dress with a full skirt, a style popular several years ago. "I'm Miss Hawthorne, dear, secretary to Vince Walsh. Mr. Walsh is one of Rip-City's talent scouts. He reports to Mr. Williams on various regional acts the company might be interested in signing. In fact," she said in a confidential tone, "he's working hard on a folk act out of Buffalo we might sign."

"I'm pleased to meet you, Miss Hawthorne. My name is Bebe Bennett, and I've come to interview for the position as Mr. Williams's secretary."

Miss Hawthorne's lips pursed. "I do hope you won't be like the others. You look like a sweet girl. I'd hate for you to be taken in by him."

"Taken in?"

Miss Hawthorne drew in a deep breath. "Mr. Williams has *a reputation*."

I smiled. "Oh, yes. I hear he's up-and-coming."

A look of shock passed over Miss Hawthorne's doughy face and she peered at me for a long moment before she seemed to relax. "What I mean, dear, is that the man chases skirts all over Manhattan."

"Oh."

"And he never misses the cocktail hour."

"I see."

"So be on your guard. Not that I think even he would stoop to seducing such an innocent young thing as you."

I could feel the heat rise to my cheeks. I knew I looked younger than I was, but it still rankled to be called "an innocent young thing." "I assure you, Miss Hawthorne, there is no way Mr. Williams could ever engage my attention other than as his professional secretary."

"I'm so glad to hear that, Miss Bennett."

"You may count on it as a sure thing."

At that precise moment, Bradley Williams walked out of his office and, without lifting a finger, claimed my heart. For a minute I stopped breathing.

Dressed in a slim-cut dark suit and thin tie, he was tall and trim, with that shade of blond hair dubbed "dirty." He had a high forehead, a thin, straight nose with slightly flaring nostrils, an angular jaw, a square chin, and the most alluring set of full lips I'd ever seen on a man. I wanted to kiss them right there. Then there were his eyes. Blue, but a shade I could hardly describe. Peacock blue would be going too far, but not by much. The only thing that saved his face from total perfection was a crescent-shaped scar under his left eye. Perversely, though, the scar made him all the more handsome.

I hardly remember him introducing himself or what happened over the next few minutes. I was on cloud nine, floating away with Bradley. Suddenly Miss Hawthorne had vanished, and I was in his office. I focused on the furnishings rather than allow myself to be mesmerized by my would-be boyfriend. I meant boss. He'd hardly hire me if he thought I was a gaping schoolgirl.

Bradley's office reflected his regard for the arts and crafts movement, a style I was familiar with due to my late aunt. The desk was made of golden oak; a matching credenza rested against the left side wall. On top of it stood a copper lamp with a mica shade. Above it were two mica-shaded sconces. The credenza held a hi-fi system in the middle. On the right side of the room was a long mission-style sofa with a coffee table and two chairs. On the floor, lush Turkish carpets in shades of light blue, dark blue, cream, and rust completed the look. A door to the left, slightly ajar, led to an executive restroom.

Sitting opposite Mr. Williams, I held on to my purse for dear life, staring at the Charles Rennie Mackintosh pewter clock.

"As you can see from my office, I'm a student of architecture," he said. His voice was low, just a touch on the raspy side.

"Oh," I replied brilliantly, forced to look at him and all his male beauty again. I guessed his age at about thirty, maybe thirty-two.

"My apartment, on the other hand, is decorated in a thoroughly modern style. I like variety."

He smiled.

I blushed.

He grinned at my blush.

"Miss Bennett, you're from a small city, I understand."

"Richmond, Virginia."

"How do you like New York?"

"I like it very much."

"You're not overwhelmed by it all, are you?" he asked, turning slightly and indicating the scene from his window.

"I find it invigorating."

"Invigorating? I like that word."

Another smile. God, he was gorgeous! Hire me! Hire me!

"I assume you have all the usual skills?"

"The usual skills?" I repeated, wondering just what he meant by that.

"Yes, typing, shorthand, telephone, keeping me on schedule with my . . . dates." This last was said with a smile that could have lit the entire Empire State Building.

"Of course, Mr. Williams."

He leaned back in his chair, a Morris piece in dark blue leather, a pencil held between his two index fingers. "I see they've sent me a girl just out of school this time. Trying to keep me out of trouble. Well, they've done their job, kid. Start on Monday."

Kid?

I spent that weekend shortening the hems on all my skirts by two inches. He wouldn't think me a "kid" for long!

The buzzer on my phone brought me back to the present. I picked up the receiver. "Yes, Mr. Williams?"

"Come in here, please, Miss Bennett."

"Yes, sir." I placed the receiver back in the cradle and grabbed my steno pad and pen. Just as I reached the office door, Mr. Purvis, the company president, walked out. I almost bumped into him, I was so excited that Bradley had summoned me.

"Good morning, sir."

"Damn if it's a good morning, girl," he said.

I eased past him into Bradley's office. He was in his shirtsleeves, a take-out coffee cup in front of him, his desk strewn with contracts.

"Would you like a fresh cup of coffee, Mr. Williams? I just made a pot."

"Miss Bennett, you read my mind." He looked up at me and smiled. I tried hard not to throw myself across his desk, and I'm proud to say I succeeded.

When I returned with the coffee, he thanked me and motioned for me to sit down.

"Miss Bennett, I don't mean to pry into your personal life, but would you like to tell me what happened last night at the Legends Hotel?"

As far as I was concerned he could *be* my personal life. I called myself to order. While he drank his coffee, I told him the whole story, not leaving out a single detail. He was a good listener, interrupting only a few times to ask questions.

Finally he said, "So you never met Keith?"

"No, but I intend to this afternoon, after work."

"Why?"

Could it be he was a little jealous? I could hope. "I'd like to get to know him before the party tomorrow night. Are we still holding the party for the band in the ballroom at the hotel like we planned?"

"That's what Mr. Purvis and I were discussing. Yes, we've sent out invitations to the media. It's too late now to cancel everything. But instead of a party, it will be more of a tribute or wake, if you will, for Philip, as well as an introduction of the band to the media. Philip's family wants his body shipped home to England as soon as the police release it. They will not even allow a formal memorial service here in the States."

"That's too bad."

"Yes. To make matters worse, the company hasn't decided yet what to do about the band's album, whether we should go forward and release it or cut our losses now. That last part's confidential."

"Yes, sir. Are you . . . I mean, because you're the one who signed the band, could you be in any trouble?"

He took a moment to look into my eyes. "You're a loyal girl, Miss Bennett," he said, making me feel like a puppy. "I'll tell you something I haven't told you before. My great-uncle is Herman Shires. Ever heard of him?"

"Doesn't he own a whole bunch of companies, including Rip-City Records?"

"Very good. You've done your homework."

I sat with my spine very straight. "It's part of my job to know all about the company."

He nodded in approval. "Uncle owns a conglomeration, you might say. He has no son to leave it all to, but he does have three nephews. I'm one of them. My cousins, Drew and Alfred, are currently working at other companies my great-uncle owns. It's a test, you see, to find out which one of us can make the most success out of himself. The one who wins is left controlling interest in all the companies when Uncle passes away."

"Wow."

He folded his arms across his chest. "So you see why Philip Royal's death is such a problem. If I make— pardon the pun—a royal mess out of this, my great-uncle will not be pleased with me. He might leave me here to molder away forever. Or send me to one of his smaller companies."

"What do you mean?"

"His plan is to move the three of his nephews around to different corporations to see how we do. Try us on for size. But he might not give me that opportunity."

My heart sank to my stomach. Bradley leave? But a voice in my head said that even if he did, he would take a valuable secretary with him. I had to find out who killed Philip Royal, not only for Darlene's sake, but for Bradley's. And I had to do whatever else it took to make sure that Bradley looked good, no matter what the company decided to do about Philip Royal and the Beefeaters.

Bradley spoke again. "Enough of my personal predicament. I need you to go down to the art department and tell Jim that we'll need a change on the album cover.

Some sort of tribute to Philip. See what ideas he can come up with, even though it's the last minute, in case we decide to go ahead and release the album."

"Yes, Mr. Williams," I said, taking notes. "I'll also check with Miss Hawthorne about the tribute tomorrow night. I'll make sure everything goes as it should."

Bradley smiled, and I noticed his gaze went to my legs. Then he looked at me and said, "Is that your kind way of saying Miss Hawthorne is forgetful and someone needs to look after her?"

"Of course not. Miss Hawthorne is a very sweet lady and competent. It's just that being in charge of the tribute is a big responsibility, and I want to help. The function must go off without a hitch, especially now."

"Miss Hawthorne is dotty, and you know it."

"She can be a little forgetful at times, that's all."

"Have it your way, kid," Bradley said in a tone that indicated our meeting was over.

I ground my teeth at the word *kid*.

In the art department, I was told Jim was busy with another project, and I'd have to wait to see him.

"Okay, Debbie," I said to the receptionist in Art. "But could I have a look at the cover for the Philip Royal and the Beefeaters album while I'm waiting?"

"Sure."

While Debbie went to find it, Vince Walsh, one of the senior talent scouts and Miss Hawthorne's boss, crept up behind me and made me jump. "Hey, cookie."

"Hello, Mr. Walsh." I didn't like him, hadn't since the moment I'd been introduced to him, and I felt bad about it. He oiled his hair, which didn't prevent dandruff from falling to his shoulders. He also smelled heavily of cheap cologne. But that wasn't why he bothered me. He said things to me I didn't like. I told myself he didn't mean anything by them. I was being oversensitive. Still, they stung.

"Or should I call you muffin-cup?" he asked, staring at my chest.

I felt my face flame. Maybe I should join in on the joke, but somehow I couldn't. I restrained myself from mentioning anything about his abnormally small feet.

"What are you doing down here in Art?" he asked.

"Mr. Williams sent me on an assignment." I needn't tell him Bradley's business.

"Oh, really."

"Here you are, Bebe," Debbie said, returning with the album.

"Thanks, Debbie."

"Philip Royal and the Beefeaters, eh?" Vince sneered. "Not anymore."

"You don't know that," I said. "And anyway, the album's all recorded, set for pressing and then release."

"What's a band without its lead singer, baby? No, Bradley's down the tubes, and he's gonna have a rough time getting out."

"That's not a very nice thing to say about your boss." *Get bent, Vince,* I thought.

Vince shrugged. "I'm just saying this whole mess with Philip is not so good for Bradley's career, if you ask me. I'm sorry I was away in Philadelphia listening to a band we might sign. I missed all the action." He walked away whistling.

Anger burned in my chest. I'd always been taught it wasn't nice to feel angry, that one must look at the positive side of people. I had a hard time doing this with Vince Walsh. Then I felt guilty about feeling so disapproving about Mr. Walsh. Maybe I would get him some Head & Shoulders and slip it into his office anonymously. That would help him with his dandruff problem. As for his remarks about Bradley, the man simply didn't know what he was talking about. I hoped.

Trying to settle myself back into a comfortable position in the chair, I spent the time while I waited for Jim reading over the demo album for Philip Royal and the Beefeaters. The words to all the songs were printed on

the back cover. I read over them casually until I came
to one. Then I sat up straight in my chair and gasped.

Get out of My Way

Well the lessons I've learned I don't really like
'Cause they just go to show you can't tell who's all
*   right*
One's like my father, listens to what's in my head
But even though he's given me shelter, now he takes
*   all my bread*

Starvin' for the good life, baby, with-out any
*   ooofff you*
Starvin' for the real thing, on my own, be-in' true
Here it is on my plate, if only I could reach it
Oh, it's so sweet, I can almost taste it—man
Get out of my waaaayyyy
Get out of my waaaayyyy

She acts like she loves me but she wants to strut
*   down the runway*
And now I know I'm a ladder and that's the only
*   reason she stays*
As for the other girls they're only there for one night
And then they're all out of my sight

Starvin' for the good life baby, with-out any ooofff
*   you*
Starvin' for the real thing, on my own, be-in' true
Here it is on my plate, if only I could reach it
Oh, it's so sweet, I can almost taste it—man
Get out of my waaaayyyy
Get out of my waaaayyyy

Then there are my mates, the ones I thought were
*   my boys*
But they're worst of all, taking my pride and joy

And turning it into something it was never meant
   to be
When all I wanted was just to be me

Starvin' for the real thing, baby, on my own, be-in'
   true
Here it is on my plate, if only I could reach it
Oh, it's so sweet, I can almost taste it—man
Get out of my waaaayyyy
Get out of my waaaayyyy

The chorus to the song was the one written on the
bathroom wall in Philip Royal's hotel room! The one
written by the killer. Did this mean the song meant
something to whomever murdered Philip? I had to tell
Bradley. And the police.

Without another word to Debbie, I raced to the elevators with the album in hand.

I paused when I reached my desk. Bradley was on his
phone. It wouldn't hurt to write the lyrics to the song
down on a piece of paper before showing it to Bradley.
That way I could have the words to help me figure out
who did Philip in.

Slipping out the little notebook I carried in my purse,
I quickly copied the lyrics before Bradley got off the
phone.

He looked up as I entered. "Yes, Miss Bennett, come
in. You look charmingly flushed."

"Thank you. Br—Mr. Williams, I was just down in
Art, like you told me to, and I was waiting to see Jim,
and I asked to see the album cover."

"Yes. Take a deep breath, Miss Bennett."

Oh, why must he persist in treating me like a child
one minute and flirting with me the next? I took the deep
breath, pushing out my 34-As as far as they would go.

His gaze dropped to my chest. I felt a wave of triumph.

"Do you feel better now, Miss Bennett?"

I could kill the man. "Yes. What I want to tell you is

I realized that what I saw written on the bathroom wall in Philip's hotel room—probably written by the killer—was the chorus to one of the songs on the album."

His right cheek puffed out and he blew out air. "Here, let me see that."

He scanned the lines, then said, "I remember this song very well. The company didn't want to include it on the album because it's an angry song. The rest of the tunes are fun and breezy. But it was a deal breaker. Philip threw a fit and insisted on including this song. This all happened recently. We already had enough invested in the band that we agreed to include it."

"What are we going to do, Mr. Williams? Shouldn't the police know about this?"

He raised his eyebrows. "I think they should. Would you call them, Miss Bennett?"

"Certainly."

"Meanwhile, I'll make sure this song is pulled from the album. I take it you didn't have a chance to talk to Jim."

"No, I wanted to tell you about the song right away."

"You did good, kid." He left the office, album in hand.

Kid. I ground my teeth. I made plans to call the police. And to meet Keith, my would-be date.

Chapter Five

To my dismay, the house phone was out of order when I reached the Legends.

"How do I know you're not just another girl wanting to meet him?"

Dealing with the snobby desk clerk to reach Keith was not my idea of fun. He was the one with the mole that looked like an earring. His name tag read Mr. Owens. "Because no one here in America even knows these guys, Mr. Owens. How many girls have you had asking for them?"

"Quite a few actually. Their picture was in the newspaper."

"Look, you saw me here yesterday. I know the band."

"Then why don't you know Keith Michaels's room number?"

"Because I didn't go up to his room."

"That's right. You went up to the dead one's room."

I gave him my brightest smile. "I know you want to help me. You're probably just going by the hotel rules. You don't have to give me the room number. If you would call Keith's room and let me speak to him as if it were the house phone, that would be good enough, okay?"

Mr. Owens glanced around the lobby. Then he discreetly extended his right hand palm up, making the universal gesture with his thumb and fingers that meant money.

So that was the way of it.

I pulled out fifty cents and placed it in his palm.

He didn't move.

I sighed heavily, took back the change, and replaced it with a dollar.

He picked up the phone, dialed a number, and handed me the receiver.

The phone rang and rang. Just when I thought I'd have to go through this whole procedure again another time, a voice with a heavy English accent said, "Hullo."

"Is this Keith?"

"Yeah."

"How do you do, I'm Bebe Bennett, the girl you were supposed to go out with last night."

Silence.

Darn, he couldn't even remember my name. "Darlene's friend."

"Oh, yeah, right. How's it goin'?"

"Well, actually, I'm downstairs in the lobby. I was wondering if you'd like to have a cup of coffee with me, so we could talk about what happened."

"Why don't you just come up?"

I'd cut out of the hotel before I went to his room. "I'm sure you're tired of being cooped up in your room with the reporters outside. A change of scenery, even if it is only the coffee shop, will do you good."

"All right, but make it the lounge."

"Okay. I'm a brunette, and I have on a navy suit."

"Be right there."

I handed the phone back to the desk clerk, who ignored me, and made my way to the lounge. Passing a policeman in the lobby reminded me of my phone conversation earlier that day with Detective Finelli. He'd told me in a bored voice that they already knew about the song, having questioned the other band members. I'd felt like an idiot. He asked to speak to Darlene, but luckily I was able to tell him I was calling from work, not home.

Before going to the lounge, I looked for Mr. Duncan, the elevator operator, but he was nowhere in sight. Maybe he had the night off. I hoped his cold was better.

The lounge was a dim area with gold cone-shaped lamps hanging from the ceiling. One could sit at the bar itself, or at one of the round Formica tables. I chose one of the few available tables and sat staring at the gold flecks in the top until a dark-haired woman dressed in a gold-and-black cocktail uniform came to take my order.

"What can I get for you, miss?"

From the swelling around her eyes and nose and the redness in the whites of her eyes, it was obvious she'd been crying.

"I'd like to order a drink, but maybe you need someone to talk to right now. I've been told I'm real good at listening."

The waitress fought back fresh tears.

"Maria," I said, reading her name tag, "is it something another girl could help with?"

"It's my boyfriend," she whispered in a rush. "He convinced me to get an apartment with him. Now we had a fight, and he moved out. The rent is due, and I can't pay it on what I earn."

I confess I was shocked. I'd never met a woman who lived with a man outside marriage. But this poor girl, surely no more than my age, didn't look like a hussy. She looked like a girl who made a mistake and was wronged in love.

"Are you working tomorrow night?"

"No. To make matters worse, they've cut my hours this week."

"Listen, I don't know how much it would help, but I'm with Rip-City Records, and we're having a gathering tomorrow night in the ballroom of the hotel. I'm sure we can use some extra staff."

The girl's jaw dropped. "Honest?"

"Honest. I'll take care of letting them know to expect you. Just be in the ballroom at four to help with the setup," I said. "The extra cash might help until you can find a roommate or another place."

"Thank you," she said. "Thank you from the bottom of my heart." She touched my hand, and I turned my hand around so I could give hers a reassuring squeeze.

"You're not in any other kind of trouble, are you?" I asked, afraid of what answer I might get.

"No, I'm on the pill."

"Gee, I've never known anyone who takes it. I'm glad it works," I said, wondering if Darlene was on it. "Now, I'd like a Virgin Mary, please." I wanted to order before Keith could get there and volunteer to buy me something else.

Maria brought the drink in seconds—with two celery stalks. "Hey, you didn't let that slimey Mr. Owens take you in about making calls upstairs, did you? I saw you talking to him, and then him handing you the phone."

"Actually, I had to slip him a dollar to ring a room for me. The house phone was out of order."

Maria shook her head. "He puts that sign on the house phone when his manager is off for the night. There's nothing wrong with it."

"Why, that jerk," I said. "He took advantage of me."

Maria looked sad. "Seems like they all do." With that she went to wait on another customer.

Soon a tall, extremely thin man in striped pants and a paisley shirt, his dark hair styled in a Beatles haircut, walked in. He immediately attracted attention. He was good-looking in a tougher way than any of the Beatles, as if he'd enjoy a good fight and a good bourbon. He had nice brown eyes, a long, aristocratic nose, and a charming smile, but his face bore a few pockmarks, left over from a childhood bout with the chicken pox, I guessed. There was a coldness about him, an aloof air that said he was already a star.

He came to my table and sprawled in the gold chair opposite, giving me the once-over. "Damned sorry I missed our date. What did you say your name was?"

"Bebe Bennett. You can call me Bebe."

Maria returned and smiled at me, checking to make sure my drink was okay. Keith ordered a bourbon on the rocks. Mentally, I patted myself on the back for guessing right. "What's that you're drinking?" he asked.

"Um, a Bloody Mary," I fibbed.

"I definitely like this Kentucky bourbon."

"Listen, let's not talk about my drink. Let's talk about Philip."

He lit a cigarette and slowly blew out the smoke. "Rotten thing to do, whoever did it."

His gaze slid away from me as if he were remembering other times, times with Philip.

"You must miss him. Had you known each other long?"

"Yeah, we'd been mates for a long time."

Then I remembered the words of the song:

Then there are my mates, the ones I thought were my boys.

"I'm so sorry. Everyone at the record company is upset. We're trying to put a tribute to Philip on the album cover."

His attention sharpened. "You're with the record company?"

"I'm Bradley Williams's secretary."

"Will you be at the tribute tomorrow night?"

"Yes, I will."

He smiled. "Good. I'll have the jump on the others 'cause I met you tonight."

I smiled back. He finished his drink more quickly than I thought was proper and ordered another. Maria frowned behind his back. In my best casual tone I said, "So how come you weren't downstairs waiting for me last night when we were supposed to go out?"

Keith passed a hand over his brow. "This is a bit embarrassing, but you see, I was boozed, and passed out. Philip would have come and got me, but . . ." He lit another cigarette.

"Had you seen Philip yesterday?"

"No, hadn't seen him at all since we landed and got to the hotel. We were given the day to rest. When we first got here we were jet-lagged, but some guy at the record company had plans to take us all around and show us the Statue of Liberty. We finally put our foot down and told him we needed a day to sleep off the time change."

"I can understand that," I said.

"When I woke up I went to Philip's room, but Darlene was there with some other bird— You're blushing. Was it you?"

"Yes, but—"

Keith smiled and leaned toward me. He smelled of bourbon and cigarettes. "You're awfully pretty."

"Thank you. I was in Philip's room after he'd been murdered. Darlene and I found the body. I wonder why anyone would want to kill him." I murmured this last bit in the most wistful way I could manage.

He sat back in his chair. "It was probably that bitch Astrid."

I almost jumped out of my seat. "Astrid?"

"Yeah, his ex-girlfriend. She thought she was still his girlfriend, even though she's with our drummer, Peter, now."

Remembering the song, I took a chance. "Isn't she a model?"

Keith snorted. "That chick wishes. The things she's done haven't exactly been the Parisian runways."

She acts like she loves me but she wants to strut down the runway.

"She's here in New York then, with Peter?"

"Yeah. Look, I don't want to talk about Philip any-

more. I need something to take my mind off his death."
He leaned closer again. He really was good-looking.
"Are you sure you don't want to come upstairs?"

Uh-oh. I looked at my watch. "No, I'm afraid I have
to go home now."

"I'll see you tomorrow, though. What about the day
after, Saturday? You have a cute accent."

"You're the one with the cute accent."

"No, you."

"No, you are."

"No, silly. You."

We smiled at each other.

"Actually, I was thinking of picking out some things
for my roommate at the used-furniture places. Her ex-
roommate took all her living room stuff."

We stood up. Keith said, "I'm the one to go with you.
I've bargained my way through the London shops and
markets at Portobello Road. We'll find some things for
you—promise."

I laughed. "Okay, let's talk about it at the get-together
tomorrow night."

"See, I've made a deal already." He winked. With that,
he showed that he knew how to make an exit, and did.

I decided to take a cab home. Cabs were a topic Darlene and I had argued about. She thought I should take
the subway more, but I couldn't bring myself to do it.
Daddy had warned me that all kinds of bad things happened down there. So I went outside and threw my arm
in the air until, as if by magic, one of the Yellow Cabs
stopped for me. I loved that feeling of power—that just
by smiling and putting my hand out, a car would stop
for me. Maybe someday I'd get up the nerve to take
the subway.

On the ride home I thought about what I'd learned,
and couldn't wait for Darlene to come home from the
Hamptons so I could fill her in.

Keith had no real alibi for the time Philip was murdered. He had said he was asleep. Of course, I knew of no motive yet, but then there was that song.

Keith was also an attractive man. Even though my heart belonged to Bradley, it wouldn't hurt to go furniture shopping with Keith. Wasn't it Bradley himself who said variety was good? *So there.*

Approaching home, I saw the wino Harry seated on a step a couple of doors down from my stoop. "Good evening, Harry."

He seemed dazed, but smiled when he saw me. "Evenin', miss. Have you got a quarter for ol' Harry?"

I was already digging in my purse and pulled out two quarters for him. I knew Darlene would have scolded me, but she wasn't around.

Walking up the stairs to my apartment, I thought back to the murder suspects. Philip had an on-again/off-again girlfriend named Astrid, a stormy romance that had maybe turned into a romantic triangle with another band member. Plenty of motive there. And again, the song. That song might hold the key to who had killed Philip Royal.

Who knew what I might be able to uncover at the tribute tomorrow with all the band members present? Not to mention Astrid. I'd get to meet everyone and try to pry out their secrets. Who would think an innocent country mouse like me would be doing anything more than showing polite interest?

The evening would be eventful; of that I had no doubt.

Now, what should I wear?

Chapter Six

"So, Keith, who do you think murdered Philip?" music critic Rolls Trank asked without sparing a thought for the lead guitarist's feelings. Rolls was short, with dark curls and glasses and a big cauliflower-like wart in the center of his chin. But he ruled rock gossip.

At five o'clock on Friday, we stood in the chandelier-lit ballroom of the Legends Hotel amid a crowd of journalists, reporters, and hangers-on, all stuffing themselves with pigs-in-a-blanket and other hot nibbles, washed down by free liquor. Philip Royal and the Beefeaters' new album played loudly over the room's sound system. A tribute to Philip it might be, but a good time was being had by all.

By everyone except the band members, who all looked rather glum. Keith was far on his way to becoming drunk. "I did it. There's a lead story for your bleeding newspaper tomorrow." He swallowed the last of his bourbon with a flourish.

Rolls took notes.

I smiled nervously. Part of my job here tonight was to protect the band from the media. "Rolls, why don't you get something to eat? Keith is just putting you on. You're wasting your time here. The band is grieving."

The music critic scowled at me over his glasses but moved away.

"What's with you, Keith?" I asked over the music.

"Rolls could very well have quoted you and made head-lines with that statement."

"Let him. I don't care. At least my name would have been out front instead of Philip's. Keith Michaels, Killer. You know," he said, leaning toward me unsteadily, "the band used to be called just 'The Beefeaters.' Later it was Nigel's idea to add Philip's name in front. Nigel always loved Philip like a son."

One's like my father, listens to what's in my head.

"Nigel's your manager, isn't he?" I asked, on the alert.

Keith nodded and then swayed on his feet. "He's the one who went along with Philip, wanting us to play this plastic pop stuff." Keith's features twisted. "I wanted to play real blues music, but no. We had to follow in the Beatles' shadow. As if anyone could."

I looked around to see if people noticed the anger in his voice, but everyone was busy with his or her own conversation. Keith sure had a temper when he drank. And from what he was saying, he and Philip had dis-agreed about the musical direction of the group. Was it enough for him to have harbored a murderous grudge?

Keith was peering at me closely. "Like those threads you're wearing, Bebe."

I looked down at my strawberry-pink Empire-waisted beaded dress and matching pink shoes. "Thank you."

Before I knew what was happening, he slipped an arm around me. "Why don't we beat it and go up to my room?"

Quickly, I slipped out of his grasp and spotted Maria, the cocktail waitress I'd befriended yesterday. "Excuse me, Keith, but I have to check on the food. My job, you know," I said, trying for a rueful look.

Before he could say a word, I was steps away from him and hurrying to where Maria was pouring Swedish meatballs from a hot stainless-steel bowl into a warming tray on a linen-covered table.

"Maria! How is everything going?"

The dark-haired girl smiled at me. "Very well, Bebe. And I have you to thank."

"I'm glad I could help."

"Has that tall Englishman you were in the lounge with been giving you trouble? I saw you talking with him just now."

I glanced over my shoulder to where Keith stood at the bar, ordering yet another drink. I sighed. "No, not really."

"He drinks too much. I know the signs. Better be careful."

"Yes, I think you're right."

"One of his friends has been running in and out of the room all evening trying to use the telephone in the booth down the hall. I noticed while I've been working the food."

"Oh, really? Which friend?"

Maria stirred the meatballs in the tray and indicated a brown-haired guy in black pants and a dark blue turtleneck, leaning against the wall near the exit. He looked cornered by a pretty blond reporter with a tape recorder and a microphone. I didn't recognize her.

"Thanks, Maria. Is Mr. Duncan here tonight?"

"The elevator operator? I think I saw him."

"Maybe someone could take him some soup. He's been sick."

"Okay."

"You take care." I made my way toward the blond reporter and the guy in the blue turtleneck. "Hi, I'm Bebe Bennett from Rip-City."

She didn't look happy to see me. In an English accent she said, "I'm Patty Gentry from *RPM* magazine in England. We're covering our local boys on their big trip to America. I guess you know Reggie Jones, the Beefeaters' bass player."

"Actually, we haven't met." I held out my hand, and he took it, looking grateful for the interruption.

"Awfully nice to meet you," he said in that same English accent that Keith had. There, though, the resemblance ended. Where Keith was all angular and sophisticated, this guy was a teddy bear, with a round face, brown eyes, and hair that fell into his eyes every couple of seconds.

"Reggie was just going to tell me whether or not the rumors that he has a wife tucked back home in Manchester are true," Patty said, frustration at my appearance tingeing her words. "It's a story I've been working on since I began covering the band a year ago."

Reggie looked like he'd swallowed a porcupine.

Out of the corner of my eye, I saw Bradley walking through the crowd. I willed him to look at me, and he did. Or maybe it was Patty, the pretty blonde, he saw. Anyway, he came over to us, looking gorgeous in a dark blue suit, a pale blue shirt that made his eyes stand out even more, and a narrow tie.

"Hello, who might you be?" Patty purred.

I reminded myself that I had already attracted the attention of the police. Kicking Patty would not help, although it would feel really good.

Bradley smiled his beautiful smile, the one that makes me want to kiss his full lips.

"Is everyone enjoying the evening?" Bradley asked after introducing himself to Patty. He eyed her white boots, shorter-than-short skirt, tiny top, and metal daisy-chain belt with an attention that even I, who was intrigued by the London fashions, had not shown. I wanted that pretty, sexy belt. And maybe even the boots.

"I am now," Patty whispered breathily.

"Jolly good time, considering the circumstances," Reggie said.

"Everything's running smoothly, Mr. Williams," I replied, barely refraining from wrapping my hands around Patty's bleached blond hair and pulling it out by its black roots.

"Can you get me a drink, lover?" Patty asked Bradley.

"Sure, anything to keep the press happy and encourage close relations between America and England," he said.

Close relations indeed!

The two moved away toward where a bar was set up, leaving me standing with my mouth open. If Reggie noticed, he was too much a gentleman to say anything. Instead, he kept glancing longingly out the exit.

Finally I realized I was being rude by staring at Bradley's and Patty's retreating backs and managed to say something. Granted it wasn't anything brilliant or tactful. "What's out the door that you want so much?"

Reggie smiled sheepishly. "You're from the record company, aren't you?"

"Yes. I'm Bradley Williams's secretary."

He nodded to himself. "It's all right to tell you then. I've been telephoning home all night trying to reach my wife. She's not answering."

"It's true then that you're married?"

"Yes. I've got a baby son, too."

"Congratulations, Reggie. Why is it such a secret?"

Reggie shifted uncomfortably. "Philip insisted it would be bad for the band's image as swinging pop stars if it were known that I'm married."

"I see. How does your wife feel about keeping the marriage a secret?"

"She and I both hate it! Why should we have to hide our love? Especially after Jamesey was born three months ago."

"Only three months ago? You must have had a hard time leaving England and coming over here while the baby's so young."

"I did. You should see how cute he is. Here, let me show you a picture." Reggie dug in his pants pocket until he produced a dog-eared black-and-white snapshot of a tyke who looked exactly like him.

"What a precious baby he is," I admired. A brief image of me holding Bradley's and my baby flashed through my mind. I made myself look at Reggie.

"Thanks. Philip and I fought about my leaving him. To tell you the truth, I never lusted after stardom the way Philip did. I would have been happy playing in England. But there you are." He shrugged and put the picture away.

I couldn't help but wonder if the two guys had fought over the decision to keep Reggie's marriage a secret too. Surely they had. How deep was Reggie's resentment over Philip's orders?

"I think Jean—that's my wife—isn't answering the phone deliberately. We had a row when I left. I'm so bummed out. Say, you're terribly easy to talk to. I shouldn't be burdening you with all this."

I touched his arm. "No, no, really. I don't mind. I'm interested in the band. I feel sorry for what's happened with Philip's death. Some welcome to America you've had."

"Thanks. It's been quite a shock." He blinked. "Oh, I shouldn't have put it that way, should I? And it doesn't help having a shark like Patty following us over, watching our every step. Heaven only knows what that chick's written for the English papers about Philip's death. She's reckless in her reporting, and one day she's going to make someone really wig out. Here's Peter. Have you met him? Peter!

"Miss Bebe Bennett, this is Peter Smythe, our drummer. Peter, this is Miss Bennett."

"Please call me Bebe," I said, extending my hand.

Peter looked a few years older than the other band members and had a receding hairline carefully concealed by a comb-over. In fact, looking closely at that receding hairline, I saw what appeared to be pen marks right at the juncture where sandy hair and scalp met. Good grief, was he marking where the hair started so that if he lost any more he'd know it?

He was dressed in burgundy-colored pants and a burgundy-and-tan-striped shirt with matching tie. His eyes were a pale blue, and the left one was twitching. Peter was a neurosis on legs, I decided.

Peter's grasp was light, brief, and shaky. "Pleased to meet you, Bebe. Reggie, have you seen Astrid?"

"No."

Peter gave the room a once-over. "She said she'd meet me down here. I don't know what's going on."

"Come on now, Peter," Reggie said. "You know you're always imagining the worst. She's probably gone and gotten her hair done or something. She'll be here."

"I expect so." Twitch. Twitch.

"Will the both of you excuse me?" Reggie said. "I have to call home again." He went out the exit swiftly.

While this conversation was going on, I found my gaze drawn to Peter's tie. Marching down the length of burgundy material was a row of different tie tacks, with one noticeably missing. Could it be the one that had found its way into Darlene's shoe? If so, that would put Peter at the murder scene.

"I see you've got a collection of tie tacks there, Peter," I said.

"Well, you've got to have a gimmick, haven't you?" he said in answer to my question. "Ringo's got the rings, hasn't he? I've got the tie tacks." Twitch.

"You're missing one, aren't you?"

"Er, yeah. Must have fallen off somewhere."

"I'm sorry about Philip."

Twitch. Twitch. Twitch. "Thank you. Bad way to go."

"Did you go to his room yesterday?"

"Me? No."

Fibber! How else would the tie tack have gotten into Philip's room and then into Darlene's shoe?

"Astrid! There you are!" Peter called.

Heads turned all around the room as a curvy girl with waist-length, straight blond hair and bangs entered the room and posed for effect. She wore a gold lamé dress that clung to her figure and screamed, "Look at me!" As she began winding her way through the room, I noticed she blew Peter a kiss but showed no intention of hanging on his arm when there was a roomful of press. No, her plans were to work the crowd of reporters.

At my side, Peter didn't seem all that annoyed. Instead he seemed proud of Astrid. "She's a lovely bird, isn't she?"

"Striking," I said.

" 'Ello Peter. You keepin' this lovely brunette all to yerself?"

The speaker was a man in his forties with a Cockney accent. He was a barrel of a man with a red nose, from heavy nights down at the pub, I guessed. His hair was a wiry gray.

"Nigel, this is Bebe Bennett. She works for Bradley Williams at Rip-City. Bebe, this is Nigel, our manager," Peter said.

"Nice to meet you, Miss Bennett," Nigel said.

"Please call me Bebe. I'm sorry for your loss."

Nigel's face got even redder. Tears sprang to his eyes. He took a long pull from the beer he was holding, and it was a minute before he spoke. "There will never be another like my Philip. Mark my words. 'E was a talent lost to the world too soon."

"You still have us, Nigel," Peter said.

"Right, that's right," Nigel said. "That is, if we still have a contract. You'd know about that, wouldn't you, Bebe, since you work for the record company. What can you tell us?"

"Me?" I asked. "I haven't been told anything. Honest. I'm here tonight to make sure everything goes smoothly. That's all."

"I'm glad you remember that, cupcake," a voice said from behind, startling me. I looked over my shoulder to see Vince Walsh joining our group. He didn't look happy. And his dark suit jacket was covered in dandruff, making me wish I'd slipped that bottle of Head & Shoulders into his desk drawer, as I'd considered doing.

"Mr. Walsh, what's wrong?" I asked.

"The cheese sauce in the fondue is lukewarm. Miss Hawthorne can't be expected to handle everything herself. See to it rather than chitchatting with the talent."

"But I was just making sure the band wasn't bothered by the press," I protested.

Vince flashed his oily smile. "I can help look after them. See to the food like a good woman should."

"I'll talk to you later, Peter, Nigel," I said, then left without another word to Vince. For a talent scout, all he seemed to do was hang around the office, doing what he considered flirting with me, and taking potshots at his boss, Bradley.

The direction of my thoughts changed when I saw Miss Hawthorne engaged in what looked like a heated conversation with a man carving a big roast beef.

Instead of bothering her, I decided to flag Maria and see if she could take care of the fondue. Spotting her with a fresh tray of cheeses, I began making my way toward her—distracted for a moment by the fact that Bradley was still talking to Patty, darn it all—and I noticed that Nigel had moved over to where Keith was falling-down drunk and making a spectacle of himself. The tribute would need to end fairly soon, before everyone was in Keith's state. Maybe I should cut off the free bar. I would have to talk to Miss Hawthorne.

"Maria, there you are. Listen, I need you to help me out with the fondue. Can you see that it gets warmed up? I've had a complaint."

"Sure." Then she leaned toward me. "Speaking of what's hot and what's not, did you get a load of that blond model, Astrid? She's going around the room talking to the reporters—all of them except that blond English reporter, I noticed. You know what she's saying?"

"What?"

"She's saying she was the dead man—Philip's— *fiancée*."

I seethed. Astrid was a publicity seeker of the worst kind, seizing the opportunity of Philip's death to put out false information that he was not around to refute.

But was she more than that? I looked over to where Astrid spoke in a cool fashion to a group of anxious reporters. Patty stood next to Bradley, gazing at Astrid with contempt. I remembered Keith saying yesterday that he thought Astrid was the one who'd killed Philip.

But then, Keith himself had motive to want Philip dead, didn't he? The two had fought over the direction of the band. Keith was playing music he didn't want to play.

Then there was Reggie, forced to keep a wife and infant son hidden away from the world at Philip's order.

What about Peter? He seemed very attached to Astrid. Could there have been a romantic triangle among the three of them?

And I had barely scratched the surface. Who knew how deep Keith's fights and jealousy with Philip went? What lengths did Philip go to come between Reggie and his marriage? What about Peter's insecurities and anxieties? Did Philip use them against the drummer?

Instead of answers, the night had brought about more questions. All I really knew was that I had to get to the bottom of who killed Philip, so I could get Darlene out of hot water and help Bradley emerge with a whole skin in front of his great uncle.

As the night drew to a close, upon reflection I realized that other than the minor fact that they were murder suspects, I liked the guys in the band. Funny, huh?

Chapter /even

Bells were ringing. Wedding bells. Bradley and I were getting married.

No, it was the phone.

I jumped out of bed and dashed barefoot to the kitchen, grabbing the receiver from the wall unit.

"Hello?"

"This is Detective Finelli. I'd like to speak to Darlene Roland."

I glanced at the kitchen clock. Just after eight in the morning. *Geez*. Where could I say Darlene was? Not in the Hamptons. My hand came up to my hair, and I sifted out a strand to twirl. I always do that when I'm nervous.

"Oh, I'm so sorry, Detective. She went for a walk."

"Is this Miss Bebe Bennett?"

"Yes, it is."

"I know Miss Roland is a stewardess. She wouldn't have left town against my instructions, would she?"

"No! I promise you, she's still in New York." *Just in the Hamptons, not in the city.*

"When did she leave for her walk?"

"You just missed her." Fibbing to the police! Darlene owed me big-time for this.

"Would you leave her a message to call me?"

This was just peachy-creamy. "I will, but our kitchen window is stuck open and sometimes messages get blown away."

"Excuse me?"

" 'Bye!"

I hung up before he could say another word. *Phew, that was close.* Darlene had better come home soon.

I went back in the bedroom and made up the bed, then had my shower and fixed my hair and makeup. I pulled out a black-and-white herringbone skirt and a white turtleneck sweater. Wearing only my slip and the skirt, I was about to pull on the sweater when the phone rang again. I went to answer it, scared it was Detective Finelli.

"Hello," I said cautiously.

"Bebe, Bradley Williams here."

My heart leaped off a fifty-foot cliff and soared through the air. "Yes, Mr. Williams," I said calmly.

"How are you this morning? Not feeling the effects of last night, are you?"

My hand came up to trace the lace on the edge of my slip. I was talking to Bradley in my underwear! "Um, no. I mean, I didn't have anything to drink. I don't drink much."

"Well, kid, that's good. Listen, I need you to go over to the Legends Hotel and settle our bill there. Evidently Miss Hawthorne forgot to do it. They called me here at home this morning."

A picture of Bradley in his pajamas ran through my mind. Silk or cotton? Checked or striped? Or did he even wear pajamas? I squeezed my eyes shut, feeling light-headed. Finally I said, "I'll take care of it right away."

"I knew I could count on you, kid. Reliable as rain. See you Monday."

Rain? "See you Monday," I said, and stopped myself before I could kiss the receiver, I was so happy to hear his voice.

I spent the next several minutes staring at the phone, then walking aimlessly around the apartment while gazing dreamily into space, wondering how Bradley would

spend his Saturday. An unwanted image of the modishly
dressed Patty, reporter, seducer, and enemy-maker,
wheedled its way into my mind. I frowned. Mentally, I
tossed her out of the picture on her ear. There, that
was better.

Instead, I saw Bradley lazily reading the papers, calling
his mother, doing the marketing, and thinking about me
in my pink dress the night before. Much better.

Finally I pulled on the white turtleneck and a short,
flaring black jacket, grabbed my purse, and left the apartment. The day was sunny and mild as I skipped down
the front steps, making me feel adventurous. I could see
Harry sleeping behind the high school that fronted Lexington Avenue. That made me frown. But you could only
help someone who wanted to be helped. And I was sure
I would continue to help Harry with quarters when I
could.

I took the bus to the hotel, congratulating myself at
navigating my way around the city—it wasn't the subway,
but Darlene would approve—and was settling the bill at
the front desk when Keith sauntered in.

"Bebe, I'm so glad I ran into you."

"Hi, Keith," I said, signing my name to the last
document.

He was dressed in a pair of jeans and a dark blue
velvet jacket over a white shirt. His long dark hair looked
freshly washed. He didn't appear to be feeling the effects
of the night before. "Bebe, I meant to make plans for
us to go shopping for your furniture today, but then I
didn't see you again last night."

That's because you were drunk, I thought. "Oh, that's
okay. I had to come by here to settle the tab from yesterday. Do you still want to go?"

"Definitely. I'm all yours," he said, and grinned,
spreading his arms wide.

"I'm game," I said, and smiled back.

Traffic was congested on the cab ride down to the
Village, and I vowed again to learn to use the subway,

but we soon found ourselves at Goodbye's Secondhand Furniture. Inside the packed store, Keith and I laughed over an old maroon-colored Victorian settee and chair. He mimicked a proper Victorian gentleman, complete with imaginary handlebar mustache, sitting very straight on the settee.

I cracked up laughing when he mimed to the butler to bring him his lady wife (making a figure eight with his hands) so that she might pour the tea. I was glad to see him up to boyish shenanigans, so I obligingly played the part of his wife, carrying the imaginary tray and serving him while he scolded that the tea was not hot enough.

"Hey, there, what are you two doing?" said an older man with gray hair and suspenders, obviously the proprietor.

"We were just having a look at your furniture, mister," Keith explained with a laugh.

The man frowned mightily. "This isn't a place for pranksters. Move on."

I spoke up. "We really are looking for some second-hand pieces."

But the owner wasn't having it. "I don't want no long-haired jokers in my store. Go along with you."

"Stuck-up man with stuck-up furniture, aren't you?" Keith sneered.

"I'll call the police!" The man moved toward the telephone.

"Come on, Keith. Let's go," I said, mortified.

"Stupid old man!" Keith shouted as we left the shop.

Once outside, I adopted a brisk step to get us away from there as quickly as possible. I wasn't used to people being rude to me in shops. Everyone was normally as courteous to me as I was to them. I glanced at Keith's angry face. Once again I thought of his temper, which was so quick to rise. I could imagine the fights he'd had with Philip.

At the next shop we went to, Favorite Things, I found a smart-looking modern bright, pink sectional with metal

legs that I fell instantly in love with. There was a cigarette burn on the right-hand side of it, near the armrest.
That could easily be covered up by, say, a gold-colored
pillow.

The price tag was more than I wanted to spend, but
Keith insisted I leave the matter to him. Call me a cow-
ard, but I moved on to look at other items while he
negotiated the price of the piece with the shop owner,
this time an older lady.

As the minutes passed and I heard no raised voices, I
dared a quick peek over my shoulder. The lady was smiling at Keith, apparently taken in by his charm. I admired
a turquoise fake-fur rug that would be striking with the
pink sectional.

Twenty minutes later Keith had arranged for both the
sectional and the rug to be delivered later that day to
my apartment, for a price I found incredibly reasonable.
I was thrilled and thought with fond anticipation of Darlene's pleased reaction to having real furniture.

"Thank you, Keith. You did a great job." I beamed up
at him. We were outside the shop in a crowd of people.

To my surprise, he leaned down and kissed me on the
lips. His mouth was warm, and he was a good kisser. I
hardly had much time to react, though, before he drew
away and smiled at me.

Embarrassed at this public display, and torn because
of my feelings for Bradley, I'm sure I blushed, which
only caused Keith to laugh and grab my hand. "I'm hungry. Let's get something to eat."

"Have you had hot dogs from a street vendor?" I
asked, anxious to talk about anything but the kiss. "You
haven't really tasted New York until you've done so."

"I do want to taste New York," he said.

"Well, come on," I said, holding his hand and racing
to the end of the block. We got hot dogs with the works
and ate them while walking down the busy streets, the
crowds of people heavy around us. Hot dogs from the

vendors who worked the street corners were one of my guilty pleasures. As I polished mine off, I grinned. I felt like a curious kitten learning her new surroundings. One day I'd be a cat who would know New York like the back of her paw. I'd wind myself around Bradley and—

"Delicious," Keith proclaimed of his hot dog, bringing me out of my daydream. "Now I need a drink to wash it down. Let's go back to the hotel."

"Um, I really should go home to wait for the furniture to be delivered."

"Nonsense. You've got time to see me back to the hotel and have a drink first. You wouldn't want me to get lost in the big, bad American city, would you?" he said in mock fear.

I smiled. "All right."

Soon we were back in the Legends Hotel lounge, where Keith ordered his usual bourbon. He told me to order a strawberry daiquiri.

"I've never tried one of those," I admitted.

"It's mostly just fruit juice, really," he said, lighting a cigarette.

"Okay." I was feeling up for anything. After all, I'd spent the morning with an English pop star buying furniture for my New York City apartment!

The drinks arrived, and Keith drank two-thirds of his in a few swallows. Mine was a pretty confection that tasted like a dessert. I drank it thirstily. Keith lit another cigarette.

Feeling the need to get back to the investigation, I tested the waters by saying, "You're really a very creative person, Keith. It's a shame Philip didn't take more of your ideas, as far as the band was concerned."

Bingo! Moody Keith's face turned into a storm cloud. He finished his drink and ordered another, blowing smoke out of his nostrils. He leaned close to me. "I tell you, Bebe, Philip was a rotter. Demanding that his name headline the band, insisting on playing only pop tunes."

"What about 'Get out of My Way'? That's not a pop tune." I opened my eyes to their widest, which was sorta easy. I was feeling very relaxed and kinda floaty.

Keith swallowed half of his new drink and stubbed out his cigarette. "Oh, yeah, that song. Philip's own personal little project. He told us we were lucky he didn't start his own solo album and put the song on that. We should feel fortunate that he was willing to let it be a Beefeaters title. Ha! It didn't go along with the others, and it was a bad song to boot. I, for one, would have been happy to let him try to put it on a solo album."

"Was he really thinking of a solo project?" I was having trouble focusing on the issue at hand. In fact, everything was bleary. I drank some more of my daiquiri to clear things up. It tasted so sweet, and I love strawberries.

"You know, I think the rotter was. He had delusions of grandeur, if you ask me. With his name out front, I think he thought he could eventually leave the rest of us behind and become a solo act. Can you believe the cheek?"

"Something's on my cheek?" I said, picking up my napkin and trying to wipe my face.

Keith chuckled. "No, luv. That's not what I meant. Not much of a drinker, are you? I find you charming, innocent, and wise all wrapped up in a very pretty package. Listen, I have my own tunes that I wrote. Real blues stuff. The genuine article."

He reached across the table and took my hands in his. Looking deeply into my eyes, he said, "Come on upstairs and I'll play some music just for you, Bebe."

"Jus' for me?" I asked, feeling like a cloud had picked me up and carried me away.

"Just for you," Keith confirmed with a sexy smile.

"Miss Bennett!"

I sat up straight in my chair, as if one of the nuns at school had just rapped me with a ruler.

Bradley Williams was standing over me, glaring at us.

Chapter Eight

"Bra—Mr. . . . Mr. Williams!" I stuttered, my head spinning.

Bradley glared down at Keith with the most disapproving expression on his handsome face. I couldn't imagine what was wrong. Everything was fuzzy, though. I took another sip of my drink.

Keith lounged back in his chair and returned Bradley's gaze.

It seemed a standoff.

Then Bradley spoke in a quiet voice. "You know she's underage."

My mouth dropped open. My brows came together. I wasn't underage. What was he talking about? I began to protest. "I'm not—"

"Be quiet please, Miss Bennett. I'll order you some coffee," Bradley said, motioning to a waitress.

Keith's face had gone pale. A telltale flash of alarm had crossed his face at the word *underage*. He rose to his feet. "I have to go. The guys and I are going down to the Gaslight in the Village tonight to hear a hot new band. We were going to ask you to go, but I expect we'd better not. See you later, Bebe."

He made tracks out of the lounge before I could say I'd go. Instead I turned to Bradley, who'd taken Keith's place at the table. "That was rude. And I'm not . . . not under . . . under . . . underage."

"Miss Bennett, I do believe you're tipsy. Here, drink this coffee."

Indignation rose in me. "I'm not tipsy. This is a fr-fruit drink."

Bradley leaned across the table and took the remains of the strawberry daiquiri away from me. He put the steaming cup of coffee the waitress had brought in its place. "Those fruit drinks can be deceptively potent. There now, drink this coffee."

Like an obedient child, I did as he said. "What are you doing here anyhow?" I asked.

He sat back in his chair. His dark brown suit with a beige shirt and a dark tie set off his blond hair nicely. In fact, he looked quite dashing. But then, when didn't he?

He looked at me with his incredible blue eyes. "I had no idea when I called you this morning that I'd be coming over here. About an hour after I talked to you, I received a phone call from one of my contacts in London. Do you know Astrid Loveday, the model Philip had dated? She's seeing Peter now, supposedly."

I squinted my eyes. Through the fog that was my brain I remembered the curvy blonde. "Yes."

"It seems that over in England she's been spreading stories. One of the tabloids had the headline 'Pinup Cutie Reveals Secret Marriage to Dead Pop Star.' "

"Oh, gosh. I wonder if that reporter Patty Gentry had anything to do with it. They don't like each other, but maybe they're using each other." The words came out slowly. I had to think hard before I could verbalize my thoughts.

"Regardless of how it happened, I'll be issuing a retraction from the record label," Bradley said grimly. "I want Astrid's explanation and her cooperation. Here she comes. Now you just be quiet, kid."

Oh! There he went again, treating me like a child. In this case, a naughty child. And what made things worse was that I should have known better about the daiquiri.

I took too big a gulp of the hot coffee and burned my tongue.

Bradley rose to his feet to greet Astrid. The blond model was dressed in a tight-fitting black skirt, pumps, and a baby-blue, low-cut sweater she had poured her generous bosom into, an outfit carefully put together to tempt men. Her long blond hair flowed down her back in silken waves. She took a chair between Bradley and me and ordered a beer.

"The boys and I find it refreshing to have cold beer instead of warm. So different," she said in a well-practiced upper-class English accent.

But Bradley was not here for chitchat. "Miss Loveday, I asked you to meet me here for a serious reason."

"Oh, what would that be?" The blonde opened her blue eyes to their widest. She had ignored me after Bradley introduced us, and now it was clear that her entire attention was on him.

To my frustration, *his* attention was on her as well. Every couple of minutes I saw that his glance strayed to the expanse of cleavage she was showing. And I was in a turtleneck! Not that I could measure up to her.

"Miss Loveday, have you been telling the press that you and Philip were married?" Bradley asked.

Astrid took a sip of her beer. "Philip and I weren't married," she said. "Is that more of the trash Patty Gentry spreads? She'll write anything to get attention."

"That's not what he asked," I said, feeling bold.

"I can handle this, Miss Bennett," Bradley said with a stern gaze in my direction.

I felt like sticking my tongue out at him. I had to clench my teeth together to avoid doing so.

He turned back to Astrid. "Did you tell the press you married Philip Royal?"

"No."

"Then why would they report such a rumor?"

"I don't know. Did they?"

"I have it on good authority that they did. Now what part did you play in this?"

"I don't know what you mean," Astrid said, trying hard for the wide-eyed innocent. "Patty or one of the others must have made it up. There are always press following us in England."

"See," I said to Bradley. "I told you Patty was involved."

Bradley ignored me. "Well, let me make it plain, Miss Loveday. The *London Reporter* ran an article with the headline 'Pinup Cutie Reveals Secret Marriage to Dead Pop Star.' "

Astrid bristled. " 'Pinup Cutie'? And that's supposed to be me? I'm a runway model."

Bradley did not let up. "That may or may not be true. But my source also told me you posed topless in *Saucy Damsels* and *Hot and Spicy*."

"Hot and Spicy?" I was almost sure they weren't talking about a cooking magazine. "What kind of magazine is that?"

Bradley pointed a finger at me. "Not now, Miss Bennett."

Astrid looked militant.

Bradley opened a briefcase I hadn't even noticed he had with him. He extracted a manila envelope and opened it to reveal what looked like a set of photographs. I couldn't really see from where I was sitting. He showed them to Astrid, though, and her lips pursed.

"Every fashion model does it to advance her career."

I half stood up, curiosity getting the better of me. The room swayed a little, but I was able to see the top photo. It was a black-and-white shot of Astrid posed in a pair of dangly triangle-shaped gold earrings, a scrap of lace, and nothing else.

I couldn't get much more of a peek because Bradley saw me looking and whisked the photos away.

"Sit down, Miss Bennett. You're weaving."

Bradley turned back to Astrid. "I still want to know what you told the tabloids."

"I might have told them that Philip and I were engaged," she admitted. "We were, you know, at one time, and he would have come back to me had he lived, so it's all the same."

Bradley shook his head. "You can't go around saying that you were married to him or even engaged to him. It wasn't true. You were broken up. What about Peter?"

"What about him?"

I remembered what it was that had been trying to come to the surface of my brain earlier. "Last night at the tribute you were telling reporters that you were engaged to Philip."

Bradley cut a sharp look at Astrid. "Is that true?"

Astrid shot me a glare. It seemed we weren't destined to be friends. "Look, a girl's gotta do what a girl's gotta do to get ahead in life. I spent a lot of time with Philip. I should be able to reap the rewards of that relationship. I use the benefits of the press when I can. God knows they aren't often kind to me, especially Patty."

"What you're going to do is issue a joint retraction with me to the *London Reporter*, saying that you were not married or engaged to Philip."

Astrid's blond hair shook like wheat in a windy field as she moved her head in the negative. "No. You say what you want, but I put up with Philip for three years. All his tantrums and the band's ups and downs. I'm making the most of things now." She got to her feet, then leaned down and placed her hands on the table, palms down, leaving Bradley with a bird's-eye view down the front of her top. "But if you ever want to get together and have an actual friendly talk, *Bradley*, you know where to find me."

With that she sashayed out of the lounge, leaving me alone with him.

Bradley put his head in his hands, mussing his perfect hair.

He quickly recovered, smoothed his hair, and said, "Come on, Miss Bennett; we need to get you home."

"I'll just get a cab." I rose to my feet and immediately had to sit back down when the room spun. I felt faintly sick to my stomach.

"You won't be going anywhere by yourself," Bradley said.

"Yes, I will. I'm capable of taking care of myself. I know I've had too much to drink, but I think I can make it to a cab on my own, thank you."

He motioned for the waitress and paid the check while I held my reeling head. How had I gotten into this state? It was only a fruit drink!

"You will do no such thing, Miss Bennett. You will come with me."

"Well, this is a side of you I haven't seen before, a bully!"

"It's for your own good. Now come along like a good girl."

I took two steps away from him. "I am not a girl!"

His gaze started at the top of my head and moved ever so slowly down my chest, my waist, and down my legs to my feet. "You could have fooled me, Miss Bennett."

Oh. Oh, my.

Bradley held my arm—oh, if only I could enjoy his touch with a clear head—and guided me through the lounge and out the front door of the hotel. It was early evening now, and the taillights from the cars all seemed to run together.

"Come on, kid, in you go," Bradley said. He held the door to a cab open. I climbed in and he followed.

Realizing he meant to see me to my door, I felt miserable. "Really, this isn't necessary. I'm feeling better."

"Yes, it is necessary. I wouldn't sleep tonight if I just sent you off on your own in your condition."

"I only had one drink!"

"Apparently that's all it took."

I gave the driver my address, and we rode in silence to my apartment. Every block that passed I was acutely aware of sitting so close to Bradley in the backseat of the cab. I could smell his delicious masculine cologne.

If only right now it weren't making me queasy.

Finally we arrived at my apartment building.

"Driver, wait here. I'll be right back," Bradley said.

"Please. You don't have to see me to my door. I can make it up the stairs," I said, humiliated.

"I've come this far, kid."

We got out of the cab. Again a wave of dizziness gripped me as I stood on the sidewalk. I placed a hand to my stomach.

I didn't notice a man standing on my front stoop.

But he saw me.

"What's going on here?" he said.

"Daddy!"

"You there, boy! Have you taken my Little Magnolia out and gotten her drunk?"

"I—"

My father punched Bradley right in the eye.

Chapter Nine

Bradley fell to the cement sidewalk.

"Oh, Daddy, what have you done?" I leaned down and cradled Bradley's head in my lap. I don't know whether it was because of the sight of my father appearing out of nowhere or that of Bradley lying there hurt, but I was suddenly sober.

Bradley groaned and put a hand over his left eye where my father's fist had made contact.

Daddy was outraged. "Bebe, what were you doing out drinking with this low-life Yankee? I knew men like him in the war. Get a girl drunk and have their way."

I looked over my shoulder at my father. By "the war" he meant World War II. A veteran and proud of it, my father was a big guy at six-feet-one. I got my height from him. He had dark hair that was now iron gray. He carried himself like he was still in the military, even though he had a big belly from drinking too much Budweiser. He had built a fallout shelter in our backyard, in preparation for any enemy attack.

Earl Bennett had always been a good father to me, if a teensy bit overprotective, as evidenced by his sudden appearance outside my apartment.

"Daddy, this is my boss, Bradley Williams. He's not a lowlife. He's vice president of Rip-City Records."

"Nice to meet you, Mr. Bennett," Bradley said, struggling to his feet. "I'm from Oklahoma, so I don't think that makes me a Yankee. And I spent two years in a foxhole in Korea."

I swung my head around at this information. Bradley in Korea?

"Your boss?" Daddy said, ignoring Bradley, disapproval dripping from the words. Daddy had on an overcoat and a hat in deference to the Northern climate. I thought at any minute he might pull a gun out from under the coat and aim it at Bradley's heart. Daddy had quite a collection of guns at home, something that scared me as a child and still did. Guns just terrified me.

I nodded my head earnestly. "Yes, the one I told you and Mama about in my last letter, remember?"

Daddy grunted.

"Besides, Mr. Williams didn't buy me the drink," I explained. "He was just seeing me home safely. Honest."

Daddy looked from Bradley to me. "Who did buy you the drink?"

"Keith."

"Who's he?"

"One of the members of Philip Royal and the Beefeaters."

Daddy got mad all over again. "Philip Royal's the one who got himself murdered by your Texas roommate. Always was something strange about that state. Thinks it's a country all to itself. I know about Miss Roland. I read the newspapers, you know. You can't keep things from me. I told you New York City was full of violence. Things haven't changed since I came through here on my way to Europe during the war. That's why I left your mother in Richmond and came up here to check on you. I want to make sure this Darlene Roland person is locked up, and you're safe from harm. You haven't been anywhere near Times Square, have you?"

"Oh, no."

"Good. Keep it that way. Place is full of drunks, dope addicts, and prostitutes."

"Daddy, Darlene didn't kill anyone. But she's out of

town right now, and you can't meet her. Let's get Mr.
Williams upstairs and put a steak on his eye before it
swells up."

"Thank you, Miss Bennett. But maybe I should just get
back in the cab and go home," Bradley said, and winced.

I turned to him. "I won't hear of it, Mr. Williams. I
have a nice porterhouse that will fix that eye right up.
Come on. Daddy, I guess you'd better come, too. Where
are your bags?"

"I wouldn't put my Little Magnolia out. I'm staying at
the Legends Hotel."

No, God. No! Did he have to stay at the same hotel
where the guys in the band were staying? I mean, really.
Of all the hotels in New York . . .

We made our way up the two flights of stairs, Daddy
glaring at Bradley the whole way. The area around Bradley's eye had turned a dark, puffy red. I needed to get
that steak on it.

But when I opened the door, it was to find Darlene,
clad in purple lounging pajamas, home from the Hamptons. She was freaking out over the new furniture I had
completely forgotten would be delivered that afternoon.

"Bebe!" Sneeze. "Oh, we've got company! And someone brought furniture."

"Darlene, this is my father, Earl Bennett—"

Daddy took off his hat, pushed his way into the apartment, and took stock of the rooms. He tilted his head
and glared down at Darlene like an eagle looking at prey.
"You're the one the papers say killed that pop singer.
Did you?"

"Daddy!"

Darlene drew herself up to her full five-foot-three.
"Pleased to meet you, Mr. Bennett. No, I didn't kill
him."

Daddy and Darlene engaged in a brief staring contest,
and when Darlene didn't back down, gazing at him stead-
ily with her big blue eyes, Daddy seemed satisfied. He

nodded. "All right, then. You seem too small to be the murdering kind anyway."

I led Bradley over to the pink sectional, which Darlene had placed in front of the fireplace. "Here, sit down and I'll get you that steak, Mr. Williams. Darlene, this is my boss, Bradley Williams."

"Hi, there," she said with a big Texas smile.

"Nice to meet you," Bradley said, sounding like he'd rather be anywhere else.

I shot Darlene a look that said, *Hands off!* and she immediately raised her palms in a gesture that cried surrender.

I hurried to the refrigerator and got the steak I'd planned to treat myself with that night. I brought it and a dishtowel over to Bradley. He leaned his golden head back on the pink couch and applied the steak.

Darlene said, "Bebe, do you mind telling me how we managed to get this furniture?"

"Keith and I picked it out this afternoon," I told her. "I wanted to surprise you with it."

"I dig it," Darlene said.

"Keith?" Bradley mumbled.

"You went out prowling the city with some man?" Daddy said.

"Yes," I replied to Bradley.

"No," I said to Daddy.

I looked from one to the other of them. To Bradley I said, "I thought it was a good excuse to talk to Keith some more about Philip. I netted some results too. It seems Keith thought Philip was a 'rotter' and harbored a grudge against him."

Daddy said, "Would someone tell me what's going on?"

"Here, Daddy, let me take your coat. Would you like a drink? I don't have any beer, but I could bring you a Coke or a whiskey."

"A Coke would be fine."

I hung Daddy's coat up and went back into the kitchen. Daddy and Darlene settled themselves on opposite ends of the sectional, with Bradley in the middle.

When I brought him his drink, Daddy said, "Now, tell me about this Keith person and why you're trying to get information out of him."

Uh-oh. "Well, Daddy, don't get mad or anything, but Keith is the lead guitarist in the Beefeaters. He might have had reason to want to . . . to . . . you know . . . do away with Philip Royal."

"What's that got to do with my Little Magnolia?" Daddy asked with a scowl.

At Daddy's lifelong nickname for me, Bradley made a noise that might have been a laugh.

Daddy took offense. "Boy, are you laughing at me?"

"No, sir," Bradley said, looking properly humbled. Well, as humble as he ever got.

Daddy's eyes narrowed. "Were you laughing at my little girl's nickname?"

There was a terrifying pause when I thought Bradley might actually answer yes, but Daddy charged on ahead. "Because if you were, youngster, that proves you don't have eyes in your head."

"Daddy!"

Bradley removed the steak from his eye. He turned his intense blue gaze on me, and I flushed. He put the steak back over his eye and said, "That's where you're wrong, sir."

I felt a flutter in the region of my heart.

Daddy made a sound that could have passed for a dog growling. "Anyway, what's this got to do with Bebe?"

Darlene spoke up. "It's got to do with me. Bebe is trying to help me, Mr. Bennett. As you know, the police suspect me of being the killer. Of course, I didn't do it, and Bebe wants to help prove that by finding out who did."

Daddy's face turned the same shade of purple as Darlene's lounging pajamas. "What! Do you mean to tell me you're up here in New York City investigating a murder?"

Bradley removed the steak from his eye and looked at me. "Is that what you're doing, Miss Bennett? If so, I would advise you to leave matters to the police."

Traitor! I looked from one man in my life to the other. "But the police aren't as close to the band as I am." Boy, was that an understatement. Keith wasn't smooching with Detective Finelli out in the New York sunshine. "I can ask questions, and they'll answer me better than they will the police. I've got to help Darlene."

Daddy set his Coke down on the floor. "What you've got to do is pack your bags and come back on the train with me to Richmond. New York is no good for you. The whole country's gone to hell in a handbasket since the assassination of President Kennedy." Daddy stopped as tears formed in his eyes, and he wiped them away.

There was silence in the room. I think each one of us was remembering where we were when we'd gotten the horrible news. I had been sitting at my desk at Philip Morris, typing. One of the other secretaries, Dorothy, told me the president had been shot to death in Dallas. Tears had begun streaming down my face, tears that would continue on and off for weeks. In the days following the assassination, Daddy, Mama, and I watched all the coverage on the black-and-white TV in our family room.

Daddy brought us all back to the present. "Now go get your things together, Bebe. We're going home."

"Daddy, I can't do that! I love it here. I love my apartment and my job and my friends." *And Bradley.*

"Then you'll stay away from police matters, young lady. Or I'll take you back to Richmond myself."

Bradley held the steak away from his eye long enough to look sternly at me.

Darlene gazed pleadingly at me.

Here was a problem. I wasn't by nature a liar. And I certainly did not make it a practice to lie to my parents.

But I wasn't going to stay out of the investigation of Philip Royal's death. I had to help Darlene. I had to help Bradley come out of this mess looking good in front of his great-uncle, whether he liked it or not. No, there was no way I could make Daddy the promise he wanted.

Of course, there was always a compromise. "Daddy, I won't get in the way of any police business, I promise."

Daddy looked skeptical. Perhaps he remembered the time when I was five and I promised not to hit Francine Mayer, the neighborhood know-it-all, then just pinched her real hard instead. Sometimes the wording of a thing could be important.

"We'll discuss it more after church tomorrow morning," Daddy said. "I'll come by and get you at seven thirty."

I barely suppressed a groan. Couldn't we go to a later Mass?

Then Daddy sat back in his place, totally prepared to wait Bradley out. It didn't take long. Bradley took the hint. "Here, Miss Bennett, I think your steak has done the job."

He handed me the meat and gently wiped his face with the towel.

"Let me wrap it up for you, Mr. Williams, and you can take it home." I hurried to the kitchen and found some Saran Wrap and packaged the steak, then washed my hands. I brought the steak back to him and noticed that his eye area had gotten no worse but still looked dark red and puffy.

"Thanks, Miss Bennett. See you Monday. Good night, Mr. Bennett, Miss Roland."

Daddy grunted again, and refused to meet Bradley's gaze.

Darlene gave Bradley a little wave from the couch, so that I could walk him to the door alone. But he only said, "Your father has a hell of a right hook."

"I'm so sorry, Mr. Williams."

"That's okay, kid. I've had shiners before."

Then he was gone.

I went back into the living room. "You should have apologized to Mr. Williams, Daddy."

"Why? I've known his sort in the army. Likes women and lots of them. Tell me, am I wrong?"

I looked at the floor. "He doesn't see me that way."

Darlene said, "He keeps Bebe at a distance because he knows that dating her would mean marriage. He's not ready to settle down yet."

My head came up at that.

"It sure would," Daddy said firmly. "My Little Magnolia is no man's toy."

"Oh, Daddy," I said.

He rose to his feet. "I'd better go get settled at the hotel. Good night, Miss Roland. I'm glad to find that you're not a murderer. I'll see you in the morning, Bebe." He bent and kissed the top of my head, and then he left.

Darlene and I looked at each other.

"Darlene, I'm sorry my father accused you of murder."

"Honey, don't worry; he wasn't the first."

"How was your trip to the Hamptons?"

"Great! Stu treated me like a princess. I've got to diet after all the food I've been eating. But, Bebe, you did a wonderful job with the furniture. It's beautiful, and this turquoise fur rug is a blast!"

"I'm glad you like it. I wanted to do something for you, since you're not charging me much rent, and your last roommate took all the furniture."

Darlene waved a hand. "I love having you here. So you've got two men on the line, Keith and Bradley."

"Hardly. Keith did kiss me, though."

"Oooooh," Darlene breathed, leaning forward to hear more. "How was it?"

"Nice."

"Just nice?"

"Keith is good-looking, and he has a cute accent, but he drinks too much, and he has a temper. I think he might well have had it in for Philip."

"So it's only Bradley for you."

I nodded. "Yes. Isn't he gorgeous?"

"He's choice, even with his eye all messed up."

"I don't think he notices me as a woman, though. All he sees is a kid."

"Come on; it's stuffy in here. Let's sit out on the fire escape for a few minutes," Darlene suggested.

We walked through Darlene's room, opened the window, and crawled out onto the iron fire escape. Darlene had placed a mat there that we could sit on. We'd come out a couple of times before.

Darlene looked at me in the light coming from the living room. "Now listen and remember what I said. Bradley doesn't impress me as being ready to settle down, and he knows you're the type of girl a guy doesn't play around with."

"You think so?"

"I do."

"Really?"

Darlene nodded her head. "Men like him eventually get tired of dating and decide to get married. When that day comes, you'll be right there, Bebe."

"Oh, I do hope so. I'm in deep where he's concerned. Thanks for the words of encouragement, Darlene."

At that moment, two male voices could be heard coming from the apartment above us. Apparently they had decided it was a nice evening too and had opened their window.

"Do you know them, Darlene?" I whispered.

"I saw a moving truck out front back in February," she whispered, "but I never saw who moved in."

Darlene and I eavesdropped shamelessly.

The first man said, "All I know is that the guy is not working for me like he should. I've had it with him."

The second voice said, "Do you want to rub him out?"

Darlene and I exchanged shocked glances.

The first male voice said, "I don't really want to—he's not a bad guy—but this is a business. He has to be eliminated."

The second male voice said, "Problem is, how are we gonna cover it up?"

The first male voice answered. "Simple. The girl. We'll use her."

I grabbed Darlene's arm and pulled her back into the apartment. She shut the window—quietly, so the men would not know they'd been overheard—and turned to me.

"Bebe, they're planning a murder!"

"Keep your voice down," I warned. "We don't know how thick these walls are. God! We have to do something, or else the man they were talking about is going to die."

Darlene put her hand on my arm. "They sounded like mobsters to me, Bebe. You don't want to mess with them."

"Darlene, are you suggesting we do *nothing*?"

"What are you recommending? Calling Detective Finelli?"

I thought for a moment. "Wouldn't that be a tea party. No, but there are other officers of the law in New York. We could call the police station anonymously and tell them what we heard."

"Okay, anonymously works for me, but we can't tell them we heard anything. If we do, the mobsters will figure out we were the ones who ratted them out."

"You're right. We'll just say that we have information that there's a murder being planned," I said. "Darlene, do you realize we're living in a building with cold-blooded killers?"

Darlene sneezed. "They won't bother us. After all, what have we done to them?"

"I hope they feel the same." I went into the kitchen. Next to our phone was a list of emergency numbers. I found the one for the police department and dialed it. Thinking back to TV shows, I decided I'd better be quick or they might trace the call. At the last minute, I grabbed the kitchen towel, folded it, and put it over the mouthpiece.

"Sergeant White speaking."

"There's a murder being planned in apartment four-B, 138–140 East Sixty-fifth Street. I can say no more." I hung up the phone, relieved, feeling I'd done what I could.

Darlene and I waited for the police to arrive. She said, "Did you know Joan Baez withheld sixty percent of her income tax from the IRS to protest military spending?"

"What does that have to do with anything?" I asked.

Darlene chewed her nail. "Nothing. Just trying to pass the time."

"Don't chew your nails, Darlene. You want them to look nice when you start flying again."

"*If* I start flying again."

I kept a lookout for the police. Then I saw a black-and-white pull slowly into a parking space across the street.

"They're here," I whispered to Darlene.

Darlene and I stared at each other, listening. Eventually we heard two sets of footsteps coming up the stairs, passing our floor and going up to the next.

After about ten minutes, we heard the same set of footsteps coming back down.

Curious, Darlene and I peeked out our door.

A stocky policeman said to his partner, "You get these types of calls all the time."

His partner said, "I never realized how many crackpots there are in New York."

"Probably a jealous girlfriend. Sarge said it was a dame who called."

Their voices faded away as they continued on down the steps.

Darlene closed and locked our door. "When that man

gets killed, I'm going to take great pleasure in telling Detective Finelli that we had warned the police and they had let the mobsters talk their way clean."

"I can't believe it! I thought we'd see two men in handcuffs being taken away by the police."

"I'll buy an extra bolt for our door Monday," Darlene offered.

"Okay," I said, and sighed. "Now if only I can get through this visit from my father. And keep the investigation going. That reminds me. I have a plan for tomorrow, once I can shake Daddy and find a costume shop."

Chapter Ten

My father and I stood in beautiful St. Patrick's Cathedral, the air heavy with the smell of incense and beeswax.

"The Mass has ended. Go in peace," the priest said in Latin. We really couldn't leave yet. There were still prayers to be said, responses to be made. I didn't mind because I loved going to Mass, although maybe not this early in the morning.

As the priest recited the first part of Saint John's gospel, I wondered how I could gracefully lose my father for the afternoon, so I could proceed with my plan. Surely nothing could keep him from the afternoon sports games on TV, nothing ever did on Sundays at home.

Everyone in church responded, "Thanks be to God." I tried to concentrate and prayed the Hail Mary and the Salve Regina, but the murder case made my attention wander again. Darn it. I supposed that Daddy and I would go out for breakfast after Mass. But heck, it was only nine o'clock in the morning. How long could that take? Then Darlene and I could be on our way. I needed to find out what floor of the Legends Hotel Daddy was staying on, so he wouldn't get mixed up in my plans.

At the end of the Prayer to Saint Michael, we were free to go. I stood up, smoothing the skirt of my toffee-colored suit. An ancient woman in a black dress and black lace headcovering in front of me turned around and stared at me.

"The young people of today," she began, shaking her rosary at me. "Just look at the length of that skirt. And in church, too," she said.

I blushed.

True, I had shortened all my skirts two inches to show off my legs for Bradley. So far Daddy hadn't noticed. Now this woman threatened to get me in trouble.

Daddy took a step away from me and leaned his head back so he could see what the old bat was talking about. His eyes narrowed, and his face turned that bad shade of purple. "Bebe, why is your skirt so short?"

"It may have happened at the cleaners, Daddy," I said. Which wasn't a lie. I said it *may* have happened, not that it did.

Daddy glanced at the old woman, arm in arm with a younger lady who appeared to be her daughter. "Well, it's too nice a suit to give to Goodwill, so don't worry about it. It's not like all your skirts are that short."

"Yes, Daddy," I said meekly, wondering if I had another skirt that wasn't this short now. Darlene had said that skirts even shorter than mine were becoming the fashion in London.

"Let's go get breakfast. They've included a breakfast buffet in my room rate at the hotel, so we'll go there."

I barely prevented myself from groaning out loud. I could only hope that none of the band were up at this hour. Pop stars slept late, right?

Wrong.

Daddy and I had just returned to our booth at the hotel restaurant, with plates of bacon, eggs, toast, and sausages, when Reggie and Peter entered the room.

I tried to be invisible, which meant that they saw me immediately and gave me a cheery wave. I waved back.

"Who are those two fairies?" Daddy asked, a forkful of eggs on its way to his mouth.

"Daddy! They are not fairies!"

"Two long-haired fairies, if you ask me."

"Just because they wear their hair long doesn't mean they're homosexual."

"Yes, it does. Couple of fruits. I was in the army; I know about these things."

I buttered my toast. "Well, you don't know in this case. Reggie, the one in the green shirt, is married and has a baby son."

Daddy wiped his mouth. "So? Lots of them queer guys get married and have kids. Don't mean they're not queer. Just means they've duped some poor woman into marrying them so they can have kids."

Mentally I counted to ten. "Listen to me, Daddy. They are in a pop band. You know, like the Beatles. They wear their hair long to achieve a certain look. A pop-star look. It doesn't mean anything else."

"Are you friends with them?" he asked, a warning tone coming into his voice. Translation: *If you are friends with them, I'm hauling you back to Richmond on the next train south.*

I swallowed some orange juice. "I know them."

Daddy leaned across the table toward me, waving a piece of toast. "These are just the sort of people your mother and I warned you about. Worldly people who use innocents to their own advantage and then, when they're done, toss them aside without a second thought. Your boss is one of them, too."

"Mr. Williams is not using me," I said firmly, and stabbed a sausage with more force than could strictly be considered necessary.

"That's because you've wisely kept him at arm's length. But I tell you I know his sort. Love 'em and leave 'em. Now, am I right or am I right?"

I could feel the bite of sausage go down and settle at the bottom of my stomach like a ball of lead. I reminded myself of what Darlene had said about Bradley waking up one day and finding himself ready to get married. I repeated the words to Daddy. "Mr. Williams just isn't ready to settle down yet, that's all."

"You keep that in mind. I don't want my Little Magnolia's reputation tarnished by that man. Oh, God, here come the fairies."

I looked up to see Reggie and Peter walking our way.

"Now, Daddy," I hissed. "Please be nice. These are my friends."

"So they *are* your friends. We'll talk about that later, young lady. They'd just better not try getting friendly with me," Daddy hissed back.

"Bebe," Reggie said. "Good morning."

"Hullo, Bebe," Peter said.

"Hi, guys," I said. "Let me introduce everyone. Daddy, this is Reggie, bass player for the Beefeaters, and this is Peter, the band's drummer. Guys, this is my father, Earl Bennett."

Reggie stuck out his hand.

Daddy looked appalled, then reluctantly took it and gave it a shake. I hoped Reggie didn't notice Daddy wiping his hand on his napkin afterward.

Peter, dressed in a shirt and tie with the usual line of tie tacks, was not to be outdone. He extended his right hand.

Daddy grimaced, then shook his hand as well, his gaze going to Peter's tie.

"I see you're admiring my tie, Mr. Bennett," Peter said, and smiled. Then the smile faded. "That is what you were doing, wasn't it? I mean, I haven't eaten anything yet, so I've not got anything on it." Peter's neurosis was in full gear.

Daddy was cornered. "I, um, *noticed* it."

Peter nodded. "It's like I told Bebe, you've got to have a gimmick. Ringo has the rings. I've got the tie tacks."

"Who are you, then?" Daddy said. "Tacky?"

"Daddy!"

Peter looked confused. His eye twitched. "No, I'm Peter."

Reggie shifted from one foot to the other. "Bebe, we didn't mean to interrupt your breakfast, but we were wondering if you could help us with something."

"Sure," I said.

"It's like this," Reggie began. "We came downstairs because the room-service menu said the Sunday breakfast buffet had everything you could want for breakfast. Yet where are the baked beans? Where are the mushrooms? Where are the tomatoes?"

"Yeah," Peter chimed in. "You'd find those in any regular English breakfast. What's wrong with this place?"

Daddy spoke before I could say a word. "You're in America now, boy. You've got everything on that buffet that any American would want for his breakfast—with perhaps the exception of some good hot grits, but what can you expect in a Yankee town? We don't cater to English folks here. Haven't since about 1776."

"Daddy!"

"What? I'm just telling the truth, is all. These boys can't expect to come here and have us drive on the wrong side of the road and serve our beer warm and replace our toilets with loos." He turned his attention back to Reggie and Peter. "Now both of y'all get back over there and load yourselves up with some good American food. Y'a'll both look like you can use feeding up. Skinny things."

I gave the guys a long-suffering expression.

They looked from me to Daddy. Clearly they recognized a stronger force.

Reggie put his hand on Daddy's shoulder. "We appreciate your explaining all that to us, Mr. Bennett."

Daddy froze. One eye turned toward the hand on his shoulder. "Did I mention I was a sergeant first class in the army during the war?"

Reggie removed his hand. "Excuse us; we'll just go fill our plates as you suggested."

Daddy nodded.

"I'll see you soon," I said to the guys.

"Oh, one more thing," Reggie said. "Bebe, do you know any groovy nightclubs around here? We're going out of our minds upstairs. There doesn't seem to be a club like our Josephine's in England."

"Have you been to the Peppermint Lounge?"

"No."

"It's on West Forty-fifth Street. Try it."

Peter smiled. "Thanks, Bebe. I don't know what we'd do without you."

Daddy grunted like a boar.

Once they had left, I quietly finished my breakfast and let Daddy eat his. It was best not to say anything that might get him started on my choice of friends. He seemed to have forgotten a lecture. And it was pointless to try to change his mind about Reggie and Peter.

Except there was that one bit of information I needed.

"So, Daddy, is your room comfortable?"

"Oh, sure. I can sleep anywhere after being in the army," he said, intent on his bacon.

"What floor are you on?" I asked casually.

"Fourteenth."

Whew. The guys were on the fifteenth. That was a near miss. "What are you going to do this afternoon? Did you want to go out and see the sights?" *Please say no.*

"What sights? There's nothing here that Richmond doesn't have, is there?"

Let's see, the Empire State Building, a matinee on Broadway, Lindy's cheesecake, just for starters. "Nothing you'd be interested in, I suppose."

"Actually I thought I'd catch the game on TV. I thought we could meet up again and have dinner. You pick the place."

"That sounds great," I said, genuinely happy. "I have some things I have to get done this afternoon. What time did you want to meet?"

"How about if I come to your place at six?"

"That's perfect, Daddy. I'd better go now. Thank you

for breakfast. It was delicious." I slid out from my place in the booth, and he immediately stood. I reached up and gave him a kiss on the cheek. "And it was very American."

I smiled at him, and he smiled back.

I bet he wouldn't have been quite so happy with me if he knew what I had planned for that afternoon.

Chapter Eleven

"This isn't right, is it?" I asked as Darlene came into my room. I was standing in front of the full-length mirror attached to the back of the open closet door.

Darlene tried hard not to laugh, I could tell, but a giggle slipped past her lips. Then another. Then a full-blown laugh. Then she was laughing uncontrollably and slapping her right thigh.

I turned to her, my voice rising. "Okay, these aren't regular maids' uniforms, are they?"

Darlene held her index fingers under her eyes to catch any wet mascara that might have gotten on her lower eyelids when she laughed herself silly. "No, Bebe. They're *French* maids' uniforms. Something completely different."

I looked back in the mirror. We were dressed in very short black cotton dresses with short sleeves. Thin white aprons tied around the waists, with matching white bibs. Black caps with white lace trim sat on our heads. Black stockings completed the sexy ensembles. They were not outfits for scrubbing bathtubs.

I sighed. "The man at the costume shop assured me they were the only maids' uniforms they had. What was I supposed to do?"

"Maybe try a uniform supply store. But don't worry, Bebe. These will do."

"Really?"

"Yes. Besides, time is a factor here. You said you wanted to search Philip's room today, right?"

"I do. Darlene, maybe we can find some sort of clue about who might have been in Philip's room the day he was murdered. I mean, we have the tie tack, so we know Peter was there. We have to follow up on that. But who else was there? And what about Philip? Is there something in his room that would tell us why he was killed?"

Darlene put her hands on my shoulders. "We can do this today, just like you planned. People will only think we're special maids, that's all. The Legends is a fancy hotel, after all."

"You're sure? I feel like such a dip."

"You're far from being a dip. Now, things will be quieter on a Sunday at the hotel. Let's go. But, uh, have you got a raincoat you can cover up with for the ride over to the hotel?"

When we put on our trench coats, I began to feel like a female James Bond. I had seen *From Russia with Love* last week and relished every minute of it. Sean Connery's voice made me melt.

At the Legends Hotel, Mr. Duncan was on duty at the elevators. "Good afternoon, Miss Bennett, Miss Roland," he said.

Well, we weren't really in disguise, I consoled myself at his instant recognition.

"How are you today, Mr. Duncan? Feeling better?" I asked. Was it my imagination or did he look at Darlene with disapproval?

"Yes, my cold is almost gone. Where are you two headed today?"

"The fifteenth floor, of course," Darlene replied.

Mr. Duncan didn't bother to hide his dismay. "Back to the scene of the crime. That won't do anybody any good."

"We'll see, won't we?" Darlene said.

Mr. Duncan shook his head.

"Don't worry, Mr. Duncan." I said. "We're going to get the matter all straightened out."

"I'm still gonna have to testify. Courts scare me," he said, looking pointedly at Darlene, "as they would anyone with any sense." Maybe it was her red hair. I don't know, but people tended to think of Darlene as a troublemaker. Kind of like a more troublesome Ann-Margret.

Fortunately, we arrived on the fifteenth floor at that moment. But I realized that we had no idea where the maids' closet was. And we needed to know so that we might appear official. We needed vacuums, dusters, cleaning products.

"Mr. Duncan, I wonder if you could help us out?"

Darlene shot me a look. I returned an expression that said, *Be patient!*

Mr. Duncan said, "Oh, no, I'm not getting involved with you two again." But he pressed his finger on the "door open" button and held it there.

I touched the sleeve of his brown uniform. "Really, all I need to know is where the maids' closet is."

"The maids' closet?"

"Yes, that's right. I, er, wanted to know what brand of air freshener the hotel uses. The rooms smell so fresh." I smiled. And prayed Mr. Duncan wouldn't wonder how I could think a room with a dead body in it—the only room I'd been in at the hotel—smelled fresh.

"Okay, I don't want to know any more," Mr. Duncan said. "You go down the corridor to the left. It's near the ice machine between rooms 1548 and 1550."

"Thank you!" I gave Mr. Duncan a little wave, and Darlene and I exited the elevator.

He gave to me what passed as a smile. At least I was still in his good graces. And I had the information I needed.

We walked down the hall, hearing the little *ding* of the elevator behind us as Mr. Duncan took the car back downstairs.

"Whew, Bebe, I don't know how you manage to sweet-talk your way into getting information, but you did a good job with Mr. Duncan."

"I just asked him, that's all. You're the sweet-talker."

"We're both sweet-talkers," Darlene said, and we laughed. "Mr. Duncan just doesn't like me."

"That's because for some reason he blames you for his having to go to court," I said.

"I guess. It's hot up here," Darlene said, as we walked down the hall. "Let's take our coats off. Where the heck is room 1548?"

I looked on the wall for signs, then heard the last voice in the world I wanted to hear.

"Confounded ice machines. Don't any of them work?"

"Daddy!" I stage-whispered to Darlene.

The ice machine on his floor below us must not be working. We looked up and saw the ice machines directly in front of us. At any second he would turn and see me dressed like this!

Darlene and I looked at each other in horror.

Darlene sneezed.

I grabbed her by the arm and propelled us into a room whose door was ajar. We stumbled inside.

A man sat in a wing chair in a very luxurious suite, a glass of wine on the table next to him. He was reading the *New York Times*. He had removed his suit jacket, leaving him in dark trousers and a crisp white shirt.

With a delighted shock I realized I was looking at Bobby Darin, one of my favorite singers! His song "Dream Lover" had played in my head constantly when it had first come out.

At my side, Darlene stood stock still, her mouth hanging open.

Mr. Darin turned a corner of the newspaper down at our appearance and raised one eyebrow, maybe at our sexy maids' uniforms. He was so handsome! "There's no need to clean up, girls. Someone's already done the room."

I could only stare.

Darlene found her voice. "We're terribly sorry to disturb you, Mr. Darin. The door was ajar, and we just didn't know whether the room had been cleaned."

He smiled. "That's okay. I left the door open because I'm expecting Sandra back any minute. She always forgets her key."

Sandra! He meant Sandra Dee, his beautiful wife.

Darlene put her hand at my waist, tugging a little, indicating we should leave now.

I turned to go, but suddenly looked at Mr. Darin and blurted out, "I love your singing. And you were wonderful in CAPTAIN NEWMAN, M.D.!"

"Thank you," he said with another smile. "I'm a very lucky man. And I'll be sure to stay here at the Legends next time I'm in New York. They have the loveliest maids."

"Thank you," I said, sure I was blushing.

Darlene and I walked out of the room backward and closed the door quietly behind us.

As one, we turned and shook each other by the shoulder, then started giggling like a couple of schoolgirls.

In unison, we said, "He's so dreamy!"

I laughed and poked Darlene's arm. "Jinx, you owe me a Coke!"

Darlene laughed too. "You've got it. Bobby Darin, Bebe! Not ten feet away from us!"

"I can't believe I just met Bobby Darin!" I said. "And that I forgot to get his autograph."

Darlene chuckled. "What were we going to do, get him to sign our aprons? Hmmm, now that I think of it . . ."

"Darlene, don't you dare! He's a married man. I wonder what he's doing in New York. I thought he liked Las Vegas."

"He plays at the Copacabana sometimes," Darlene said.

"Too bad we don't have dates to take us there," I bemoaned. Then, "At least we got to meet him, talk with him, and find out he's just as nice in person as anyone could want him to be. I'll never forget it!"

"Neither will I. But we'd better pull ourselves together and get back to what we were doing."

I took a fast look down the hall, but there was no sign of Daddy. "I think Daddy's gone. Let's go find the maids' closet."

I couldn't help but do a little dance. "Darlene, we just met Bobby Darin! We just met Bobby Darin!"

"I know. I wonder what he's like in—"

"Sshhh! You know he's married. You mustn't think like that!"

"What about you, Miss Pious? Hmmm? Does the name John Lennon ring a bell? He's married too, you know."

I punched her in the arm. "Point taken, but I'm not changing my feelings for John. Oh, look, there's the maids' closet, right where Mr. Duncan said it would be." The closet was not locked. I pulled out a cart with soaps, shower caps, towels, toilet paper, and cleaning products. Darlene got out the vacuum.

We rolled the cart down the hall toward Philip's room. My mind was still on Bobby Darin. I started to sing "Dream Lover."

"Bebe! Bebe! We're here at Philip's room."

"Oh, good."

"Bebe, snap out of it! We've got a locked door here and not much time before we call attention to ourselves. Come on!"

"Don't look at me. What are you waiting for? Isn't that the master key hanging off the cart?"

Darlene made a dive for it. "If you aren't the limit, Bebe Bennett."

Darlene turned the key in the lock.

The door of the dead man's room swung open.

Chapter Twelve

We entered the room with the cart and closed the door behind us. All was eerily still inside. Dust motes hung suspended in a slim line of sunshine beaming in from a crack in the curtains. Otherwise the room was dim. There had been no crime-scene tape outside the door. Maybe the hotel wasn't renting it out until the police finished their investigation.

"Can we turn on the lights?" I asked.

Darlene reached for the wall switch. "We'll have to if we want to see what we're doing," she said. It looks like the room has been cleaned since the police were in here. The bed's been made, the beer cans and pizza boxes are gone, and there's no fingerprint dust anywhere."

"Thank goodness for that. We'd have a hard time explaining ourselves if the place were still supposed to be untouched." Luckily, no one has cleared Philips things out of here.

"No one is going to bother us. Come on; let's get to work. It's a big room. I'll take the closet. You start with the bedside table."

I sat down on the edge of the bed. The bedside table was littered with guitar picks and a guide to New York City. I shook out the guide to make sure there was nothing in it. Then I opened the drawer to the table. Several red square foil packets met my gaze. I picked one up and examined it. In tiny print I read the word *prophylactic*.

I dropped the packet like a hotcake. So that's what they looked like! Hard on the heels of this realization came the vision of Bradley standing in front of me holding one in his hand, a smile on his handsome face. *Oh!*

My face got hotter, but my lips curved into a devilish smile.

Then, as if to remind me of my upbringing, there was a Gideon's Bible right next to the little square packets! I took a quick look through the rest of the drawer, which mercifully held only some earplugs and tissues. I slammed the drawer shut and fanned myself with a little complimentary hotel guest pad that was lying next to the telephone.

"Find anything?" Darlene called from the closet.

"No!" I responded.

"I'm going through Philip's pockets. Why don't you try the desk?"

I took a deep breath. "Okay."

Starting with the smaller drawers on the side, I went through the desk. Empty. The larger center drawer was a different story, though. I was running my fingers through a generous supply of hotel stationery I'd lifted out of a box, enjoying the feel of the fresh paper. In the middle of it, my hands stopped over the smooth surface of a black-and-white photograph. I took it out and saw a picture of Reggie with a young girl in a school uniform sitting on his lap. He was smiling at her. Another photo revealed her again sitting in his lap, but this time with her arms around his neck and him laughing.

And then on the hotel's stationery there was a letter scrawled in nearly illegible handwriting. Actually, there were a couple of different drafts of the letter. I picked one up and began to read:

> Dear Jean,
> I know we're not the best of friends, but I still think you've a right to know what's going on while we're on the road. If you'll look at these

photos, you'll see that Reg is not the adoring, faithful husband he wants you to think he is. Sorry about that.

Philip

What a horrible letter! I looked again at the pictures. Surely Reggie would have an explanation for this. Him cuddling with schoolgirls didn't match up with the man I'd met, the one who was so anxious to call his wife, or the proud father holding out pictures of his son.

But that didn't take away from the fact that Philip was trying to torpedo his bandmate's marriage. "Darlene!"

She joined me, wiping her hands on the front of her apron. "What?"

"I think I found something."

Darlene looked over the photos and the letter and raised her eyebrows. "What a terrible thing for Philip to do. I wonder if it was the first time he'd tried to come between Reggie and his wife."

"Probably not," I said. "But if you're thinking that Reggie killed Philip, you're wrong. He's a nice family guy."

Darlene looked at me. "Look, Bebe, some of the prettiest plants are the poisonous ones. We can't rule anyone out, including Reggie."

"I suppose."

"Anyone is capable of murder if they're pushed hard enough. If Reggie thought his family was threatened, we don't know what he might have done."

"You're right. I guess I just don't want to look at Reggie that way. But I will, since—"

The sound of male voices outside the room interrupted me.

Darlene heard them too. "Quick, Bebe, hide the photos and the letter on the maid's cart."

I buried the evidence among the clean towels.

We heard the key turn in the lock.

Darlene threw the covers back on the bed, then pretended to be tidying them.

I got out the Windex and sprayed a big blue splash on the mirror above the desk.

Two uniformed New York Police Department officers entered the room, clearly startled to see us.

I thought for sure we would be thrown out, maybe even taken in for questioning. It would be bad for Darlene, who was already a suspect. My heart rate increased, and my chest tightened painfully.

"Good afternoon, Officers," Darlene said in her Texas drawl. "How are y'all doing today?" She patted the bed.

The taller of the two policemen grinned. Lean and lanky, with sandy-colored hair, he was clearly halfway in love with Darlene already. His partner, a balding, stocky fellow with a paunch, looked leery as he stood with one hand hovering above his nightstick.

Balding spoke first. "What are you two doing in here? The room was already cleaned."

"We're just doing our job, cleaning all the rooms on this floor," Darlene said with another killer smile.

"Yes," I chimed in. "We just finished 1556 and came down here because the room was unoccupied." Best to let him think we knew nothing about any murder. "Is there a problem?"

Sandy Hair spoke next. "Didn't you girls know a guy was murdered in here?"

Darlene allowed her glossy lips to part in an astonished O.

I dropped the Windex on the desk. "Lord have mercy! And I haven't even vacuumed yet." With that statement, I went to the vacuum cleaner and began unwinding the electric cord from its holder. "What happened? Was he shot? I don't see any blood on the carpet. I hope I don't have to clean up any blood."

Balding stared at me. "He was electrocuted in the bathtub."

Darlene and I both moaned dramatically.

"That's awful," I said. "I guess you got the person who did it."

"Not yet, but some dame is the most likely suspect," Balding replied.

Darlene sneezed.

I plugged the vacuum into the electrical outlet. "May we finish up here, Officers? We'll be out of your way in just a few minutes, believe me. We don't want to get in any trouble with the head of housekeeping. And being in here now that I know someone was killed . . ." I gave what I hoped was a convincing shudder.

Balding eyed me unfavorably. "I guess it's all right if you hurry. We have work to do in here."

"Okay by me," Darlene said.

I nodded, then turned on the vacuum and began running it around the gold carpet.

Balding went to stand outside the room, but Sandy Hair stayed and watched as Darlene dusted. With each swish of the feather duster, her bottom twitched, completely holding the young officer's attention. He didn't pay the slightest attention when a *ching* sounded in the vacuum cleaner. Darlene heard it, though, and gave me a look. I kept on vacuuming as if nothing had happened. She dusted harder.

Soon we were finished. I rewound the vacuum cleaner cord, and Darlene put the feather duster on the maids' cart. With another big smile for Sandy Hair, who looked decidedly dejected at her departure, Darlene drove the cart out the door I held open for her.

We wasted no time returning to the maids' closet, passing only a family with a squirming toddler in the hall. Once in the closet, I slammed the door behind us.

"That was close. Did you hear that sound?" I whispered, reaching down to the vacuum bag compartment.

"Yes. Let's see what we have."

I retrieved the bag and opened it, letting loose a faint cloud of dust. "Thank God those policemen let us off so easily."

"I think it was the short skirts," Darlene said, and sneezed because of the dirt exposed in the bag.

I split the bag down the center and pawed through the gray dirt.

Darlene sneezed again.

Then my hand felt something slick and metal. I pulled it out. "Here, I've found it."

Sneeze. Sneeze. "What is it?"

I wiped away the dirt from the object and recognized it at once.

It was a triangle-shaped dangly gold earring.

Exactly like one of the ones Astrid had been wearing in those naughty photos.

This proved Astrid had been in Philip's room sometime on the day of his death. Had she been the one to put the fatal amplifier plug into the socket and end the pop star's life?

Chapter Thirteen

"Now we can place Astrid at the scene of the crime," I said, turning pancakes in a skillet. It was early Monday morning, and Darlene and I were in our minuscule kitchen. I was clad in my pink chenille robe. Darlene sat at the small green-and-white-speckled Formica table, wearing her purple lounging pajamas and painting her fingernails with Cutex's new spring color, Hot Pink.

I had survived dinner with Daddy the night before and managed to dodge all directives about staying out of police investigations. By now Daddy would be on the train back to Richmond, content in believing his daughter innocent of meddling in police business.

Darlene yawned, then used the long, white-ridged applicator brush to polish her left pinkie. "From what you've told me about Astrid, I think she's our prime suspect. Say, do you want to use this nail polish?"

"No, thanks. It's a little bright for me. You're just saying that about Astrid because I told you she came on to Bradley."

"No, really. She's Philip's ex, and an ex-girlfriend always has a motive. And you know what they say on *Dragnet* about motive, opportunity, and means adding up to the killer. Seems to me like Astrid fits all three."

I put a plate of pancakes on the table, along with a bottle of Vermont Maid maple syrup. The farm maid smiled at us from the label. "If Astrid is guilty, she put on quite a performance when she appeared at Philip's tribute. She's one cold woman."

Darlene pointed a newly varnished nail at me. "And that's exactly the type who could walk casually into Philip's bathroom, see an opportunity to get rid of him for good, and seize the moment."

We both looked down at Astrid's gold triangle earring lying on the table between us.

I said, "We need to take this to the police and tell them where we found it."

Darlene checked her nails, put the polish aside, and then carefully pulled a stack of pancakes in front of her. "And as quickly as possible. I can't put the airline off much longer. I've coughed my way into a couple of days off, but it won't be long before they get suspicious. Besides, I'll go stir-crazy being on the ground and sitting in this apartment. I have to clear my name. What do you say I go to the police today while you're at work? Or could you meet me there on your lunch hour?"

I poured syrup generously over my pancakes and then reached for some coffee. "I could meet you. I'd like to be there—"

The sound of the buzzer from downstairs startled us both.

"Who could that be at this hour?" I asked.

Darlene stood up, holding her hands out so her nails wouldn't rub up against anything and smudge. "I'll go find out."

She went to the intercom next to the front door with me following behind her. "Who is it?" she asked, pressing the button.

"Detective Finelli for Miss Roland," his authoritative voice sounded over the speaker.

Darlene and I exchanged dismayed glances.

Into the intercom, Darlene said, "Come on up. Third floor, apartment B."

When she made sure the button was off, Darlene

turned to me. "What can he want? We're the ones who want to show him Astrid's earring."

"I don't know, but I don't like this. I've never even had a policeman come to my door, let alone a detective. And I'm in my robe!"

There was a knock on the door.

"Don't worry about it. He's the one who's coming over at such an early hour," Darlene whispered, walking over to the door.

"Good morning, Detective," Darlene said, letting Detective Finelli in. "Would you like some coffee? Or do you think I might poison it?"

So much for the good-Southern-girl approach. Manners never fail to disarm, Mama had taught me. Darlene had never spoken about her mother to me.

The detective held his hat in his hand and ran his other hand over his crew cut. He nodded to me. "Miss Bennett, Miss Roland. I'll pass on the coffee. I'm here on official business."

"Won't you sit down?" I said, indicating the pink sectional.

We all took seats, Darlene and I sitting next to each other, not exactly huddled together for comfort but close to it. Detective Finelli got out his pocket notebook, leaned forward on his left leg, and looked Darlene straight in the eye. "Miss Roland, do you know Astrid Loveday?"

Darlene swung an arm out over the back of the sofa. "No, I can't say that I do."

Finelli's gaze did not waver. "Think before you answer. Are you sure you do not know Astrid Loveday?"

Darlene reached up and patted a red curl. "I meet a lot of people in my job as a stewardess. It's possible I could have served her on a flight and not known it was her, but I'm certain we've never been formally introduced."

Detective Finelli made notes. "Do you know who she is?"

Darlene looked at her nails. On the index finger of her right hand the polish had smudged. She tried to pat it into place. "Since the death of Philip Royal, I've heard that she used to be his girlfriend."

"You didn't know that fact *prior* to Philip Royal's death?"

Darlene looked up. "No. Why?"

"I'll ask the questions, Miss Roland. Now once again, did you know that Astrid Loveday was Philip Royal's girlfriend prior to his death?"

"No."

I watched the interplay between the detective and Darlene with growing concern. Was this the time to bring out Astrid's earring? Somehow I didn't think so. Where was he trying to lead Darlene? Because it sure seemed he was trying to get her to say something. Was it some sort of trap?

Detective Finelli's next words confirmed my worst suspicions. He turned to another page in his notebook, glanced over the words on the page, then fixed Darlene with a steely gaze. "Miss Roland, I have a statement here from Astrid Loveday. She says that before his death, Philip Royal told her he was seeing a red-haired American stewardess."

Darlene leaned forward on the sofa. "What? That couldn't have been me, if that's what you're thinking. I just met Philip on the flight over from London."

"Are you absolutely sure about that, Miss Roland? Think before you answer."

"I don't have to think," Darlene said, offended. "Of course I'm sure. It must have been some other stewardess he was seeing. We do get around, you know."

"I don't think so. Miss Loveday says that Philip Royal had been dating this red-haired"—here he looked pointedly at Darlene's flaming locks—"American stewardess and was going to break off the relationship upon his arrival in America. Didn't you tell me Philip Royal stood you up for your date?"

"That's because he was dead!" Darlene protested.

"Would you have been angry if he broke off the relationship, Miss Roland?"

"There was no relationship."

"You were dating."

"We'd known each other less than twenty-four hours."

"A lot can occur in that amount of time, especially between a stewardess and a pop star."

Darlene folded her arms across her chest and glared at the detective.

"And it would have hurt if Philip Royal abruptly stopped seeing you for another woman, maybe broke some promises, wouldn't it, Miss Roland? It would have hurt, and you would have been angry."

"No," Darlene said, but was ignored.

"How angry would you have been? Angry enough to kill Philip Royal in a fit of jealousy when he told you that he wasn't going to go through with your date that night at the Legends Hotel?"

Darlene jumped to her feet. "That's not true. He was dead, I tell you."

Detective Finelli rose slowly to his feet and took a step toward Darlene. "How did it happen, Miss Roland? Did you come up to his room and find him playing his guitar in the bath? Did he tell you then that there was someone else? That he was going back to his girlfriend? Did you see the plug for the guitar lying on the floor? Imagine in a flash that if you just plugged the amp in, life would be over for Philip Royal? That he couldn't waltz away with another woman?"

"Stop it! Stop it right now!" Darlene shouted.

I stood next to her, holding her by the arm, and said, "That's enough, Detective Finelli. You don't have any right to come here and make all these wild accusations against Darlene based on some floozy's statements."

Detective Finelli's sharp gaze pinned me. "So you know Astrid Loveday?"

Happy to take the heat off Darlene, I said, "I met her

at Rip-City's tribute to Philip Royal. The one where the media met the band members. Miss Loveday was present." No need to tell him about the confrontation Bradley had with Astrid at the Legends Hotel lounge over those tabloid reports.

Detective Finelli closed his notebook and put it in his inside coat pocket. He looked at Darlene again. "Are you sure you want to stand by your statement, Miss Roland? I can check with the airline and see how many times you've flown in and out of London in, say, the past six months."

Darlene's chin came up. "Go ahead. It doesn't matter how often I've been in London. I'm telling you I just met Philip on this flight over. We got together on the plane, we had one date—if you could call it that—once we landed, and then we were supposed to go out that night—the night he was murdered, by someone *other* than me. That's the truth, and I won't lie, no matter how much easier it would make your job."

He shrugged and put on his hat. "I'm just trying to get to the truth. I'll be going now, but you can be sure I'll want to talk with you again, Miss Roland."

We all walked to the door. Darlene slammed it after the detective walked out. "Can you believe that witch Astrid? Lying like that."

"Darlene, don't you see what this means?" I said.

"What?" she huffed.

"It means that Astrid must be feeling the heat of the investigation. That's why she deliberately made up a story to turn the focus back to you. There's no other explanation for what she did. Astrid must be guilty."

"You know what else this means?" Darlene said, her cheeks flushed with anger.

"What?"

"It means we can't turn that earring over to the police now."

"Why not?"

"Because it will look like we planted it in Philip's room

to get me off the hook. In the end, I'll look even more guilty. No, we have to keep that piece of evidence to ourselves. We have to continue investigating until we can find out who the murderer—or murderess—is ourselves and we have proof. Then we go to the police."

Darlene's blue eyes sparked fire, but I could see that her chin trembled.

"Darlene, are you okay?"

She stood up straighter. "I'm a Texas girl. I've shot rattlesnakes before. Detective Finelli just shook his rattle at me, and now I mean to take aim."

"What are you going to do?"

Darlene took a deep breath. "I'm not sure," she admitted. "I think I'll call Stu and see if he'll take me to lunch today. Maybe he'll have an idea. We need to find out more about Astrid. Stu knows people in London. Let's see what he can come up with."

"That sounds good. I have to get ready for work. Do you mind cleaning up the kitchen?"

"No, honey, you go ahead. Make yourself pretty for Bradley. Wear that royal-blue suit of yours. Men love royal blue."

I took Darlene's advice and laid out the royal-blue suit on my bed, then went to my records and pulled out *Meet the Beatles*. I spared a fond glance for the guys in their turtlenecks before carefully letting the vinyl album slide into my hands, gently holding the record by its edges. I put the black LP on the turntable and found the groove for "It Won't Be Long," one of my favorite John Lennon vocals. I hummed along as I put on the royal-blue suit, matching heels, and white gloves. Soon I reluctantly told John and the boys good-bye—carefully replacing the album in its sleeve before I headed for the office.

Once I reached the tall building in Midtown that served as headquarters for Rip-City Records, I headed to the heart of the office: the coffeepot. Noticing it was already empty, I started a fresh pot and went to check on Bradley. He was in his office, sitting behind his golden oak desk, and, bless him, his eye looked just as bad. Still he took my breath away in a gorgeous dark suit, white shirt, and blue-and-gold tie.

"Good morning, Mr. Williams," I said, trying hard not to drool. "How is your eye today?"

He looked up, giving me a blast of his incredible blue eyes. "Good morning, Miss Bennett. Thanks for asking about the eye. Your steak helped a lot. The eye probably looks worse than it feels. Didn't slow me down at all Saturday night after I dropped you off," he said, and winked at me with his good eye. "Which reminds me. See that this bottle of perfume is sent to the address on the attached card."

A bottle of Chanel No. 5! If Bradley were to get *me* any sort of scent, it would probably be Budding Beauty Little Girl Toiletries by Tussy. I fumed.

He was looking at me looking at him. "Er, is there coffee, Miss Bennett?"

I tossed my dark hair. "I just made a fresh pot. Let me get you some." I took his cup, a Saint Louis Cardinals mug—doing my best to ignore the remark about his evening and the ensuing bottle of perfume, darn him!—and filled it with the steaming beverage. The crease between Bradley's eyes did look very pronounced this morning. I pushed aside the possibility that the crease was caused by his having frolicked with females. Something was bothering him.

"Here you are, Mr. Williams. What else can I do for you this morning?"

"Thank you, Miss Bennett. That will be all for now. Just take care of the usual filing. I'll have some letters to dictate in a little while."

I hesitated. "I don't mean to pry, but you seem preoccupied for so early on a Monday morning. Is there anything I can do to help?"

"That's a pretty suit you're wearing," he said.

I felt a warmth go through me at his words. Nevertheless, I trained my gaze on him, willing him to take me seriously.

He looked at me, then sat back in his chair, a pencil balanced between his two index fingers the way he always did when he was thoughtful. "All right, Miss Bennett, I don't see why you shouldn't be among the first to know, although it won't be official until later today."

I sat down on the chair opposite him, waiting expectantly.

"You see, kid, Rip-City has decided not to release Philip Royal and the Beefeaters' album after all."

Chapter Fourteen

I felt a sick sensation in my stomach for the guys in the band. All they had worked for! "Not release the album? But the guys—when was this decided?"

Bradley held my gaze. "Early this morning at a breakfast meeting. I trust you to keep the news to yourself for now."

"Of course. But why has the label decided not to release the album? The record is finished and ready to go."

The sunshine in the room hit Bradley's golden hair, making it shimmer. "Go where, kid? The band has no lead singer. There's no way to send the guys out on the road for concerts to promote the album, no way to get television gigs lined up. Think of it. Are we supposed to put just Reggie, Keith, and Peter on *The Ed Sullivan Show*? Who's going to sing the songs?"

"I see what you mean, but does the band have to go out and perform in public? Can't you just release the album and get the songs played on WABC and other radio stations across the country to boost album sales?"

Bradley leaned forward and put the pencil down on his desk. "It's critical that the girls—and they're the bulk of the paying audience—*see* the guys behind the songs. You know that, Miss Bennett. They want singers they can idolize, ones they can dream of meeting and marrying. Without Philip, it's best to cut our losses now by not pressing and releasing the album."

I thought of my own feelings about John Lennon and the rest of the Beatles and felt a blush rise to my cheeks. Bradley was right. But the band! What would happen to Reggie, Keith, and Peter? They would be crushed. Everything they had worked so hard for would go down the drain. "When are the guys in the band going to find out, and who's going to tell them?"

"I'll be calling a meeting with their manager, Nigel, for tomorrow morning at eleven. That's the first opportunity I have, my schedule is so tight. I'll explain matters to him, and it'll be up to him to tell the band." He regarded me closely. "Look, Miss Bennett, I don't want to have to be the messenger bearing the bad news, but it's part of my job."

"I know that. It's just that I keep thinking about the guys. All their hopes and dreams will be dashed. They'll have to deal with that along with their grief over Philip's death."

"I know, kid, but what can I do? The word came from Mr. Purvis. This is a business, and the big guys want a profit."

An idea came to me. "What about your great-uncle? Could you go to him?"

"Only if I can come up with a viable plan to save the album, and I don't have that right now. You see, I agree that it's not in Rip-City's best interests for the album to be released. It's not that I don't understand the band's position, but I'm a businessman too. Uncle Herman is as big a shark as the rest of them. What could I say to him? He always looks at the bottom line."

"I guess things are pretty bleak."

"Not really. Try to remember this: A British record label is bound to pick the album up. The boys already have a name over there. The album will be released to the British public. All is not lost."

"I suppose you're right, although the guys wanted to make it in America."

"That's just not going to happen."

"I guess they'll want to go back to England now." I thought Reggie wouldn't be sorry to return home to his wife and baby son.

"I don't think they'll be allowed to go until the murder investigation is cleared up," Bradley pointed out. "Now, you'd better get Nigel on the phone for me, please."

He was right. I went back to my desk feeling down in the dumps. If only there were something I could do. I flipped through my Rolodex and found Nigel's number. The thought came to me that it might be a good idea to talk to him about the murder before he got the news about the album not being released. Afterward, he might not be so willing to talk to someone from the record label.

He answered the phone sounding like I'd woken him. "Hullo."

"Hello, Nigel, this is Bebe Bennett from Rip-City Records. How are you this morning?"

"Too early to tell, luv."

I forced a chuckle. However he felt was bound to be better right now than he'd feel at this time tomorrow. "Mr. Williams would like to set up a meeting with you for tomorrow at eleven. Would that be a good time for you?"

"Sure. I'd be glad to meet with 'im. There're some things I think the label could be doing for the boys that I 'aven't seen 'appen yet. We need to 'ash things out."

I barely suppressed a groan. "Very good. We'll expect you at eleven. Oh, and Nigel, I wonder if I might speak with you privately about Philip. I, um, want to get some information together for a bio for him. Can you meet me for coffee after work today?" I crossed my fingers at the lie. I wondered how many Hail Marys the priest would assign me at confession this week.

"Right. Where do you want to meet?"

"I could come to the hotel coffee shop, say around five thirty?"

" 'Ow about the lounge, luv? A fella's got to have something to wet 'is lips around that time o' day."

"All right. The lounge it is. See you then."

I hung up the phone to find Vince Walsh standing over my desk, having listened to every word I said. The shoulders of his dark suit were peppered with white flakes of dandruff, and he smelled of that darned cologne. "Good morning, Mr. Walsh."

"Hello, babycakes. Here's a report for Bradley."

"Thank you. I'll see that he gets it."

Vince lingered like a bad cough. "So tomorrow is when ol' Nigel's gonna get the big news, eh?"

"I don't know what you mean," I said stiffly, remembering my promise to Bradley to keep quiet about the album not being released.

"Play it your way, muffin-cup, but America won't be playing it at all. The album, that is. I'll have to be sure to hang around so I can see Nigel's red face when he comes out of Bradley's office. What time's the meeting?"

"I'm not allowed to give out information about my boss's schedule." I turned to my typewriter and inserted a sheet of paper. I didn't have anything to type at the moment, but if I had to, I'd make something up.

He laughed. "Never mind. I heard you say eleven." He leaned closer to me, forcing the smell of his cheap cologne into my nostrils. "Say, how about you and me go out sometime? I'll take you to the pictures and afterward to the Automat. Whaddya say? This Friday night sound good? Or would you rather catch an act with me?"

"I'm sorry, Mr. Walsh, but I make it a rule never to date anyone I work with," I said. It was true, Bradley and I had never been out on a date. Except in my dreams. Still, confession this week was going to be grisly.

"I think you can make an exception for me," he said, and leaned over the typewriter so close to me that I felt a wave of nausea from the cologne.

Bradley came out of his office as I was stumbling for a reply. "Miss Bennett, I'm ready for that dictation now."

"Yes, Mr. Williams," I said, grabbing my steno pad, tripping over my chair, and putting as much distance as I could between myself and Vince Walsh.

"Hey, Bradley, why don't you tell your secretary to come with me to the Bitter End this Saturday night to hear that guy you're so jazzed about," Vince said.

I looked at Bradley, sure he would decline Vince's offer.

But instead the beautiful traitor looked from me to Vince and said, "That might not be such a bad idea, since I can't be there myself. I have other plans, and I'd value two opinions. You don't mind, do you, Miss Bennett?"

"Oh, no, I'm keen on the idea," I said, my voice dripping sweet sarcasm, my hands folded across my chest, my gaze on Bradley.

Vince grinned in triumph. "I'll pick you up at eight."

"Since this is business, Vince, not a date, I'll meet you at the Bitter End at eight," I corrected. "Now if you'll excuse me, I have to take dictation for Mr. Williams."

"I'll catch you later, kitten," Vince promised. Then he turned to Bradley. "Hey, Bradley, that's some shiner you've got there. A jealous husband? We know how good you are with the ladies."

"You've got it all wrong, Vince."

"Do I? Not over a chick, huh?"

Bradley's expression reflected a warning.

Vince beat a hasty retreat.

Bradley shut the door. "I hope you don't have to break a date for Saturday night to go with Vince. No, wait, I don't mean to pry into your personal life."

Pry all you want! "That's all right. I'll handle Vince Walsh. You know, I think Mr. Walsh is jealous of you, Mr. Williams, and that he speaks out of turn. He certainly seems to relish what he thinks is a failure for you. Maybe he wants to move up into your job."

Bradley shuffled papers on his desk. "Yes, he's made no secret of the fact that he wants my job. Maybe he's fool enough to think this mess with Philip Royal is his chance to get it. I'm a patient man, but even I have my limits. If Vince doesn't start bringing in talent for Rip-City soon, he'll be out on the street."

"Good— Um, I mean, that makes sense. You've done absolutely nothing wrong in the situation with the Beefeaters." I found I was gripping my steno pad so hard the metal rings were digging into my skin, leaving marks.

"I'm glad to have such a champion on my side, Miss Bennett." Bradley's eyes twinkled. "I'm pleased you made it clear to Vince that your going with him to the Bitter End is not a date," he said in an overly professional tone. "We can't have office romances, now, can we?"

I barely refrained from throwing the steno pad at his head. "You said you had some dictation for me, Mr. Williams. If so, I'd like to take it now. Otherwise I have things to do."

I crossed my legs and made sure my skirt hiked up several inches above my knee. He deserved it.

Chapter Fifteen

I called Darlene from the shiny telephone box down in
the lobby of the Legends Hotel. I wanted to tell her I
wouldn't be home after work. I also wanted to find out
what happened during her lunch with Stu. She answered
on the second ring.

"Hi, Bebe, lunch with Stu was a blast. He took me
uptown to a great little place called EE's. They had a
wild beef roast in mushroom sauce."

"What about Astrid?"

"Stu thinks he can find out about Astrid in London."

"He has contacts?"

"Yes, but the darling is going to fly over there himself
and prowl around. Isn't he wonderful? I told him not to
flirt with any of the stewardesses, but I might have saved
my breath. My minty breath, get it?"

I smiled at her reference to Stu's being the Minty-
Mouth Breath Mints heir. Stu might flirt, but he'd come
back to Darlene.

"Listen, Darlene, I called to tell you that I'm having
drinks with the band's manager after work. I won't be
home."

"Great! Why don't you arrange for us all to go out
later? I know a fabulous club called Rocket-a-Go-Go.
All space stuff. I need to see the guys in the band and
dig up some dirt. How about it, Bebe?"

"Okay, I'll see what I can do. They'll probably be glad of a chance to get out and have some fun."

"You'll need to come home and change. I have an outfit you can't believe that I think would fit you. Very boss."

"Me wear one of your outfits? This I've got to see to believe. I'll call you after I meet with Nigel."

I hung up the phone and made my way to the lounge.

Maria was waiting on Nigel, who was seated at the bar. Nigel wore tweed pants with a red-and-blue wide-striped shirt. His nose was the perpetual red, full of the broken capillaries common to heavy drinkers. Sure enough, from the look of disapproval on Maria's dark features, I could tell Nigel had already consumed a couple of beers before my arrival.

" 'Ere you are, luv. I remember you now from dear Philip's tribute. A right 'elp you were with the press, especially that terror, Patty Gentry. That bird's always out to get something dirty on me boys. Wants to make a name for 'erself."

I settled myself awkwardly onto the adjacent bar stool, bar stools not being my favorite chairs. Taking off my gloves, I asked Maria to bring me a Virgin Mary. I remembered Patty Gentry paying more attention to Bradley than the guys in the band. "I didn't do that much, Nigel, but I'm glad to help in any way I can. I'm fond of the guys."

He grinned and lifted his beer. "That's part of their charm. People are drawn to 'em. It's what'll make 'em famous."

Maria brought my drink, which Nigel eyed without comment, and I began my questions. "So, Nigel, how are you doing, you know, since Philip's . . . death?"

He raised bushy eyebrows. "You mean since some common American criminal callously did my boy in?"

I perked up. "How do you know an American killed him?"

"Wouldn't bloody likely be an English gent. No proper Englishman would do such a thing."

"Oh."

He pounded his fist on his chest. "My boys were loved and admired by everyone in England. Then we come over 'ere to the colonies and before you can say 'Bob's your uncle,' my boy is sitting in a tub of electricity, frying like your mum's fish on Friday night."

"I have to disagree. The murderer may not have been an American."

"Eh? What?"

"How long had you known Philip?"

Nigel took a swig of beer, then sat back in his chair in the manner of one about to embark on a long story. "Since they was kids I've known the lot of 'em. They all come from broken homes. Fourteen-, fifteen-year-olds, angry and without a place to go with their guitars and music. Reggie's mum is dead. I saw that Philip 'ad a gift. I encouraged them to play. They played in my garage, slept on my floor, and rattled about the English countryside in my old van, playing gigs wherever they'd 'ave us."

"You were like a father to them," I said, remembering the lyrics of that song, "Get out of My Way."

"That I was. They're like my sons, and I'll stick by 'em no matter what 'appens. I wasn't much for coming over 'ere to America, but it's where the big money's to be made, and that's what Philip wanted. The big money and the fame. He wasn't 'appy with being known just in England. I got them that, you know. Top of the charts in Britain."

"I know they're grateful."

"They are. That's why I paid no attention to those silly rumors about them getting a fancy new manager now that they 'ad an American record deal. That was just Philip spouting off when he was in 'is cups—that's English for drinking, luv."

"I see. So Philip threatened to get a new manager?"

Nigel waved an expansive hand. "Never mind about

that crap. The boy didn't mean it. My boy wouldn't have left me behind after all I done for 'im."

I was quiet for a moment, allowing Nigel to nurse his beer and blink back the tears that threatened. I didn't believe for a moment his theory of an American killer. No one here knew the guys, much less wanted to kill one of them. As for Philip wanting to have a new manager, perhaps one more skilled than down-home Nigel, this presented interesting possibilities, and I wouldn't put it past Philip for a second. Did Nigel? Could Nigel's grieving-father act be just that? Could he have been shoved out at the last moment, and in an angry rage murdered the man he considered his son? But there was someone else I needed to ask Nigel about.

"Nigel, what about Astrid?"

He snorted. "What about 'er?"

"What do you think of her?"

"Pain in the arse, that girl, but Philip loved 'er. What can a body do?"

"So you think they would have gotten back together had he lived? What about Peter?"

"The thing with Peter is nothing, poor boy. No, it was always Philip and Astrid. Those two were a case of 'can't live with you, can't live without you.' "

I didn't know about that. Astrid seemed to be getting along just fine since Philip's death. Perhaps Nigel was romanticizing Philip and Astrid's relationship.

"So where's this bio going to be published?" Nigel asked.

"I'm not sure. It's something I'm doing for the record company." Another Hail Mary. "What are you and the guys doing tonight? My roommate knows a cool place to go where we could get some drinks and hang out. How does that sound?"

"Sounds like the best offer I've 'ad all day. I'll round up the boys and meet you back down 'ere at eight?"

"Make it eight thirty," I said, wondering how an outfit that belonged to petite, buxom Darlene could possibly fit taller, small-breasted me.

It wasn't long before I found out.

"What do you mean 'no'? I think it would be darling on you, Bebe. Just try it on."

We stood in the doorway of my bedroom, Darlene holding up a fuzzy sweater dress.

"Darlene, it looks like a tight sweater, only longer."

"That's because that's what it is," Darlene said, and grinned. "Come on, live a little. Pink looks pretty on you, and even you have to admit the style is modest."

"The style is modest—it's really just an Empire waist with sequin trim around the collar and cuffs—but the material is bound to cling all over. Not to mention the fact that it's going to be short on me."

Darlene thrust the hot-pink angora number on my bed. "Put it on and let's see. I'm going to throw something on myself. Wait until you see what the dancers at the club wear. You'll be Miss Modesty herself, I promise."

A short time later, after I sprayed some Emeraude cologne on—I wanted to be the woman who dared to be different, like the ads said—I studied my reflection in my full-length mirror. The dress was deceptively sexy. The style was simple, but boy, did it hug every one of my curves. And it ended well above my knees, giving the viewer quite a gander at my legs.

"Darlene, I don't know about this," I said, turning a shocked eye to the back view. "Oh, dear."

"You sound like that old Miss Marple character," Darlene scolded, coming into the room wearing a navy wool cocktail dress with a middy top, pleated skirt, and rhinestone banding around the low waist and exaggerated vee neckline. The dress was sleeveless, showing off Darlene's creamy freckled arms. "Do you like it? I just got it this afternoon at Bonwit Teller."

"Bonwit Teller! Darlene, you didn't! It must have cost a fortune."

"Actually, Stu paid for it. He saw it in the window and said it had to be mine."

I needn't worry about attracting attention in my dress when Darlene was around in that outfit.

She eyed me critically; then a slow smile came over her face. "If only Bradley could see you now."

That wasn't very likely. Then I thought of the recipient of the bottle of Chanel No. 5. That settled it. I would wear the dress. The fact that Bradley would never see me in it was of no import. I would be out on the town in New York City in a very sexy dress.

After meeting the guys at the hotel, we all cabbed it over to Rocket-a-Go-Go, which was, as Darlene said, done in a space motif. Neon outlines of rockets lined the blue walls, and a small stage had been set up where glittering planets were hung. Everything was done in silver, white, and blue, and the room was quite dark. The guys were in an upbeat mood for a bunch who'd just lost their lead singer, and I was glad. Tomorrow would be a different story when they found out their album wasn't going to be released. Let them enjoy themselves tonight.

As soon as we took off our coats, Keith was at my side. "Hey, Bebe, you look really cool." His gaze lingered on my legs.

I remembered our kiss outside the secondhand store. Unfortunately I also remembered Keith's temper. Tonight he wore striped corduroys and a black shirt with his blue velvet coat. All right, he was a sexy man with a temper.

"Hello, Keith. I'm happy to see you, too." I thought about how he had practically run away at the possibility that I was underage. Tonight I would prove to him that I wasn't by ordering a drink. But I would *not* get tipsy like I had before.

The waiter came by and took our drink orders. When he got to me, he said, "I'll need some identification, please."

I felt my face grow warm.

Keith watched as I pulled out my Virginia driver's

license—no need to get one here in New York—and
handed it to the waiter.

Keith grinned at my stormy expression.

The other guys flocked around Darlene. From the way
she skillfully handled them, it was clear she was used to
lots of male attention.

There was one surprise guest: Astrid, who had
slipped into the second cab with Peter. Now she sat at
Peter's side in a black dress with a deep rounded neckline. Every once in a while she'd shoot Darlene a poisonous glance, which Darlene ignored with aplomb.
Obviously Darlene was not going to call Astrid on her
story of Philip dating a red-haired stewardess weeks
before his murder.

I was wondering what we could do to further the investigation when, after our drinks arrived—I had ordered a
champagne cocktail—Keith announced, "Nigel said I'll
be singing lead now that Philip's gone."

I nearly choked. "Really."

"Yeah. It's not that surprising, when you realize I've
got quite a good singing voice."

"I'm sure you do."

"And I've convinced Nigel that when the band plays,
we can introduce some of the blues tunes I've written.
That way, when we include them on the next album, our
public will be ready."

"Sounds like a good idea," I said, and forced myself
to smile.

"It is," he replied in a smug tone. "I've had to take
over as leader now that Philip's gone."

"What about Nigel? He's the manager. Shouldn't he
be making decisions like the direction of the music?"

Keith's lip curled, and he lowered his voice, leaning
close to me. "Nigel was all right when we wanted to be
a pop band in England, but now we're in America."

I opened my eyes to their widest and took a sip of
my champagne. The bubbles got in my nose and tickled.

"Keith, you aren't saying that you need another manager, are you?"

He shrugged, carelessly turning his back on the older man at the other end of the table. Keith's voice was for my ears only. "We need a high-powered manager now. Nigel will understand he's taken us as far as he can."

"Will he?"

"He'll have to."

"Is this your idea?" I pressed.

"Well, Philip talked to me about it on the plane over, and it made sense to me."

"Did he tell Nigel?"

"Yeah, Nigel knows. He's just hanging about now because of Philip's death. Soon we'll start looking for someone else. Or someone will come knocking on our door after the album takes off."

"Yes, after the album takes off," I echoed, taking a long sip of my champagne despite my earlier caution to myself not to drink much. Nigel certainly did not know the band was serious about replacing him as manager. At least, he didn't appear to from our earlier conversation. Or was that just a ruse? Did he know, and was he concealing how angry he felt about it?

"Hey, you're not underage after all," Keith said, eyeing my drink. "Not like that Mr. Charming said last Saturday. Isn't that him over there with that blonde?"

My head swung around so fast my hair stuck to my mascaraed eyelashes and had to be pried loose so I could see.

Yikes! There was Bradley, looking mouthwateringly sexy in a midnight-blue silk suit, white shirt, and tie. His blond hair was combed perfectly in place, as always. He sat at a table for two on the next tier up from ours with a sophisticated-looking blonde decked out in a strapless, ice-blue cocktail dress. Miss Chanel No. 5?

My heart plummeted as I took in Bradley's handsome face—still with the redness around his eye due to Daddy's punch. Somehow, although it seemed stupid, that punch made me feel connected to Bradley. I wanted to walk up to him, put my arms around him, and stroke his head until he turned his lips to mine.

He must have felt me staring at him, for at that moment he turned and saw me in that tight hot-pink sweater dress nestled cozily between Keith and the other guys in the band.

Chapter Sixteen

I gave Bradley a carefree little wave—just a wiggle of the fingers on my left hand. *Here I am,* the wave said, *no big deal, me out with my pop-star friends. Not pining for you at all.*

Bradley waved back, short and businesslike.

I ground my teeth together. There he was with a blonde draped over him like a fur coat in twenty-degree weather. Not that I minded, I told myself sternly with a toss of my hair. I took another sip of champagne and smiled brilliantly at Keith, who was smoking and drinking bourbon.

"When are they going to start the show?" he asked, indicating the stage.

"I don't know. It's my first time here." I forced my head to remain centered, not turning my body so I could stare at Bradley and Miss Chanel No. 5. What I needed was a distraction. Oh, yes, the murder investigation. That might be a good thing to focus on instead of letting my jealousy get the better of me. I needed to question Reggie about those photos we'd found in Philip's room. I needed to ask Peter about the tie tack, although I didn't relish trying to talk to him while Astrid was glued to his side. And let's not forget Astrid's earring and her accusations about Darlene. But not now. Reggie it was.

We were crowded around a small round table with a blue neon ring circling it, I guessed to resemble a launch pad. I caught Darlene's eye and slid back in my chair so I could talk to her. We moved our heads together.

"I need to question Reggie about the photos," I whispered.

"No problem. I can handle Nigel and Keith. Astrid is monopolizing Peter."

"Okay."

Darlene began to speak to Keith, using her considerable Texas charm. Keith seemed willing to be dazzled.

I turned to Reggie, who was looking deep into the bottom of a glass of beer.

"Reggie, how are you? Did you get in touch with your wife?" I tried for a friendly, confidential tone, which wasn't hard because I liked him. I still couldn't imagine a big teddy bear like him in those poses with that girl, but I had the proof right in my pink purse.

Just now, the bass player was looking morose. "No, Jean still isn't answering the phone. I know she's angry with me."

Here was my cue. "Reggie," I began, touching his sleeve, "do you think Philip succeeded in sending her any of those photos of you and that fan?"

His brown eyes widened, and I felt him jump under my touch. "What do you mean?"

"Reggie," I said as softly as I could with the music playing, "I know about the photos Philip was going to send Jean. Did Philip often interfere with your marriage?"

To my surprise, the teddy bear's expression became that of a grizzly ready to attack. "The bastard," Reggie said through clenched teeth. "I don't know how you found out about it, Bebe, but yeah, Philip delighted in getting fans to pose with me and then sending the snaps to Jean. He wanted to put me in the worst light with her, hoping she'd divorce me."

"He wanted you free because of the band's reputation?"

He swallowed a heavy gulp of his beer. "You got it.

So we could be 'swinging' pop stars, not married men with children. At first he just hinted to Jean that I was misbehaving on the road; then he tried to get incriminating photos. What rubbish! I've never been unfaithful to Jean. Those girls posed with me at Philip's urging. It meant nothing. At the time, I thought I was just going along with what Philip wanted. I never dreamed he'd use the photos as evidence against me."

Sweat was breaking out on Reggie's brow, and his fists were clenched.

"Calm down, Reggie. I believe you. And I think it was a terrible thing that Philip was trying to do. Surely Jean didn't get upset?"

Reggie drained his beer. "That's the rub. You see, Jean's the jealous type, and Philip knew it. He knew how to play on her insecurities. I'll never forgive him for it. Never!"

I felt a chill at the passion in Reggie's voice.

People turned their heads our way. Keith said, "Quiet, Reggie; the show's about to start. Whatever's got you worked up will have to wait."

In a low voice I said to Reggie, "I promise you the pictures will never find their way to Jean now."

He looked at me with an intense stare, then nodded tersely, turning his gaze to the dance floor. He was obviously shaken and angry. How angry? Angry enough to have killed Philip for trying to come between him and his wife? Maybe he'd been trying to get the photos back before Philip could send them to Jean, and an argument had followed. One in which Reggie felt he must take desperate action.

I stole a look at him. Though girls were cavorting on-stage in skimpy outfits that were supposed to pass as space suits, Reggie's gaze seemed far away. He glanced at his watch as if calculating the time difference between America and England. I found myself feeling sorry for him. Then I quickly pushed the feeling aside. There could be no room for personal feelings in a murder investigation. Reggie had a reason to want to see Philip dead. That was what I had to keep in the front of my mind. Now, did he have an opportunity to be in the room with Philip the day he was killed? I'd have to find out.

When the stage show was over, general dancing began. Keith stood up and put his hand at my elbow. "Come on, Bebe. Let's dance."

The song was "Heat Wave" by Martha Reeves and the Vandellas. I got to my feet rather reluctantly at first, not being a great dancer, but then I got into the beat and threw myself into the music. Breathless, I was caught up in the song, the lyrics making me think of a certain blue-eyed man who happened to be my boss. Glancing around, I didn't see him on the dance floor. In fact, the steps of the dance enabled me to view the table where he had been sitting with the blonde. It was empty.

Darlene came onto the floor with Nigel, who proved to be a wild dancer, doing the Frug with the best of the younger people. Astrid and Peter remained at the table with Reggie.

When the song ended, I wondered if maybe Keith would ask Astrid to dance, and I would have an opportunity to question Peter.

I was halfway back to my table, to the strains of Bobby Vinton singing the opening notes of "Blue Velvet" when out of nowhere, Bradley appeared.

He held out one long-fingered hand. "Our dance, Miss Bennett."

I don't think I even answered him, I was so surprised. All I felt was my heart leap and my body tremble. The next minute he was guiding me by the elbow back to the dance floor. Couples were in each other's arms for the slow dance. The houselights dimmed even more. My heart was going to jump out of my chest!

When we reached a space in the swaying couples, Bradley turned me into his arms. Could he smell my Emeraude cologne? Oh, he held me a respectable distance away from him, but his left hand was in mine—

skin to skin touching for the first time since he shook my hand at the job interview—and his right was at my waist. Was it my imagination, or was he gently massaging my lower back?

While all this was heaven, I found myself wanting more. Wanting him to pull me all the way into his arms and kiss me right there on the dance floor. A long, deep, satisfying kiss.

Instead, I looked up into his blue eyes and said the first thing that came to mind: "Where's your blonde?"

He chuckled. "She had to leave."

"Oh." *What a dunce!* Why couldn't I think of something clever to say? We were dancing, though, and my brain apparently couldn't function on more than the naughty thoughts that were flowing through it like Niagara Falls. I felt more than a whisper of a thrill at his touch. I looked down, afraid I couldn't control my emotions.

"Are you proceeding with your investigating, Miss Bennett?"

I had to look at him again. God, he was beautiful. And he was a divine dancer. "Yes, I am."

"You promised your father you wouldn't get involved."

"Well, that's not exactly what I said."

"I see. Twisting the truth a bit, are we?"

"It's for his own good. He'd only worry."

"So what have you found out?" Bradley asked in a casual tone.

"Peter was in Philip's room the day of the murder," I heard myself answering. I felt mesmerized by Bradley's eyes, the touch of his hands, and the closeness of his body. He smelled so good. I wanted to taste him. I'd tell him anything he wanted to know.

"Are you sure? That's a damaging statement."

"I have physical proof."

"What proof?"

"Let's not talk about that now," I murmured into his

ear, as if I were trying to be heard above the music, but really so I could get even closer to him.

To my delight, I felt his breath on my skin. "Oh, come on."

"One of Astrid's earrings, found in Philip's room."

"That is damning. Anything else?"

I snuggled into his arms. "Philip was trying to break up Reggie's marriage. He had photos taken of Reggie with adoring fans and then showed them to Jean, Reggie's wife."

"Not a very nice thing to do."

"No, and Reggie didn't take it well."

"Could he be your man?"

You're *my* man, I thought. "I don't know. There are too many suspects. Nigel even had reason to be angry with Philip. He was being phased out of the band's management."

"They thought they'd gotten too big for him already, didn't they?"

"Yes. How did you know?"

"I heard talk. Well, Miss Bennett, you have been a busy girl."

"Thank you."

"I wasn't praising you. You must stop before you place yourself in any danger." His blue eyes stared at me.

"What? What do you mean?" I asked, drawing back.

"Exactly what I said. We are dealing with a killer here. Someone who's killed once won't hesitate to do so again. Stop your investigating now and stick to being my secretary."

The music ended. He dropped his arms. We stood facing each other on the dance floor. I was steamed at him now. "You got all that information out of me on purpose, didn't you?"

"Perhaps."

"You just wanted to know what I'd found out. Then you could tell me to quit, just like my father!"

"It's for your own good. Let's leave matters to the police."

"To the police? They think Darlene did it. And what about you? You don't exactly look good to your uncle."

"Let me worry about Uncle Herman. As for Darlene, if she's innocent, the police will find that out."

"What do you mean, *if* she's innocent? Of course she's innocent. I'll tell you this, Mr. Williams; I'm not stopping my investigation just because you told me to. I will get to the truth. I'm smart and capable of finding out who murdered Philip Royal!"

Bradley adjusted his cuff. His gaze went down the length of my tight dress. "I'll be keeping an eye on you, kid. No one transcribes my writing as well as you do. I won't be put to the trouble of training a new secretary."

Oh! With that infuriating remark, he practically marched me back to my table and turned to leave.

I followed him and poked him on the shoulder. When he turned around, I said, "Listen here, Mr. Williams, I'm an independent career woman, and I can do as I please. What pleases me is to find out who killed Philip Royal. There's nothing you can do to stop me."

He raised his hand and ran a finger across my left cheek. I felt a shudder run through my body. "Okay, have it your way. Just be careful." With that, he turned and left the club.

I stood there for a moment longer, still angry. I'd show him. I'd show Bradley Williams that Bebe Bennett could solve a murder. Then he'd be forced to eat his words!

Chapter Seventeen

I sat on the floor of my bedroom, my hair in curlers and under the dryer cap. I had used Lustre-Creme shampoo, and had had to lather only once. The dryer was turned on high so I could finish my hair and get to work.

Darlene ambled into the room wearing a blue terry-cloth robe and drinking a Sego weight-control drink. She perched on the edge of my bed. "Bebe, what happened last night?" she asked, raising her voice to be heard over the noise of the hair dryer.

"You mean about Reggie and the photos?"

"We could start there," Darlene said.

"He claims it's all innocent. I believe him. Philip was just out to cause trouble."

"Even if Reggie wasn't doing anything wrong with those girls, Philip was sure taking advantage of it. That's motive for Reggie to want to see Philip stopped."

I adjusted the hose of the dryer so I could turn my head and see Darlene better. "See Philip stopped, but I don't know about killing him to do it."

Darlene made a noncommittal nod of her head.

"What did you find out from Peter?" I asked.

Darlene rolled her eyes. "What a weirdo. Do you know he draws pen marks on his hairline to keep track of his hair loss?"

"Yes, I noticed that too."

"And they say women are vain. Anyway, I asked him

about the tie tack, and he said he isn't missing one. He acted like he didn't know what I was talking about when I said I'd found one in Philip's room, but the whole time his right eye was twitching and blinking more than a traffic light in a hurricane. You know he and Astrid are each other's alibi. She claims she was with him the night Philip was murdered."

"Great."

"Stu's going to London today to find out what he can about Astrid."

"That's wonderful, Darlene! Stu really cares about you."

"Yeah, me and every other Skyway stewardess."

"No, Darlene, he really likes *you*. He wouldn't be going to all this trouble otherwise."

"You're wrong, Bebe. Stu just likes an adventure. Anyway, honey, what are you wearing for Bradley today?"

"Hmpf. Nothing in particular."

Darlene raised an eyebrow. "He'd like that."

"I mean I'm not dressing to attract his attention. I'd have to be blond to do that, and I'm not bleaching my hair."

"What's got you in such a snit about Bradley? You two looked cozy on the dance floor."

I whipped the hood of the hair dryer off my hair and began unpinning my rollers. "He treats me like a child! He warned me off investigating the murder."

"Maybe he's just being protective of you."

"Or maybe he thinks I'm too stupid to solve the case."

"Bradley wouldn't have a stupid secretary. Now wear the emerald-green suit with the gray velvet buttons. It makes you look like a forest nymph. He'll be distracted all day."

"I said I wouldn't wear anything just for him."

"Honey, looking good is your best revenge. Now be your prettiest and your nicest, and it will drive him wild. Trust me. And stop scowling. You'll get wrinkles."

"Oh, all right. But only because the green suit needs an airing."

Darlene laughed.

Later at the office, I stood at the duplicating machine, watching the paper reel off in purple ink, when Nigel arrived for his eleven-o'clock meeting with Bradley.

I closed my eyes for a moment, knowing what would happen when Nigel went into Bradley's office.

"Hullo, there, Bebe. Thanks for arranging for us to go out last night. The boys needed some entertainment. That was some club."

"You're welcome. I hope they enjoyed themselves."

"As much as can be expected with our Philip not joining us. A great partier Philip was. 'E would have been up there with those girlie dancers, you know. 'Ad a way with women."

I stacked the mimeographed sheets on my desk, hardly knowing where to look. "Can I get you some coffee, Nigel?"

"You 'aven't got a nice cuppa tea, 'ave you? That would go down right nice."

"I'm sorry; all I have is coffee."

"Well, don't bother, luv. 'Ere's Bradley come to get me 'imself. See you've got yourself a shiner, Bradley. Noticed it last night, but you didn't 'ave time to talk to us then."

This last was said with a significant look at me.

Heat flooded my face despite my effort not to blush. I hated this weakness of mine. Mama always told me ladies blushed regularly, but I thought it had more to do with my fair complexion.

Bradley had been quiet this morning, keeping busy with paperwork. I knew he dreaded telling Nigel the album wouldn't be released.

"It's starting to fade," Bradley said, touching the spot around his eye.

"Fight over a bird, I'd wager," Nigel said. He let out a booming laugh.

"No. A simple misunderstanding. Now, has Miss Bennett offered you coffee?"

"Yes, I have," I said tartly.

"Of course, ever efficient. Sometimes she can be dangerous, Nigel," he teased.

"The lot of women are, Bradley. Surely you've learned that," Nigel responded with yet another booming laugh.

"Don't worry, Nigel; I harm only those who threaten me," I said, hoping Bradley knew I meant him. Warning me off the investigation!

With a knowing look in my direction, Bradley waved Nigel into his office. The moment the door closed behind him, I put my head in my hands and grieved over what was about to happen to the remaining members of the Beefeaters. How would they take the news? I was sure they'd want to leave immediately for England, just as I was sure Bradley was right in that the police wouldn't let them.

"Pining for me, baby? Here I am." Vince Walsh walked up to my desk. I remembered he'd promised to be nearby when Nigel was told the bad news.

"Mr. Walsh, what can I help you with?" I said with little patience.

"Now, there's something we can talk about at my place Saturday after listening to the band, muffin-cup," he said.

"I told you, Mr. Walsh, I don't date coworkers. Saturday night will be strictly business."

"That's a shame. I'm going to continue to try to get you to change your mind. So, how long do you think it will be before—"

"You can't do this to us!" Nigel's voice thundered from inside Bradley's office.

Bradley's voice could be heard in a lower tone.

Then Nigel: "We've got a contract! We've come all the way from England to make it 'ere in America. You 'ave to release the album!"

Bradley said something else; then Nigel yelled, "Go ahead and call security. I won't 'ave you do this to my boys!"

Vince, obviously enjoying the exchange, took the opportunity to open Bradley's door. "Any trouble in here?"

I heard Bradley's clearly annoyed voice say, "Nothing that concerns you, Vince."

Nigel said, "I'll give you a shiner to match your other if you don't take back what you said and release the album, Bradley."

Then there were sounds of a scuffle. I ran to the door to see Nigel leaning across Bradley's desk, grabbing him by his suit collar. Bradley removed Nigel's grip and Vince took hold of Nigel's arm.

"I suggest you leave now, Nigel," Bradley said. "Before I do call security."

Nigel broke away from Vince and pushed past me to the elevators. His face was mottled red.

Back in Bradley's office, Vince beamed. "That's one unhappy limey. He was going for your throat, Bradley."

"Well, he didn't get it," Bradley said in a calm tone as he smoothed his suit jacket. The expression on his face told me of the mixed emotions he had concerning the scene with Nigel. Bradley wasn't happy with what he'd had to do, or with Nigel's violent reaction.

The only person who seemed pleased by it all was Vince.

Chapter Eighteen

At lunchtime I still felt bad for the guys in the band and decided to skip eating. Vince hung around on the flimsiest of excuses.

Around quarter to one, a tall, handsome, graying man walked proudly into the office. I recognized him at once: Sal Vitelli, the singer who had stolen Mama's heart with his searing ballads. I had loved his music as well, ever since I was a young girl. I knew he was one of Rip-City's artists, but never thought I'd get to meet him.

"Mr. Vitelli!" I cried, a bit breathless. "How exciting to see you in person."

The older man, surely in his early sixties by now, smiled at me. "I'm here to see Bradley Williams, sweetheart. Is he in?"

"Oh, no, Mr. Vitelli. He's at lunch."

Vince, who, if you ask me, didn't do much more than wander around the office letting Miss Hawthorne take messages for him, came up to Sal. "How's it going, Sal? I heard sales of your last record weren't so hot."

Sal's nostrils flared. "I have a large, devoted fan base. This company's distribution leaves a lot to be desired."

How rude of Vince! I thought. He thrived on meanness. *Poor Mr. Vitelli.*

"Sir, if you'd like, I'm sure Mr. Williams wouldn't mind if you waited in his office. I could bring you a nice cup of coffee," I said, smiling in an effort to take the sting out of Vince's words.

Sal turned back to me. "Sweetheart, that's exactly what I'll do."

"Great! How do you like your coffee?" I asked, rising from my chair.

Mr. Vitelli walked past me to Bradley's office. "Nice and sweet. Three sugars, cream."

"I'll be right in with it," I promised.

Going toward the coffeepot, I was glad I had just brewed a fresh pot. Sometimes Bradley liked a cup when he returned from lunch.

I chewed my bottom lip. I'd heard the rumors that Sal Vitelli's albums weren't selling like they did in his heyday in the fifties. But surely he was right in that he still had plenty of loyal fans.

"Hey, cupcake," Vince said, coming up behind me.

I almost scalded myself with the coffee.

"Yes?" I measured three teaspoons of sugar into the hot liquid and then reached for the cream.

"Why don't you go into Bradley's office with Sal and make the old guy happy? He looked you over pretty good, and I think he'd enjoy the pleasure of your company, if you know what I mean."

"Well, sure, I'd be glad to wait for Bradley with him if you think Mr. Vitelli would like it."

"Oh, I'm sure he'd like you." Vince winked and chuckled.

I stirred the coffee and brushed past Vince. He followed me, and when I was in Bradley's office handing Mr. Vitelli the coffee, Vince closed the door behind us. I wondered why he did that, but then figured he didn't want the star being bothered by any of the Rip-City staff who happened to wander by and see Sal in the office.

Mr. Vitelli was seated on the sofa. I chose the chair opposite. "Vince said you might like some company, Mr. Vitelli."

The older man's eyebrows rose. "Did he?"

"Yes, but if you want me to leave, just let me know. I don't want to be a bother. I would like to tell you how much I've enjoyed your music over the years."

Mr. Vitelli sipped his coffee. "Thank you."

"I know you must hear this all the time, but you have the most soulful voice. Sometimes hearing you sing has brought me to tears. I know Mama cries all the time when she listens to you. In fact, Mama would die if she knew I was sitting here talking to you. She just loves you! She has all your albums. She's the one who introduced me to your singing. I'm not boring you, am I? Like I said, you must hear this all the time."

Mr. Vitelli slowly smiled. "Sweetheart, you've made my day. I needed a little ego boost just about now."

"Well, good! Could I press my luck and ask for your autograph? It would be for Mama. I'd like one, but Mama would kill me if she found out that I'd gotten your autograph and didn't get one for her."

"You can have two."

"Wow, that's so nice of you! Here, I'll get a pad and pen off of Mr. Williams's desk." I did so and handed them to him.

"What's your mother's name?"

"Noreen."

"And where does she live?"

"Richmond, Virginia."

He scribbled a note to Mama and handed it to me. It said, *To Noreen, the prettiest gal in Richmond. Yours, Sal Vitelli.*

"Oh, this will make Mama so happy!" I squealed. "Thank you."

"And what's your name?"

"I'm Bebe."

Mr. Vitelli wrote out another note and handed it to me. It said, *To Bebe, who makes a great cup of coffee. Best of luck, Sal Vitelli.*

"I feel like the luckiest girl in Manhattan today, Mr.

Vitelli. If you only knew the nights Mama and I would spend washing up the dishes listening to you sing 'Beautiful Brown Eyes.' Thank you so much for your kindness."

Impulsively, I got up and gave the older man a brief hug and a peck on the cheek. He laughed and called me a good girl.

Suddenly the door to Bradley's office burst open. Bradley stood in his overcoat with a steamed look on his face. "What exactly is going on in here?"

I couldn't figure out why he was mad, but he sure was. Maybe it was because I let Mr. Vitelli wait in his office instead of the reception area. But Mr. Vitelli was a star and deserved special treatment. I found my voice. "Mr. Vitelli arrived to see you. I thought it would be okay to let him wait in here."

"And why are you in here, Miss Bennett? With the door closed."

Sal Vitelli answered for me. "She was just making me feel like I was still appreciated by my audience. She asked for my autograph. That's all there was to it."

A look passed between the two men, one I couldn't understand. Then Bradley said, "I'm back now, Miss Bennett, so you can return to your desk."

I rose, confused by Bradley's attitude, and exited the office. Before I did so, I said, "Mr. Vitelli, I hope to say good-bye to you before you leave today, but if I'm not at my desk when you go, let me say now that it was an honor to meet you."

"Thank you, Bebe. You take care. Don't let New York take away your Southern charm."

"No, a part of Virginia will always be in me. But I want to be a New Yorker!" I smiled and closed the door.

Much to my dismay, Vince was leaning against a file cabinet. "So how did it go?"

"He's such a nice man. Not stuck-up like you'd expect some stars to be. I got his autograph. One for me, and one for Mama."

"Is that all?"

I looked at him. "Yes, what else would there be?"

Vince shook his head. "I can't figure you, babycakes. But anyway, Sal Vitelli doesn't have much time left with Rip-City."

"What do you mean?" I asked, sitting at my desk.

"His sales have progressively dropped over the last two albums. Especially the last one. People don't want to hear aging crooners anymore. They want the Beatles and Motown, the new stuff. Sal is old news."

"Are you telling me that Rip-City might drop Mr. Vitelli from their list of artists?"

"You got it, babe. In fact, I wouldn't be surprised if Bradley isn't telling Sal that unless the new single rises on the charts, he's history. Bradley called the meeting, you know."

"No, I didn't," I said in a soft voice. I couldn't believe it. Rip-City would never drop Sal Vitelli, even if his last few singles hadn't made the top ten on the charts.

After I ignored Vince, busying myself with papers on my desk, he finally took the hint and wandered away.

As it turned out, I was at my desk when Mr. Vitelli and Bradley came out of Bradley's office. Bradley didn't look pleased. Sal Vitelli's proud bearing had slumped. He didn't forget me, though. He leaned over and patted my hand, then walked swiftly to the elevators.

I looked at Bradley. He said, "Come into my office, Miss Bennett."

I got up and followed him.

He sat at his desk, a pencil between his two index fingers. "Now suppose you sit down and tell me what was going on in here between you and Sal Vitelli."

I took my place in the seat across the desk and repeated what I'd told him earlier.

"And that's all?"

"Yes, what else would there be?"

"Vince told me he'd sent you in here to 'make the old guy happy.' Do you know what I'm talking about, Miss Bennett?"

"I think Mr. Vitelli was happy hearing that Mama and I like his music so much. He said I'd made his day."

Bradley dropped the pencil on his desk. He got out of his chair and came around the desk to perch on the edge nearest me. "That's not what Vince had in mind when he sent you in here."

"Just what are you saying?" I asked, an idea beginning to form in my mind.

"When I saw you kiss Sal on the cheek, I thought maybe you did understand what Vince meant."

"Let's stop beating about the bush. What did Vince mean?"

Bradley looked at the ceiling. "The expression 'to make him happy' was meant as a sexual reference." Bradley looked back at me.

My face flamed. "Are you trying to say that Vince wanted me to . . . to let Mr. Vitelli . . . for me to—"

"Yes, that's exactly what I mean."

I rose from my chair. With him leaning on the side of his desk we were almost eye-to-eye. "That can't be what Vince meant. He knows I'm not that type of girl. *You've* been spending too much time at the Playboy Club."

"I assure you, that is exactly what Vince meant for you to do when he sent you in here."

"And you thought I would comply with such a request?"

Bradley looked down at his expensive shoes. "I didn't know what to think when I saw you on the sofa kissing Sal."

"On the cheek! I didn't know you had such a low opinion of me, Mr. Williams." I was mad now. I turned to march out of his office.

He caught my arm in a snug grasp. "I'm sorry, Miss Bennett. I should have known better. I lost my head when I saw you kissing him. You're not that kind of girl at all. I respect you, kid."

His hand on my arm was making my heart beat faster.

While I was glad to hear he respected me, I wished there were more to it than that.

"Okay, I accept your apology because you said you know I'm not that type of girl."

"I know it all too well," Bradley said in a low voice.

We stood almost toe-to-toe, looking at each other. I wanted to touch his hair, to keep staring into his eyes. But mostly I wanted him to slide his arm around my waist, pull me to him, and kiss me with his sexy mouth.

My heart almost stopped when it seemed like that was exactly what he was going to do. His gaze dropped to my mouth and stayed there for a long moment.

Then he turned away and muttered, "I'd better get back to work. I have things to accomplish before I get ready for my date tonight. I'm taking her to the 21 Club right after work, so I'll be changing here."

It's amazing how fast the drop is from heaven to hell.

I held my head high as I left the office without another word. Inside, the lyrics of Sal Vitelli's "Beautiful Brown Eyes" went through my head. The song was about a man who couldn't resist his girl's beautiful brown eyes.

If only Bradley felt that way about my brown eyes.

I was sitting at my desk, sorting through the filing, when I thought again of what Bradley had feared was going on between me and Sal Vitelli. Bradley had been *angry* when he saw us on the sofa.

Could it be that Bradley had been jealous? What a delicious idea!

A smile crossed my lips, and I began to hum Dusty Springfield's "I Only Want to Be with You."

Chapter Nineteen

Bradley had gone for the day on his stupid date, smelling like heaven and looking like anything but an angel, when Darlene called.

"Hi, Darlene, I was just about to finish a report, then leave for the day."

"Honey, you aren't gonna believe what Stu just called and told me."

"I thought Stu was on his way to London to dig up some dirt on Astrid."

"Exactly. He was at LaGuardia airport and guess what he saw happen?"

I was all ears. "Tell me."

"It seems Nigel was trying to leave the country and go back to England. There was a big fuss with the cops all over him, dragging him back from the London gate."

"You're kidding!"

"Nope. Nigel wants out of America. Don't you think that's strange? That he would try to leave to go home without the guys in the band, as close as they supposedly are?"

Thoughts of Keith telling me Philip wanted another, more powerful manager went through my head. Had the guys fired Nigel? Or was it worse than that? Was Nigel running from the police?

"Bebe, are you still there?"

"Yes. I was just thinking."

"Well, if you're thinking what I'm thinking, it looks really bad for Nigel. Stu says that the police will take this as direct disobedience of their orders not to leave town. It will make them look harder at Nigel as a possible suspect."

"That's what I was thinking."

"Maybe this will take some of the heat off of me, but somehow, Bebe, I can't picture Nigel as the murderer. He loved Philip too much."

"True, but remember, Darlene, Philip was talking about getting another manager. That could have put Nigel into a murderous rage. And just this morning Bradley let Nigel know that Rip-City isn't going to release the album."

"Oh, no! Are you going to tell Bradley about how Nigel tried to run?"

I sighed. "Yes, he'd better find out before it hits the newspapers in the morning."

"That Patty Gentry will be sure to get the story. Both stories—the album not being released and Nigel's trying to leave the country. That woman is slippery."

"Okay, I'd better go tell Bradley."

"Is he still there at the office?"

"No, he took a date to the 21 Club."

"Groovy! I've been there with Stu. It's some fancy place. I'll say this much for Bradley. When he wines and dines them, he goes all the way."

"Ouch. I wish you hadn't put it quite that way."

Darlene laughed. "Sorry."

"I have no choice but to interrupt Bradley and his date. A pity, isn't it?"

"Will you phone him at the club?"

I twirled a piece of my hair. "Oh, dear, no. I really think this news is best given in person, don't you?"

Darlene laughed. "Indeed, I do."

I looked off into space. "Sadly, the news will probably end their date."

Darlene snickered. "Yeah, I'll bet you're sorry about

that. Listen, Bebe, how about after you do that, we go to the guys' hotel room and commiserate with them about not having the album released? They might be in a talkative mood right now."

"True. Angry and talkative."

"Exactly. We might learn more. And we can tell them about Nigel before they hear it from anyone else. We can get their reaction to Nigel's trying to leave."

"You do think the police are holding Nigel? That he's not back at the hotel?"

"I wouldn't be surprised. Giving him the grill, you know."

"Okay, I like your plan. What about Keith?"

"You leave that to me, honey. After you've told Bradley the news, why don't you come home and put on something sexy? Then we'll go see the guys."

"I don't see why putting on something sexy has anything to do with the guys. Bradley's the one I wish I could come home and change for."

"Bebe, trust me on this."

"Okay. See you then, Darlene."

I hung up the phone, my nerves on edge. Why had Nigel tried to run?

"What's the matter, muffin-cup? Bradley making you stay late?"

Vince stood with his overcoat on and his briefcase in hand. Having done all he could to ruin everyone's day, he was now headed home.

I saw no reason to tell him about Nigel. The news would be all over the company and in the newspaper in the morning, if he didn't hear it on the late news tonight. "No, Mr. Williams doesn't force me to stay late. If I want to finish up work, I decide on my own to put in extra hours."

"I'm sure that makes him very happy," Vince said with a leer.

I felt like hitting him over the head with my purse. At the least.

I waited for the next elevator to arrive so I wouldn't have to ride with Vince. Okay, I also took a moment to powder my nose and freshen my lip gloss, so that while I was ruining Bradley's date I could look good.

I cabbed it over to the 21 Club, where, wide-eyed with awe at the posh décor, I was led to a room upstairs that was lined with beer steins. There, I found Bradley cozy with a blonde I felt sure I'd seen between the covers of a magazine. She had her hair teased high in a bouffant hairdo. Her low-cut gold-and-silver dress revealed a generous bosom.

I approached their table, which I noticed contained two glasses of champagne. Evidently they had not ordered any food yet. I felt a little guilty for being so pleased to interrupt their date. But all's fair in love and war. "Mr. Williams?"

Bradley looked up, startled. "Miss Bennett, what are you doing here?"

"I'm afraid something has come up at the office that I felt you should know about without delay."

"What is it?"

I looked pointedly at the blonde. Bradley got the message.

"Elkie, would you excuse us for just a moment, please?"

Elkie rose from her seat. "Of course, darling. I'll just go powder my nose." Behind Bradley's back she glared at me, but slunk away. I took her place at the table.

"All right, Miss Bennett, what's this all about?"

I pushed Elkie's champagne glass to the side and leaned toward Bradley. "Darlene called me. A friend of hers is flying to London to try to find out more about Astrid. When he got to LaGuardia, he saw Nigel, handcuffed, being led away by the police. He recognized Nigel from the picture in the newspaper when the band first arrived in America, I suppose. Anyway, the point is that Nigel was trying to leave the country and return to London."

Bradley let out a weary sigh. "Damn. Kid, this doesn't look good. Nigel will probably tell gruesome stories about Rip-City."

"I agree. I thought you'd want to know before it hits the papers or the evening news."

"You did right. I'd better call the corporate attorney and see if I can get him down to the police station. We don't want this looking bad for Rip-City. And we don't want Nigel talking about how the album isn't going to be released."

"That may already have happened. He has a love-hate relationship with that reporter from London, Patty Gentry. Nigel might have been so angry with us for not releasing the album that he told her."

Bradley frowned. "Maybe I'd better go down to the police station too."

"I think that would be wise," I said.

Elkie returned to the table. I thought it prudent to leave. I had done what I'd come to do. It was time to go back to the apartment and meet up with Darlene.

I said good-bye to the pair, trying really hard not to look happy that their date was ruined. I glanced back once and saw Elkie with a furious look on her face. I skipped out to the street.

Back at the apartment, Darlene was ready to go, decked out in a sky-blue dress that was almost the same color as her stewardess uniform.

"How did Bradley take the news?" she asked, as I examined my closet for something to wear.

"He was anxious to get to the corporate lawyer. And he decided to go to the police station himself."

Darlene grinned. "His date was over then?"

"Oh, yes."

"You are bad, Bebe Bennett," she teased.

Darlene and I looked at each other and fell into a fit of laughter.

Once we regained our composure, I pushed my clothes

to one side of the closet, then slowly moved items across the rack so I could contemplate them. I was studying my herringbone skirt when Darlene reached past me and pulled out a simple burgundy velvet A-line dress.

"Wear this. You want to look good for the guys. We'll get more information out of them that way."

"I thought you weren't supposed to wear velvet after Valentine's Day."

"Velvet is *always* appropriate. So sexy," Darlene opined.

"Okay."

At the Legends Hotel, Mr. Duncan was on duty at the elevators. He returned my smile but regarded Darlene warily. "Good evening, girls. Can I take you upstairs?"

"Thank you, Mr. Duncan, we'd appreciate it," I said with a smile. "How's your family?"

"Fine, thank you."

Darlene asked for the fifteenth floor, being sure to enunciate her words carefully. I was pleased to see how considerate she was about Mr. Duncan's hearing problem.

Once we arrived, I ignored Mr. Duncan's disapproving look and my own doubtful feelings about going to the guys' hotel room, and followed Darlene.

She knocked on a door, and Keith opened it. He waved his hand expansively. "Come on in; might as well join the party."

Keith had a suite—I wondered how he'd managed that when Philip only had a regular room—and the other band members were present. Reggie sat next to the telephone. Peter was perched sideways in a chair with his feet dangling over the arm, his right eye twitching. Astrid was noticeably absent.

The air was full of tension. You could barely see the tables, they were so covered with glasses and bottles of Jack Daniel's. Overflowing ashtrays were scattered throughout the room, and there was the smell of marijuana in the air.

"Want a drink?" Keith said, a cigarette dangling from one side of his mouth.

"Sure," Darlene said, sitting down and crossing her legs.

"What about you, Bebe? Maybe you'd better not unless your knight in shining armor is planning on showing up here too. After he axed our record."

"I proved at Rocket-a-Go-Go that I know how to drink," I protested, ignoring the remark about the album. Still, he didn't pour me one.

Darlene accepted a drink from Keith. "Look, that's why we're here—about the record. We wanted to tell you how sorry we are that the album isn't going to be released in America."

Keith swallowed the contents of his glass in one gulp. "Bastards, bloody bastards. We're all broken up that Philip's gone, but that doesn't mean the album can't go on. I can sing lead."

"Maybe you killed him, thinking that you'd finally be the front man," Reggie said in a deceptively mild voice. "God knows you think this band belongs to you."

Keith rounded on him. "Bloody hell! What a thing to say. And the band *was* my idea from the beginning. Nigel just liked Philip more and made him the lead. But I didn't kill Philip."

Reggie shrugged. "One of us did it. And I know it wasn't me."

Keith sneered. "How do we know it wasn't you? Philip was trying to break up your marriage. All you ever do is sit by the phone, pining for Jean and that snot-nosed kid."

Furious, Reggie shot out of his chair and moved toward Keith.

Darlene came between them. "Soon you'll be able to go home to London. The album will be released in Britain to great success."

"Keith can be the lead singer," Peter said. "He's got

the talent." His right eye twitched violently. "We'll be all right. Won't we?"

Darlene said, "Why were you in Philip's room the day he was murdered, Peter? I know you were there because we found this tie tack on the floor." She pulled the tie tack out of her purse and held it up.

Keith looked at it and then at Peter. "That does belong to you, Peter. You said you hadn't been in Philip's room."

Cornered, Peter threw up his hands. "All right, I was there. I wanted to talk to Philip about his latest round of threats about getting a new drummer. But he was in the tub singing. There was no talking to him, so I left. I left him *alive*."

I said, "You'll have to tell the police, Peter."

"Why? Astrid and I were together when Philip was killed. I have an alibi."

I wondered about that alibi. Darlene and I needed to get to Astrid, show her the earring, tell her about Peter's being in Philip's room, and see how she reacted. Or get Peter alone and get him to crack.

I said, "There's something you all should know. Nigel was caught at the airport trying to board a plane for London. The police have him in custody."

"That's not possible!" Keith burst out. "He wouldn't leave us."

"He might if he was the one who killed Philip," Reggie said. He seemed a little drunk. He was certainly not his usual mild-mannered self. "Or maybe he just didn't see the need to stick with a bunch of losers who can't get an album out."

Peter was literally shaking with nerves. "Stop it! Stop saying these evil things. No one here killed Philip. Nigel wouldn't try to leave without a good reason."

"Oh, shut up, Peter," Keith said. "No wonder Astrid's been coming on to me lately. It's clear you're nothing but a bag of nerves. I'm the new leader of the band."

Peter swung a fist, but Keith easily blocked it. Peter said, "You always think the birds are after you. Well, Astrid is not!"

The drummer left the room in a huff, slamming the door behind him.

Keith poured himself another drink.

Reggie went back to dialing the phone.

I looked at Darlene and signaled that we should leave.

We had heard enough here. It was time to see if we could break Peter's and Astrid's alibis. Although suspects and motives were plentiful, considering the troubles and petty rivalries in the band, Astrid remained the chief suspect in my mind. Philip had tossed her aside, and Astrid would not tolerate him being with another woman. Ever.

Chapter Twenty

The next morning at work, Bradley didn't come in until ten. I was worried about him. Had he gone back to Elkie when he was finished at the police station? Or had he just had a late night trying to control Nigel?

"Good morning, Mr. Williams," I greeted him. The windy day had left a lock of his hair hanging over his forehead.

"Good morning, Miss Bennett."

Bradley explained that Nigel was under control. He had just flipped out and decided to go home. The police had yet to decide whether to press charges.

The explanation left me wondering about Nigel's real motives.

Bradley spent most of the day on the phone, leaving me to my work. I had a lot of filing to catch up on.

That night Darlene and I discussed our next move. We wanted to get to Peter, to break his alibi with Astrid. But we couldn't be sure when he would be alone.

The problem solved itself when Peter called early in the evening. Darlene and I had just finished dinner—Darlene griping because the airline was pressuring her to come back, and the police wouldn't let her—when the phone rang. I went to answer it.

"Hello?"

"Bebe?"

"Yes, who's this?"

"It's Peter. Can you come over here? We've got trouble."

"What is it?"

"I wouldn't have bothered you, but Astrid is out talking with Patty Gentry again. You see, Reggie's wife, Jean, is here."

"There at the hotel? I thought she was in England."

"Can you just come over? Jean and Reggie are really going at it, and we think maybe another female could help."

"I'll be right there."

I hung up the phone, related the news to Darlene, and we grabbed our coats and headed for the hotel.

In Keith's suite, Peter and Keith were trying to calm an obviously distraught ruddy-faced blonde, a bit on the plump side, who was holding a wailing infant.

"You've been playing around on me, Reggie!" she accused.

Reggie stood in front of her. "Jean, I never have!"

"Philip showed me the photographs."

"What are you talking about? Philip never got a chance to send them."

"Then there are *more* of them?" She cried harder, which made the baby cry harder.

I stepped forward, pulling a tissue out of my purse. "Excuse me, Jean. I know we don't know each other. My name is Bebe. I think I can clear some of this up."

"And I can help too," Darlene said. "I'm Darlene."

Jean looked suspiciously at me, but accepted the tissue and blew her nose. She popped a pacifier in the baby's mouth. "I've seen you with Reggie. I saw you both with him at that space club. But you, Bebe, were cuddling close to him."

"We were only talking, I promise," I said. "Um, when did you get to America, Jean?"

Reggie's eyes widened.

Jean lowered her head, but addressed Reggie. "I followed you over directly. I didn't trust you here with an ocean between us and you with those fans."

I couldn't believe what I was hearing. Jean had been dogging Reggie since his arrival in America. Reggie had certainly understated the case when he'd said Jean was the jealous type. She hadn't been answering the phone back in Manchester because she was here in New York!

"Jean," I said, "Reggie and I are only friends. I work at his record company, that's all. I know Philip was taking pictures of Reggie with fans, but I also know that it was all Philip's doing. He wanted to break up your marriage. He had some weird idea that pop stars shouldn't be married."

"She's right, Jean," Reggie confirmed. "It was all blasted Philip's doing. You must know how much I love you and Jamesey."

Jean blew her nose again. "It's just that when I saw those photographs, and then I knew you'd be all the way over here, I couldn't take it."

Darlene said, "A woman's got to trust her man or there's going to be trouble. Reggie and I just met, but I can tell how much he loves you and the baby."

I nodded. "He's been frantic trying to telephone you ever since he got here. He thought you were too mad at him to talk."

Reggie bent down in front of Jean and the baby. "I know we had that row before I left; that's why I kept trying to call. I swear there's not been anyone else, Jean."

"Well, now that Philip is dead, you can come back home to England where you belong," Jean said. "Dirty rotter deserved what happened to him. I'd like to thank the person who did it."

A thought went through my mind. If Jean had been in America the whole time the guys had been, could she have killed Philip? She certainly wasn't very emotionally stable.

Just then Reggie put his arm around her. "Here, luv, don't cry anymore. We're together again." He kissed her temple. "Let me hold Jamesey. It feels like forever since

I've held him. If someone hadn't already done it, I'd kill
Philip myself for the trouble he's caused."

Jean passed him the baby, and Reggie's face glowed
with happiness.

Keith moaned like the scene made him sick. He
stalked off to one of the bedrooms.

My head whirled. So many people wanted to see Philip
dead! Reggie, Keith, Peter, Nigel, Astrid, and now Jean.

I sensed it was time to leave the couple alone, while
there was a chance to talk to Peter. Astrid was out with
Patty Gentry. I wondered about that for a moment, re-
calling that the two women weren't exactly friends, but
then I figured that Astrid wouldn't let that fact stop her
if she wanted to use the press. And Patty needed her
as well.

"Peter," I said, "let's leave them. I want to talk to you
anyway. Can we go to your room?"

Peter's eye twitched. "Sure."

After murmuring good-byes, Peter, Darlene, and I left
and went to Peter's room.

"What a mess," Peter said, flopping down on the bed.
"Jean's never going to make Reggie's life easy. He
shouldn't have married her."

"He obviously loves her," Darlene said. "And being
married to a pop star can't be all that easy."

I wished I were Cynthia Lennon, I thought.

"*Being* a pop star isn't all that easy," Peter said.

Darlene began the attack. "Neither is being a murderer. You admitted that you were in Philip's room. Why
don't you tell us what really happened the night Philip
was killed?"

Peter jumped up off the bed and began to pace. "I
already told you. I went to see Philip. He was singing in
the bath. He was in no mood to talk, so I left. That's
the end of the story."

I said, "You just decided to drop the whole idea that
Philip was threatening to replace you as drummer for
the band?"

"What else could I do? He wouldn't talk."

"What did he say?" Darlene pressed on. "That you were too old to be in the band?"

Peter's face reddened. "I'm not too old. I'm just as good a drummer as Ringo. Philip knew he couldn't get anybody to replace me."

"Did he?" I said. "Philip seemed to want to make some changes. He wanted Reggie divorced. He wanted Nigel out. Nigel, of all people, who'd helped the band from its infancy."

"I tell you, he wouldn't have fired me."

"Then why were you so anxious to talk to him?" Darlene pressed.

Peter's nerves were out of control. His voice turned whiny. "I just wanted some reassurance, is all. Philip could be so cruel."

"And when you didn't get it, you came back to your room and spent the rest of the evening with Astrid," I said.

"No, she was out. She's never around when I need her."

Darlene and I exchanged looks.

"Peter, what did you just say?" I asked.

"I said I came back to my room and cried in my beer all night. Philip could really rattle me," Peter said.

"No, the other part." I took a step closer to him. "About Astrid. She wasn't with you that night, was she?"

Peter's eyes grew huge. "I didn't mean that. She was here."

"No, she wasn't," Darlene said. "She just made you promise to tell anyone who asked that she was. Wasn't that the way of it, Peter?"

"You're wrong. I don't know what I was saying," Peter cried as he backed into the wall. "Astrid and I are a couple. We were together. We're each other's alibis for that night."

"Astrid's only loyalty is to herself, Peter," I said.

"We showed her the tie tack, Peter. She confessed

she wasn't with you that night," Darlene fibbed. I held my breath.

Peter began to cry. "All right, we weren't together. I don't know where she was. She begged me to say she was with me. That as Philip's ex-girlfriend she'd be the most likely suspect. I love her. How could I turn her down?"

Darlene didn't let up. "Plus, without your saying you were with Astrid, *you* don't have an alibi either for the time of Philip's death."

Peter was panicked. "I swear I didn't kill him. I left him alive, I tell you. I was tired from the photo shoot earlier and still had some jet lag. I came back to my room and stayed here alone all evening."

"What time did Astrid return?" I asked.

"I don't know. I fell asleep. She was with me the next morning," Peter said miserably. "What are you going to do? Are you going to tell the police?"

"I don't think you killed Philip, Peter," I said, not mentioning that I didn't think he had the gumption to do it. "At this point, I see no need to tell the police you were alone."

I didn't promise not to tell the police that Astrid's alibi had been blown to bits. And now with these new developments, maybe we could tell the police that we'd found her earring in Philip's room.

We just had to wait for whatever information Stu brought back from London. And we might have our killer.

Chapter Twenty-one

The next night Stu called. Darlene spoke to him.

"Wait, slow down, Stu. I've got Bebe here and I want her filled in on this. I'm going to repeat everything you say," Darlene said.

"You found Astrid's sister, Penny. Okay, go ahead. What did Penny have to say? Astrid is determined to be a fashion model. Right, we know that. Oh! Nasty magazines. *Those* kind of pictures. And Philip had pictures of her trying to get an all-over suntan? What was he going to do with those?"

Darlene listened carefully. "What a sweetheart. He just wanted something to hold over her to keep her in line. He knew she was using him as a ladder, hanging with a pop star to further her career as a model. No, Stu, you're right; he never cared for her the way he pretended to. So after the breakup, Astrid begged Philip to take her back? Penny remembers the long weeping phone calls. Astrid was *stalking* him? And that's why she took up with Peter? To keep an eye on Philip. The song lyrics in 'Get out of My Way' are about her, in Penny's opinion?"

Darlene looked at me to be sure I was getting all this. I rolled my eyes to indicate I was.

"Stu, did Penny say whether she thought it was possible that Astrid killed Philip in a fit of jealousy? She did! And Astrid is going to what? File a claim against Philip's estate? On what basis? Oh, that's okay. You couldn't have found out everything. You did great, Stu. When are you coming home? Good, then I can see you tomorrow? Great, give me a call when you've had some sleep. In your bed, waiting for you?" Darlene giggled.

I moved away, thinking I'd heard enough.

Darlene hung up the phone and came into the living room, where I was sitting on the pink sectional, staring at the turquoise fur rug.

"Did you get all that?" Darlene asked.

"Yes, and I'm thinking that it all makes Astrid look extremely guilty. I know Nigel tried to run away, but the evidence against Astrid is more pressing."

"What are we going to do?" Darlene asked.

"I think we should force a confrontation with Astrid," I said.

"If you're thinking she might confess, forget it. She's one cool customer."

"I think if we have an opportunity to get her alone, we should do it."

"Okay, it's worth a shot."

Tuesday morning when I went to the office, everyone was in an uproar. I quickly made coffee and took Bradley a cup. It was really an excuse to see what was going on in his office. Vince was there, as was Mr. Purvis, the company president. Bradley was holding a copy of the newspaper in his hands.

"This makes our company look incompetent," Mr. Purvis said.

"Everything that's happened weighs on my conscience," Vince said.

Conscience! Vince had no conscience.

Bradley looked at Vince as if he were a worm. Which he was.

"There's nothing we can do about it now," Bradley said. "The damage is done. All we can do is release a press statement confirming that Rip-City will not be releasing the album."

"Handle it, Bradley. Make this mess go away." Mr. Purvis turned to leave and noticed me standing there.

I hurried out of the room, feeling like an unwanted eavesdropper. Vince fled to his office.

Curiosity filled me. What had been in the newspaper to make the men upset?

I had on my red suit, which Darlene said made me look sexy. My nails were painted red too.

I stood in Bradley's doorway. "Mr. Williams? May I come in?"

Bradley had been turned in his chair, staring out at the New York skyscrapers. He swiveled around at the sound of my voice. "Yes, Miss Bennett. Come in and sit down."

"What's happened?"

For an answer, he passed me a folded section of the tabloid, the New York *Daily News*. The headline screamed, "Inside Scoop on Rip-City's Beefeaters Blunder" by Patty Gentry.

Imagine it. Rip-City's handsome Bradley Williams goes to London and finds what he thinks will be the next big British Invasion pop band, Philip Royal and the Beefeaters. He proceeds to offer the band a solid contract. The band is elated at this big break in America, land of opportunity, and—more important—fame and money.

The band packs its bags and crosses the pond, bringing along their small-time manager, Nigel Evers. Philip Royal reputedly has plans to fire Nigel once the band hits it big. Philip also works to cover up the fact that the bass player has a wife and infant son. Married pop stars are so boring.

But what Philip doesn't know is that someone really hates him. Hates him enough to kill him. He's found electrocuted in his bathtub shortly after his arrival in America. The police have yet to make an arrest, possibly because they have so many suspects.

There's Astrid Loveday, his ex-girlfriend. She had taken up with the band's drummer, Peter Smythe. But as Miss Loveday confided to me in an exclusive interview, this was all a ruse to stay near Philip. Miss Loveday herself does not have a squeaky-clean past. In England, she's posed for the equivalent of *Playboy*, although she calls herself a fashion model. I've yet to hear what runways she's appeared on.

Then there's Nigel, who hears that he's about to be tossed out on his ear. One can only guess how this made him feel. He made the band a Royal success in England, taking the boys from homeless, pub-playing nobodies to the top of the charts. Making himself look guilty, Nigel was caught trying to flee the country after the police specifically told him he must remain here until the matter of who murdered Philip Royal has been cleared up.

Philip had no friends within the band either. Besides the marital issue with Reggie, Philip often threatened to fire Peter Smythe, the band's aging drummer. And then there's Keith Michaels, whose temper is as legendary as is his desire to shift the band's musical direction to blues.

Besides Philip's death, what's the result of all this chaos? Rip-City is dropping the album from its release in America.

I'm betting Bradley Williams wishes he never set foot in London the day he met Philip Royal and the Beefeaters.

Who exactly did plug in the guitar that fatally electrocuted Philip Royal? This reporter has done some investigating on her own and thinks she knows. And when that person's identity is revealed, it will be the most shocking event in rock since Elvis's grinding pelvis.

Stay tuned as this hot story explodes in the next few days.

I handed the tabloid back to Bradley. "What a nasty article! And Patty Gentry claims to know who the killer is."

"She certainly knows how to get her byline in the paper," Bradley pointed out.

"It makes me angry that she mentioned you the way she did. I mean, how could you know what would happen when you signed the band? Are you a fortune-teller? I don't see a crystal ball on your desk."

That made him smile. Then he looked down at the newspaper. "I wonder if Patty Gentry will go to the police with her so-called knowledge instead of teasing the public to sell newspapers."

I thought of Detective Finelli. Shouldn't he be questioning Patty? Maybe it was time to pay him a visit. I'd put the idea before Darlene and Stu and see what they thought.

And I knew where I was going tonight when I got off work—straight to the Legends Hotel to see what the guys in the band thought of Patty Gentry's article.

Chapter Twenty-two

At the apartment, it was hard prying Darlene away from welcoming Stu home, but I managed it by not leaving them alone where they could kiss and cuddle. I stood next to them, studying my nails and humming "My Boyfriend's Back" by the Angels. Darlene shot me an exasperated look, but got ready to go.

When we arrived at Keith's suite, everyone was there, including, to my surprise, Nigel. The atmosphere was one of doom and gloom, with the dreaded tabloid article prominent on the coffee table.

We were admitted, but not greeted with any great enthusiasm.

Astrid sat next to Peter. She glared at Darlene, but said nothing.

"I'm so sorry about the article, guys," I said.

"That Patty Gentry is a bitch. She's followed us for the past year and never had a kind word. Now this," Keith griped.

"And she had to throw in that bit about Jean and Jamesey," Reggie complained.

"Where are they?" I asked.

"Jean's trying to put Jamesey to sleep in our room. Poor tyke's been feeling the tension," Reggie replied.

"He's not the only one," Peter said. "How dare that Gentry woman call me 'aging.' Makes me seem like I'm thirty."

"You don't look anywhere near thirty, Peter. I promise," I said. He nodded and hung his head.

"I just want to get the 'ell out of this godforsaken country," Nigel said from where he sat away from the others looking out the window. "This is what comes from greed. If we'd been 'appy at the top in England, none of this would 'ave 'appened. Our Philip would be alive."

"I'm sure the police will let you go soon, Nigel," I said.

"They have to catch the killer first," Darlene pointed out.

Nigel said, "According to the Gentry bitch, she knows who 'e is. Let 'er put some proof in front of the police so we can all go 'ome."

"She didn't put on to me like she knew the killer," Astrid said, speaking for the first time.

"Maybe that's because she thinks you did it," Keith said with a snarl. "Why you had to open your mouth to her, I don't know."

Astrid bristled. "I thought that if it were in the papers that Rip-City had dropped the band, there would be a public outcry for the record."

"You always were just a dumb blonde," Keith said. "Now look what you've done."

Peter shot Keith a look. "She couldn't have known how Patty would twist things around. Astrid was only trying to help. Why must you always stir up trouble?"

Keith shot a look at Peter. "I don't know why you're defending her when it says right there in the paper that she was only seeing you to follow Philip."

Peter reddened. "Well, Philip's not here now, is he? And Astrid is still with me."

"Aren't we all lucky," Keith spat.

Astrid rose, looking down her nose at Keith. "I'm going downstairs for some ciggies."

Peter said, "Look, when Astrid comes back, let's all of us go out to a club. The Village is the happening place. We'll go to another coffeehouse there, listen to some bands."

Everyone agreed to Peter's plan, instantly ready for a fun time. Reggie hung back, saying he'd stay in the hotel with Jean.

"I won't be but a minute," Astrid said.

I glanced at Darlene. This was our chance to get Astrid alone.

I stood up. "Well, we just wanted to come by and say how sorry we were about the article. And who knows what the future holds? I've got some ideas—too soon to discuss—but maybe they'll work out."

"Take care, guys," Darlene said, and we made our exit.

Astrid had gone ahead of us in the elevator.

"We'll have to catch her downstairs," I said.

"I noticed a cigarette machine down the hall leading to the telephone booth the night I tried to call up to Philip's room. Maybe she's gone there," Darlene said.

The elevator seemed to take forever to get to us. Mr. Duncan was not on duty. A younger man was working. We told him to take us to the lobby fast, but we ended up having to stop twice to pick up other passengers. Darlene let out a growl of annoyance each time. I put my arm around her and said, "Don't worry; we'll catch her."

Downstairs, we did catch Astrid walking back up the hallway from the cigarette machine.

She looked militant upon seeing us. "What do you two want?"

For an answer, Darlene grabbed her by the arm and dragged her into the nearby empty ballroom. I followed, unable to believe what happened next.

Astrid turned around and slapped Darlene across the face. "Don't you touch me, you dirty Yank! If it hadn't been for you screwing Philip—"

Darlene grabbed Astrid by her long hair and pulled her head down until the woman was bending over backward looking up into Darlene's face.

"You told the police those lies about Philip and me. I

never had a relationship with him before we met on that plane and you know it. Admit it! Admit you lied!"

"Darlene!" I said. "Be careful!"

She ignored me.

Astrid took her right hand and shoved Darlene in the stomach as hard as she could. Darlene stumbled backward, releasing her hold on Astrid's hair. Astrid lost her balance and fell to the ground, her skirt hiking up to her thighs.

Darlene got up, grabbed both sides of Astrid's exposed garter straps, and snapped them hard. Astrid howled with pain. She reached up and clutched Darlene by the knees, knocking her to the floor. The two of them rolled around on the hotel's elegant carpet.

A wild thought of throwing cold water on them, like Mama used to have to do with two of our cats, flashed through my mind.

Astrid had Darlene around the throat, both women huffing and puffing for air.

"Astrid, let her go!" I shouted.

In a lightning-fast move, Darlene used both arms to knock Astrid's hands from her throat. She stood up, dragging Astrid with her, and twisted one of Astrid's arms behind her back. Astrid moaned in pain.

Darlene gasped for air and then said, "I told you to tell me you lied to the police. Are you ready to talk now?" She pulled Astrid's arm harder.

"All right, you American hellcat," Astrid said, breathing hard. "I told them Philip was seeing a red-haired American stewardess."

"And?"

"And that he was going to break off the relationship when he arrived in America. I said I thought it was you."

Darlene said, "I'm going to tell the police you confessed to lying to them. I have a witness right here."

Astrid kicked Darlene with her right foot, forcing Darlene to release her hold and stumble backward. But she did not fall. The two women stood glaring at each other.

"I have to preserve my looks for my modeling. I could kill you for manhandling me like that," Astrid hissed.

"Like you killed Philip?" Darlene challenged.

"I did not kill Philip!" Astrid insisted.

"Oh, yeah? Bebe, have you got it with you?"

I opened my purse and pulled out the gold triangle earring. "What about this, Astrid? We found it in Philip's room. You said you hadn't been in Philip's room the day he was murdered."

"Give me that," Astrid said, making a lunge for the earring.

I held it out of her reach.

Darlene stepped between us. "You lay a hand on her and I'll beat you until the only photo shoots you'll do will be for horror movies."

"You can't prove that earring belongs to me," Astrid said.

"Yes, I can," I replied. "Mr. Williams has a picture of you with these earrings on, remember? He showed them to you that day at the Legends lounge."

"I remember."

"It would be quite a coincidence that another woman with the exact pair of earrings dropped one in Philip's room the day he was murdered."

"Okay, so you can prove I was in Philip's room. That doesn't mean I killed him," Astrid said.

I put the earring back in my purse.

"You had the motive—he'd dropped you—and the opportunity when you came in his room and saw him in the bath playing the guitar," I said. "You killed him."

Astrid shook her head. "I was there *before* he got in the bath. We were going to reconcile. In fact, we made love that afternoon."

"That's impossible. He was with me that morning," Darlene said.

"Don't you know anything?" Astrid sneered. "Men can be with one woman in the morning and another in the afternoon."

Darlene glared. "Why did you go to Patty Gentry if not to plant the idea of another killer and take any heat off yourself? You know you look guilty."

Astrid tossed her hair. "I didn't think she'd turn on me. Patty was a good way for me to get publicity. She never let me down in England. Any publicity is good."

"This is a murder case, not an opportunity for you to further your career," I said. "Don't you have any respect for the dead?"

Astrid snorted. "Patty's been useful in the past. But I know not to trust her now."

"Fat lot of good that does the band and Rip-City, doesn't it?" Darlene said. "Besides, Patty says she knows who the killer is. Maybe she thinks you did it."

Astrid picked up her cigarettes from where they'd fallen to the floor. "I'll take care of that."

With those menacing words, she flounced out of the room.

Chapter Twenty-three

"Oh, God, that feels good. Mmmmm. Aaaahhh."

"Darlene, you've been in that tub for half an hour," I said, talking from the other side of the bathroom door.

"Bebe, I have muscles aching I didn't know I had. This hot water is heavenly. And the way the water turns cold in this apartment I'm lucky there was enough to heat the whole tub."

"Are we still going through with our plan to see Detective Finelli?"

"Absolutely. Stu's joining us. He's meeting us here at nine. Have you called Bradley to ask for the morning off?"

I twirled a piece of hair. "No. I guess I'd better do that now. I hope he won't be difficult about it."

"Just pour on that Southern charm, Bebe. Bradley will melt like a stick of butter in the Texas sun."

"Okay."

Officially the office didn't open until nine, but Bradley, hard worker that he was, usually arrived around eight thirty. I'd made it a practice to be there at that time as well—it was nice to have that half hour alone with him before coworkers began to arrive—so he might have noticed my absence already. I called on his private line.

"Bradley Williams."

"Mr. Williams, it's me, Bebe Bennett."

"Good morning, Miss Bennett. How are you?"

"I'm fine, but I have a favor to ask."

"Oh, what's that?"

"Well, you see, Darlene and I have to do something this morning. I need the morning off. I'll be in at lunchtime, though."

"Does this *something* that you and Miss Roland have to do involve the murder investigation?"

I twirled my hair again and chewed my bottom lip. I could hear the disapproval in his voice. "Actually, it does. We want to meet with Detective Finelli and bring to his attention some evidence in the case," I said defiantly.

"That's all you're going to do? You're not going to put yourself in any danger?"

"Oh, no. We'll be at the police station. What safer place could we be?"

"You could be here in my office, where you should be. But go ahead and see the detective. I'll expect you at noon."

"Thank you, Mr. Williams. You can count on me."

We hung up, and I went to my closet to get dressed. I could hear Darlene moving around in her room, so she must have managed to pry herself from the tub.

We were both dressed by the time Stu arrived promptly at nine. Darlene had on a horizontally striped pink-and-green knit dress. I wore a camel-colored suit with leopard-patterned buttons.

Stu was his usual exuberant self. He looked like the self-assured heir he was in a deceptively simple navy suit with light blue pinstripes. I was willing to bet it came from Saville Row in London. Stu was the type who would take time to shop while in London.

"Hey, doll," he greeted Darlene, and wrapped her in a big hug.

She groaned.

He pulled back and looked at her. "What's the matter with my favorite girl?"

"She got into a catfight with Astrid yesterday at the

hotel." I reported primly. "Darlene came out on top, but Astrid got in a few blows." I gave Darlene a look of severe disapproval.

"Gee, I'm sorry I missed that," Stu said. "Did either of your clothes get ripped and reveal some skin?"

Darlene gave him a playful punch in the arm.

"Seriously, doll, are you all right? If not, remember I know some people who could expose information on Miss Astrid Loveday that would make her long blond locks frizz up like a Halloween wig."

"I'm fine, Stu. But thanks for your concern. I managed to get Astrid to admit she'd made up those statements about me seeing Philip before his flight from London to New York. And Bebe is my witness."

"Great. You're a doll, with many talents," he said, and winked at her. "We can include that in our talk with Detective Finelli. Anything else?"

Darlene looked at Stu with a seductive smile. "I have bruises all over me. Maybe you could give me a massage—"

I interrupted her. "Astrid claims she and Philip reconciled the afternoon of the day he was murdered. They were . . . uh . . ." I stumbled for the right words.

"They'd been screwing," Darlene piped up.

I blushed.

Stu looked thoughtful.

"Well, that's what Astrid said they'd been doing. I don't know that I believe her one little bit," Darlene added.

"Astrid also said that Patty Gentry had been her ally. She didn't seem to understand how Patty could have turned on her and written those nasty comments in her article," I explained.

"Speaking of Miss Gentry, I thought we might also want to pay a little visit to her, so I took the liberty of finding out what hotel she's staying at," Stu said.

Darlene and I smiled.

"You're mint, Stu, and I don't mean because of the

Minty-Mouth company," Darlene said, and again gave him that sexy grin. "I can almost forgive you for all the stewardesses you probably flirted with on the trip over to London and back."

"Nobody who can hold a candle to you, doll. Come on; let's go," Stu said, holding the door open for me and putting an arm around Darlene.

We arrived at the police station, and a desk sergeant took our names. A few minutes passed. I could see Detective Finelli through a glass wall. He glanced up at us from where he sat at his desk. The desk sergeant returned and opened the door to us.

The room was crowded with detectives and police on the phone or writing reports. It seemed to me that all of them looked up at our appearance. Darlene flashed her big Texas smile, causing the men to grin back.

Detective Finelli walked over to us. "Miss Roland, Miss Bennett. What can I do for you?"

"This is Stu Daniels, a friend of ours. He's just returned from London," Darlene said. "We have a number of things to go over with you regarding Philip Royal's death."

"Is that right?"

"Yes, and I think you'd better hear us out," I said.

Detective Finelli looked wary, but he said, "All right, come with me down to the conference room, where we can be private."

We reached a big room with orange-upholstered chairs arranged around a large table. I was relieved to see it. I had thought for a minute that we would be led to a room with a small table and a bright light hanging over it.

Detective Finelli closed the door and motioned for us to be seated. "Now, what's this all about?"

I took the lead. "First we'll tell you some facts we found out; then we'll tell you who we think killed Philip Royal. And you'd better believe us, because we're right."

Detective Finelli got out his notebook and looked at me skeptically.

I took a deep breath. "The other members of the band are not above suspicion. Keith, for example, has quite a temper. He held a grudge against Philip because he says he was the original leader of the band. Also, Keith did not like the direction the band was taking musically. They argued a lot. Keith resented the fact that the band used to be called just the Beefeaters, and then Nigel changed it to Philip Royal and the Beefeaters."

Darlene said, "Philip told me that Keith was a hothead with a huge ego who drank too much and had tried cocaine."

I looked at Darlene in surprise. She hadn't told me about the cocaine. Good thing I didn't go out on any dates with him.

Stu said, "You know how crazy people get when they're on cocaine, Detective. The two could have had a fight and Keith did him in."

Detective Finelli looked up from his notes. "That all you got on Keith?"

"Yes," I said, feeling frustrated. Detective Finelli didn't seem to think it was much. "Then there's Peter, the drummer. Evidently Philip thought he was getting too old to be in the band. He routinely threatened to fire Peter. And we know for a fact that Peter was in Philip's room that day." I looked at Darlene.

Out of her purse, Darlene pulled the tie tack. "Peter wears these as part of a gimmick. While I was in Philip's room the night of the murder, it stuck to my shoe. You know Philip had just checked into the hotel that day. This puts Peter at the scene of the crime. And he had motive if he thought he was going to be cut from the band. We interviewed Peter, and he's a nervous wreck. He admitted to being in Philip's room and trying to talk to Philip while he was in the bath. Peter claims Philip wouldn't talk to him, so he left. But Peter might have plugged in the guitar before he went."

Detective Finelli continued to take notes with that

maddeningly expressionless look on his face. "Why didn't you turn that tie tack in to me?"

Darlene looked militant. "I am now."

"You should have before now, Miss Roland," Detective Finelli said, and scowled.

"While I hate to say it, because I like Reggie, he also had motive to see Philip dead," I began, to keep Darlene from scratching the detective's eyes out. "You see, Philip didn't like the fact that Reggie was married with a son. He thought it was bad for the pop-star image. So he had photos of Reggie taken with young female fans sitting on his lap. He wrote to Jean—that's Reggie's wife—and insinuated that Reggie was having affairs. Reggie was furious."

Detective Finelli looked up from his notebook. "Is that all you've got?"

The detective was starting to sound like a broken record.

Darlene stood up. "Wait a minute. We've been doing all this investigating. We've come up with suspects who have motive and opportunity. Are you still so determined to pin this on me?"

"The investigation is going forward here at the precinct as well, Miss Roland. We haven't charged you with anything yet."

"I guess I'm supposed to be grateful for that." Darlene fumed as Stu put a soothing arm around her, and she sat back down. "But I'm going to lose my job if you don't lift this ridiculous ban on my flying."

Detective Finelli rolled his right shoulder in a mannerism I took to indicate his frustration. "No one leaves town until we make an arrest."

"Well, let me tell you who you should be arresting," Darlene said, standing up and leaning over the detective, hands on hips. "Astrid Loveday. All three of us agree that she's the one who killed Philip."

Chapter Twenty-four

"Sit down, Miss Roland. We're having a civilized conversation here," Detective Finelli said. "Or, if you'd prefer, I can have you arrested for withholding evidence."

"You don't seem interested in anything we're saying," I complained. "We've done a lot of work on this."

"I'm sure you have," the detective replied grimly. "Now, what is it about Astrid Loveday that's got you so worked up?"

Darlene looked about to burst, her red hair clashing with the red flush of her face, so I stepped in.

"Astrid had the motive, the opportunity, and the means to kill Philip. That's what it says on *Dragnet* is needed to catch a killer. Now, Astrid and Philip had broken up. She desperately wanted him back, to the point of taking up with the band's drummer in order to be close to him."

Stu said, "That fact can be confirmed by Astrid's sister, Penny, whom I interviewed personally in London."

"You have been a busy group," the detective said, smoothing his hand over his crew cut.

I dug in my purse and pulled out the golden triangle-shaped earring. "This belongs to Astrid. We have a photograph of her wearing it. We found the earring in Philip's room—"

"Wait a minute," Detective Finelli interrupted. "How did you get into Philip's hotel room?"

How we got in there isn't important," I said. "What is important is that Astrid was there the day he was murdered. Plus, we've spoken to Peter, Astrid's alibi. He admitted that he lied to cover up for her. He doesn't know where she was when Philip was killed."

Darlene said, "Astrid told me and Bebe that she was in Philip's room. She claims she and Philip reconciled and that they made love. That's her story. I think the earring dropped off when she was in the room killing him."

"Let me have that earring," Detective Finelli commanded. "Why didn't you bring this to me immediately? And I ask you again, what were you doing at a crime scene?"

"I have to try to clear my name any way I can!" Darlene said, her eyes the color of blue flames. "And we didn't bring it to you right away because you scoff at our findings, that's why."

Stu said, "Apparently Astrid is quite a character. According to her own sister, Astrid stalked Philip when they split and finally hooked up with Peter to stay close. Philip allegedly has pictures of Astrid in the buff. She wanted them back, and he wouldn't give them to her. I don't know why she was worried. In England, she's posed for racy pictures that have appeared in several magazines."

"And to top everything off," Darlene said, "Astrid confessed that she lied to the police about Philip seeing a red-haired American stewardess—me—before his flight over to London. Bebe is my witness. Now, Detective Finelli, what have you got to say in light of all our evidence?"

"I'd say you've got a lot of *circumstantial* evidence here. Not enough to charge Miss Loveday," the detective said.

"What do you want, a taped confession?" Darlene cried.

"Look, I believe Miss Loveday had reason to kill Philip Royal. I believe we can place her at the scene of the crime the day it took place. I'm still waiting for fingerprint evidence to come back from that electric plug."

"Aren't you even going to bring Astrid in for questioning?" I asked.

"Yes, I am. The investigation is ongoing, as I told you at the beginning of this meeting."

"All you have on *me* is 'circumstantial,' as you call it," Darlene protested.

"But I have you at the crime scene at the time of the singer's death, Miss Roland. And I haven't charged you with murder yet."

Darlene put her head in her hands. "So you still won't lift the ban on my flying?"

The detective shook his head. "Not at this time."

"You realize I could lose my job?" Darlene said, looking at him.

"I'd be sorry if that happened. If it turns out you're innocent, I'd be happy to try to make it right for you with the airline."

"When do you expect to have the fingerprints back?" Stu asked.

"Another week maybe. These things take time. Now, if there's nothing else, I need to get back to work," Detective Finelli said, rising from his chair. "Let me warn you all, getting involved in a police investigation is dangerous. I suggest you stop your amateur detective work now, before the killer decides to stop you himself."

"But you'll use the information we've given you," Stu said, holding the detective's gaze.

"Yes, I will."

I walked out of the police station feeling defeated.

"There's a Chock Full o' Nuts," Stu said. "Let's grab a cup of coffee and some of those white doughnuts."

As we sat at the counter a few minutes later, I could tell that Darlene was really down. She barely touched her doughnuts and took only little sips of her coffee.

Stu noticed it too. "Look, doll, police investigations

are slow. We've done everything we can to prod this one along."

"You'd think that with Philip being a star of sorts, they'd move their butts a little faster," Darlene complained.

"Nah. That only slows them down. They have to be sure they've got their facts right, and that they've nailed the real killer."

"Speaking of getting her facts right, are we going to go by Patty Gentry's hotel? Because if we are, we need to go soon, so I can get to work," I said.

"That's the spirit, Bebe. Let's keep on rolling," Stu said, with a grin at Darlene. He put a bracing arm around her shoulder, and we left.

Patty Gentry's hotel, the Biltmore, was beautiful but not nearly as luxurious as the Legends. And Stu had said Patty had a penthouse suite.

"What exactly are we going to say to get Miss Gentry to talk to us?" I asked in the elevator.

"Leave that to me," Darlene said. "The main thing is that we get her to tell us who she thinks the murderer is and why. Remember in her article she said she thought she knew who he or she was. We want whatever evidence she has. It might be enough to convince Detective Finelli of my innocence."

We walked to the very end of the hall.

"This is it," Stu said, pointing to a door marked 811A.

We could hear loud music, "He's So Fine" by the Chiffons, coming from the only other suite on the floor, 811B. The song made me think of Bradley.

The door to Patty's suite was open, a room-service tray wedged between the door frame and the door. Patty hadn't finished her scrambled eggs, or eaten any of her bacon. A half of a slice of toast remained as well.

Stu put out a hand in front of Darlene and me. "This is odd. Why would Miss Gentry leave her door open like this? Why didn't she just put the tray outside the door and close it?"

"Who cares?" Darlene said. "Maybe the maid left it like that. Let's see if Patty's here."

Stu turned and faced us. "Look, girls, I'm going in there first."

"What if she's not dressed?" I said. "You can't walk in on a woman getting dressed. It's not proper."

"I'm not standing around here all day discussing it." Darlene brushed past Stu, pushed the door to the suite open all the way, and stepped over the breakfast tray. "Patty Gentry, I want to talk to you!"

Stu and I quickly followed her into the room. Newspapers were scattered all over the living room, which was decorated in earth tones. At the desk, a portable typewriter sat, blank paper in the roll.

"She's not answering us," I said. "She must not be here."

Darlene pulled open a door that turned out to be a closet. A coat and three suits hung neatly. "Her coat's here."

"Darlene," Stu said, "let me do the looking."

But it was too late. Darlene opened another door, which led to the bedroom. She let out a piercing scream.

Stu and I rushed to her side.

There, lying on the floor, was the body of Patty Gentry. Her mod metal daisy belt, the one I had so coveted, was twisted around her neck.

Stu stepped over to the body and felt for a pulse.

Darlene and I stood together, our arms linked, our gazes unable to move away from the scene in front of us.

Stu looked up with a grim expression on his face. "She's dead."

Chapter Twenty-five

Needless to say, Detective Finelli was not pleased to find us sitting in Patty Gentry's suite with her dead body. Stu had made the call to the police. He had stated that the killing was connected to that of Philip Royal, so the detective was sent right over.

"I just told the three of you to let the police do the investigating," Detective Finelli said, his normal composure slipping. He had already taken our statements as to what we had found when we came in. "What exactly were you doing here?"

As a team of police filled the bedroom where Patty lay, the detective sat with us in the living room. He ran a hand over his crew cut, waiting for our answers.

Stu said, "Miss Gentry made it clear in her newspaper article that she knew who killed Philip. We came by to find out what evidence she had and against whom. Astrid Loveday told Miss Roland and Miss Bennett that she was going to 'take care of Patty.' Killing her might have been her way of doing so. Remember all the evidence we have against Astrid."

"The killer must have come here to collect the evidence," I said, feeling cold though the room was a moderate temperature. "But you must see if you can find anything left behind, Detective. I know you can do it."

Detective Finelli looked at me. "Thank you, Miss Bennett. Let me ask you this: What if you had arrived while the killer was doing his work? Do you see how you are placing yourself in the path of danger by continuing to meddle in police business?"

"We aren't going to quit 'meddling,' as you put it," Darlene said. "You refuse to clear my name. Do you think I killed Patty too? That my friends and I came over here after talking to you and wrapped that belt around her throat? Can't you see that Astrid is your most likely suspect?"

"I'm not going to comment on this new case to you, Miss Roland," Detective Finelli said. "You are already under orders not to leave the city."

Darlene got up and stood over the detective. "You've got a lot of nerve, mister! Accusing me of two murders. How dare you think I'm capable of such a thing. I'm going to report you to your superior, because I can't punch you a good one."

"Darlene!" I exclaimed.

Stu stood and took Darlene's arm. "That's enough. Let's go, doll."

Detective Finelli was still looking at Darlene. "I didn't accuse you of anything, Miss Roland. But I wonder if you always react with violence when things don't go your way."

"Don't answer that, doll," Stu said.

Stu and I led Darlene from the room. We stood in the hall to wait for the elevator.

Darlene was shaking with anger. "I can't believe that man."

"He's only doing his job, doll. Try not to take it personally," Stu said.

"How can I not when there's been a second murder, and I'm at the scene of that crime too? Detective Finelli is just waiting for an opportunity to arrest me," Darlene said.

"He can't arrest you," I replied. "You didn't do anything."

The elevator came, and we went down to the busy

street. The clouds over the skyscrapers seemed to be moving fast. Rain threatened. As usual, cabs and cars drove down the street in no particular lane.

"I have to get to work," I said. "Darlene, I'll see you tonight. Try not to worry." I leaned over and gave her a hug.

"I'll take care of her," Stu said. "I'm taking her to the Plaza for lunch."

Darlene turned to him in surprise, and he put his arm around her.

I hailed a cab to the office. It was a little after two, later than I had told Bradley I would be. A lot later. *Uh-oh.*

I slipped around the frosted-glass partition to my desk, and put my purse and gloves in the bottom desk drawer as silently as I could, thinking that maybe I could pretend I'd returned earlier.

Bradley had a letter he wanted typed. I put the dictating machine's headset on, pulled out a piece of paper, and rolled it into the typewriter.

Immediately Bradley came out of his office. I made my expression as innocent as possible, but I could tell I was in for it now.

"Miss Bennett, come into my office." His body was stiff as he pointed to the doorway.

"Yes, Mr. Williams," I said sweetly, taking the headset off, smiling at him, trying to defuse the situation.

We went into his office. Bradley closed the door. He did not motion for me to sit down, so we stood there facing each other. Boy, did he look mad. I'd never seen him like that.

"Where have you been? You told me you were going to see Detective Finelli and would be here by noon. You're over two hours late." His blue gaze never wavered, and he pointed at me when he said *two hours late.*

I swallowed. I couldn't lie. But gosh, I really didn't want to tell the truth. What a pickle! Instead I said, "Have you been busy? A lot of phone calls?"

"Yes, as a matter of fact. Since word has gotten out that we're not releasing the Beefeater's album, industry people are ringing me nonstop. But that's not what had me concerned. I didn't know where you were."

So he was concerned about me, was he? *Hmmm.* I pressed my lips together and smoothed my lip gloss.

"Don't think you can distract me from the issue at hand. What happened at the detective's office?"

Okay, I could answer that. "Stu, Darlene, and I presented Detective Finelli with the evidence we have against Astrid Loveday. Darlene and I had even found one of her gold triangle earrings. You know, like the one in the picture you showed her that night at the Legends' lounge?"

He nodded tersely. "When did you find the earring?"

Darn, I was digging myself in deeper. "Darlene and I searched Philip's room last Sunday."

Bradley's jaw dropped. "How on earth did you do that?"

"We posed as maids. The earring came up when I was vacuuming." Maybe he'd see now how clever I was. Not just a 'kid.'

"When you were vacuuming?" He put one hand to his brow. "You realize how much trouble you could have gotten into if hotel personnel had caught you?"

Or Daddy. Or if those police officers hadn't believed us. "Well, nobody caught us. It all turned out okay. And we got some evidence against Astrid."

Bradley's hand dropped to his side. "You are one stubborn girl."

Girl! My chin came up at that. "I am one *loyal* woman. I'm loyal to Darlene. I want to see her name cleared. And I want to help you out of this sticky situation with the band and Rip-City."

"I don't need your help, Miss Bennett."

That cut it. "Well, you're getting it whether you like it or not."

We stood staring at each another. Then he said, "So you've been at Detective Finelli's office the entire morning and two hours into the afternoon?"

My heart rate increased. My hands twisted. "No, we went somewhere else afterward."

"Where exactly was that?"

Darn him! "Patty Gentry's hotel."

"Patty Gentry's hotel . . . Wait, don't tell me you went there to talk to her about that article she wrote."

"All right, I won't." I could feel myself getting angry at him. He was treating me like a naughty child.

"You will tell me," he said, contradicting himself.

"You know, Mr. Williams, this really isn't any of your business. I apologize for being late. It won't happen again."

He looked stumped, and almost guilty, but still, he pressed me. "I think it's my responsibility to know where you are during working hours. Now tell me."

Maybe he did care about me. "Fine. I went with Stu and Darlene. Patty had written that she knew who Philip's killer was. We wanted to find out what evidence she had. Maybe she could clear Darlene's name."

"And what did she tell you?"

I closed my eyes. "Nothing."

"What do you mean 'nothing'? How could that be?"

Oh, God, transport me to another planet right now.

"I'm waiting, Miss Bennett."

I shifted from one foot to the other. Then I opened my eyes and said, "She told us nothing because she was . . . um . . . dead." My voice finished on a squeak.

"What!"

"When we got to her suite, the door was open. We went in and found her strangled on the floor of the bedroom." I had to stop myself from cringing at his look.

"She's dead? *Murdered?*"

"Yes."

"And you found her? After all my warnings about

staying out of this investigation? How could you put yourself in danger like that?" He was breathing hard now and pointing his finger at me again.

"I'm a modern woman, as I've told you before. I have free will to investigate this crime if I want to!"

"What if the killer was still in the suite when you came in? You could have been hurt, if not killed, you silly girl."

Silly girl! "I wasn't hurt or killed. I'm not as naive as when I first got to New York," I said, my own voice rising.

"I can't believe you keep getting in deeper and deeper. And you've ignored my warnings. I am so angry with you right now, Miss Bennett, I could throttle you myself."

"But you won't. And you know why?"

"Why?" he yelled.

"Because you'd have to touch me to throttle me, and you'd never do that!"

"Is that right?"

"Yes!"

In a flash he swung one arm around my waist. His other hand came up and held my chin. He lowered his beautiful head and kissed me right on the lips, a long, leisurely kiss. His lips were incredibly soft, then demanding as he deepened the kiss.

Shocked and drowning in pleasure, I took a moment, then put my arms around his neck and began to kiss him back.

That was when he abruptly dropped the embrace and moved back a step.

Gone was the angry Bradley. Gone was the passionate Bradley. In his place was a cool, composed businessman.

"I'm terribly sorry. I lost my head. It won't happen again, Miss Bennett."

To my mortification, I felt tears behind my eyes. He regretted kissing me. Was I not a good enough kisser for him?

He went on: "If you feel you would like to be transferred to another department, I won't blame you. I'll give you an excellent recommendation. Rip-City doesn't want to lose a good secretary over my foolish behavior."

Gathering every ounce of strength and pride I could muster, I said, "That won't be necessary. Your apology is accepted. Now, if there's nothing else, I have work to do."

"Thank you, Miss Bennett," he said, moving to sit behind his desk. "I think that's an excellent idea. I've spoken to you too much about your private life. My only excuse is that you are young and new to the city. I've felt protective of you. But as you have pointed out to me, you don't need my concern. We must therefore keep this a business relationship."

I turned and walked out of the office at a normal pace. I managed to make it all the way to the ladies' room before the tears fell.

Chapter Twenty-six

Although there was plenty of work to do, and normally I would have stayed and finished it, I couldn't. I had to get out of the office and away from Bradley.

So I left right at five. Bradley had closed his door for the remainder of the afternoon. I hadn't seen him after that kiss.

I took the bus home, thinking the whole time of Bradley's lips on mine. And how Bradley regretted it, called it foolish. Tears burned in my eyes again. I had to fight them back lest I disgrace myself on the bus.

At my stop, I got off and made my way up Sixty-fifth Street to my apartment. Harry, the wino, was hanging around the apartment building. I sighed and reached into my wallet for some change.

"I knew I could count on you, Miss Sweet Face," Harry said, smiling at the money. "I need this tonight."

He wasn't drunk, but he was shaking badly. "Get yourself something to eat, Harry," I said in a sad voice.

He scratched his head. " 'Man does not live by bread alone,' " he quoted. He turned to leave, but then stopped. "Say, you don't look so good."

"I don't feel so good."

Harry narrowed his bleary eyes at me. "Trouble with a man?"

"Yes. Is it written on my forehead?"

"Nah, but I know only a man can put that kind of gloom on a woman's face. I don't know what kinda fella would treat a lady like you bad," Harry mused.

Wearily I sat down on the front steps. To my surprise, Harry sat on the step below me. He said, "Want to talk about it?"

Great, here I was discussing my love life, or lack thereof, with a wino. "There's not much to tell. I love somebody who doesn't love me back."

"Ah," Harry said, shaking his head. "There's a problem. How do you know he doesn't love you back?"

"He kissed me and then said he regretted it. That it was foolish."

"Kissed you, eh? Must feel something for you then."

I relived the kiss once again, closing my eyes against the late-afternoon sunshine and remembering how Bradley had held me tight, kissed me like he would like nothing better than to keep on doing so.

"Maybe he does," I said in a small voice. "But he pulled away and apologized for kissing me. He said it would never happen again."

"Never's a long time."

"I don't know."

"Not married, is he?" Harry asked.

"No! In fact, he's quite the dashing bachelor."

Harry slapped his knee. "That's it then. He likes you so much he doesn't dare kiss you again. Might give him thoughts of marriage. Threatens his bachelorhood. But he'll come around. Wait and see."

I remembered that was Darlene's theory—that Bradley wasn't ready to settle down. Though I didn't think Bradley would "come around" anytime soon.

Rising from my seat, I said, "Thanks, Harry."

He got up. "Anytime. I'm always here in this block. The police kinda pass me by because I don't give anybody trouble."

"Harry, I don't mean to pry, but have you thought of getting a job?"

Harry scrambled down the steps. "I gotta go now, miss. Hey, I don't even know your name."

"Call me Bebe." Obviously Harry wasn't going to discuss with me the reasons for his living on the streets. Maybe someday.

I unlocked the apartment door and headed straight for my bedroom. Food would have made me sick, so I skipped dinner. After a long, hot bath, I crawled into my pajamas and went to sleep with my fingers touching my lips.

I spent most of the next day, Saturday, eating Fig Newtons and hanging around in my bathrobe, feeling sorry for myself. Darlene was with Stu. Around six in the evening I remembered I had to meet Vince down at the Bitter End in the Village. What a bummer.

I changed into a simple black dress with a neckline to my throat. I took a bus down to Bleeker Street—still afraid of trying my hand at the subway—and entered the coffeehouse.

As I scanned the crowd for Vince, a man came up to me.

"Hi, gorgeous, I'm Fred Weintraub. Can I help you?"

"I'm sorry, Mr. Weintraub, but I'm meeting someone here," I said, wondering if he was trying to pick me up.

Suddenly Vince was at my side. I had to hold back a giggle. Dressed in a black beret, black turtleneck, and black slacks, Vince was trying hard for the beatnik look. Pushing forty, he looked ridiculous.

"Hey, Fred, I must've missed you when I came in. Good to see you," he said enthusiastically, shaking Mr. Weintraub's hand.

Mr. Weintraub ignored Vince and looked at me. "Are you with him, miss?"

"Well, we're both from Rip-City Records," I said, not wanting to give any wrong impressions. "I'm Bebe Bennett, secretary to Bradley Williams. Vince and I are going to check out a new act, a Mr. Neil Diamond."

Mr. Weintraub smiled. "I'm happy to hear it, Miss Bennett. Neil is a fantastic singer. And please, while you're with us, be my guests. Drinks are on the house."

That was when it dawned on me that Mr. Weintraub was the owner of the Bitter End. Otherwise why would Vince be groveling and Mr. Weintraub be offering us drinks on the house?

I smiled at him. "Thank you, Mr. Weintraub."

"Please," he said, "take a table at the front of the house. Just ignore any 'reserved' signs."

"That's very kind of you," I said.

"Great seeing you, Fred," Vince said.

Mr. Weintraub went to welcome some new arrivals.

Vince led us to a table, placed the reserved sign face-down, and began his attack.

"So, babycakes, you sure are looking wicked tonight," Vince oozed, his tacky cologne in full evidence.

I pulled my skirt down over my knees. "This is an interesting place," I said, changing the subject. "I'm anxious to hear Mr. Diamond."

"And I'm just happy to be with you."

Saved! A waitress came up and took our orders. Vince requested a Manhattan. I asked for a Coke.

Vince's eyebrows went up. "Babycakes, just a Coke? Come on, you're in one of New York's hot spots. Live a little."

"I'm here on business, and I have to get home later. I have no intention of getting blitzed."

Vince sighed dramatically.

The houselights went down, leaving a spotlight on a bar stool in front of a redbrick background.

A tiny, terrified girl with short brown hair, no more than seventeen, came on first. She wore a long cotton dress with a cactus print all over it. Despite her little-girl appearance, her strong voice, singing about the civil rights movement, held the audience captive. When she finished, she whispered that her name was Adele, and thanked everyone. A respectable round of applause

made her smile and give a timid bow before she exited
the stage.

Vince whispered to me, "She's got no looks. No one's
gonna sign her."

"I thought she had great potential. Do you always sign
acts based on their looks?"

"Yeah."

No wonder Vince hadn't gotten very far at Rip-City.

A man came up to the bar stool next. I caught my
breath. Handsome, with thick, dark, wavy hair, he wore
a dark red turtleneck underneath a navy jacket.

He smiled at the audience, making a shiver go up my
spine, and said, "Hi, everybody, I'm Neil Diamond."

A hearty round of applause met these words. Either
Mr. Diamond had played the Bitter End before, or he
was simply well-known among the Village coffeehouses.

The room got quiet as he took his acoustic guitar and
strummed a few notes. Then he opened his mouth and
began to sing. The song, called "Solitary Man," was
about a man who kept falling in love with the wrong
woman and decided to remain on his own until he could
find the right one.

Totally entranced by his beautiful, rich voice and the
lyrics of the song, I was sad when the song faded away
with, "Mmm hmmm, solitary man."

The crowd burst into loud applause.

I grinned at Vince. "We've got to sign him. He's going
to be a star!"

"Girls don't go for his type. He's from Brooklyn."

"Well, I'm a girl, and I think he's handsome and sexy,"
I countered, outraged at Vince's line of thought.

"I'm tellin' you, babycakes, Neil Diamond will never
amount to anything."

I stood. "I've heard Mr. Diamond sing. He has enor-
mous talent. I'll be giving my report to Mr. Williams."

Vince looked surprised. "You're leaving me?"

"Yes, I am. And in the future, Vince, don't call me
'babycakes' or 'muffin-cup' or any of those other offen-

sive terms or I'll report you to Mr. Williams." So saying,
I marched out of the Bitter End, feeling proud of myself
for finally standing up to Vince—the devil with the
consequences—and took the bus home.

I stayed up for two hours writing my report to Bradley
about Neil Diamond before going to bed exhausted.

Sunday, I went to Mass, then came home and crashed.
I couldn't get that kiss Bradley had given me out of my
mind, or my heart.

Monday at the office was torture. I was behind in my
work because of my absence Friday, and Bradley kept
giving me more, plus I had to type the report on Mr.
Diamond.

Although his door was open, Bradley rarely spoke to
me unless it was to give instructions regarding this letter
or that chart or a phone call he wanted made.

I decided I would not show him how miserable I was.
If he could be businesslike, so could I. I kept a professional, pleasant manner, even though it was killing me.

At lunchtime I escaped the heavy atmosphere, took
the elevator downstairs, and ran out to the street for my
daily guilty pleasure, a hot dog. Hoards of people seemed
to be in a rush to get somewhere. Cabs honked. The air
smelled like different foods cooking, mixed with exhaust
fumes from trucks unloading goods. The excitement of
New York City was all around me.

I stood against my building, eating my hot dog and
watching people go by. I treated myself to a bottle of
Coke and took it back upstairs with me. No matter what
happened with Bradley, I couldn't go back to Richmond.
I loved New York City.

There was a note on my desk from Bradley, saying he
was going out to lunch and not to expect him back until
around three. I held the paper in my hand and reread
the words. Bradley often had business lunches that went
on until two, but three? I wondered if he was meeting
some woman for a few hours of pleasure. *Stop!* I crum-

pled up the piece of paper, threw it in the trash can, and told myself not to think such thoughts.

I was transcribing a letter from dictation when Darlene called.

"Hi, Bebe, how are you?"

"Fine," I said, unable to share my sadness with her. After all, she was a suspect in a murder investigation. What were my bruised feelings about Bradley compared to that?

"You were asleep last night when I came home," Darlene said, "so I didn't get to tell you that Stu and I are planning to go for drinks at the Legends tonight. We just want to see what's going on over there since Patty Gentry's death. Want to come with us?"

"I don't want to be a third wheel," I said.

"Bebe, don't be silly. Come on and meet us. You don't have other plans, do you?"

"No, I don't have other plans." What other plans would I have?

"Well, then, come on."

I sighed. "Okay, but it's going to have to be late, because I have so much work to do. I probably won't get out of here until seven."

"Stu and I will be waiting for you in the lounge."

"All right," I said, and hung up the phone. At least I wouldn't be alone with my thoughts tonight.

Bradley came back to the office at three fifteen. A faint odor of alcohol followed him. I heard him using his electric shaver in his executive bathroom. About twenty minutes later he emerged from his office with a fresh shirt on.

"I'm leaving for the day, Miss Bennett."

Already? She must be very enticing. I held back a sniffle. "Very well, Mr. Williams."

"Have you finished the report I gave you?"

"No, but I'm planning on staying late to catch up on all my work."

"Fine. Just remember to lock the door when everyone else leaves at five."

Then he was gone. In the bottom drawer of my desk I had an emergency Hershey candy bar. Now was the time for it if there ever was one.

The afternoon went on, and slowly people began to leave. An idea formed in my mind, a childish one, but I couldn't help myself. When everyone was gone, I went into Bradley's office. In a half closet next to the executive bathroom hung several of his shirts. I opened the door and stood there gazing at the neat rows of cotton. Of its own volition, my hand crept up and touched the cuff of a white shirt. It was heavily starched.

Suddenly I realized what I was doing and dropped the cuff. This was not the eighth grade! I was a grown woman, and grown women did not moon over their would-be boyfriend's shirts.

I marched back to my desk and dug into work.

It was when I was working on a letter from Bradley to Patty Gentry's boss when the lights in the office suddenly went out, leaving me in pitch blackness.

For a moment I was too stunned to move.

Then it hit me: I had forgotten to lock the door to the office. Someone had come in and turned out the lights!

I couldn't see who was there. Frozen at my desk, I called out, "Who's here?" My voice sounded weak and frightened despite myself.

My heart started beating hard. I could sense a figure coming right up to the glass partition next to my desk.

Then a voice with a heavy English accent whispered, "You'd better watch yourself, bitch. Stop investigating or you'll be the next one to die."

I sat there unable to move or speak, I was so terrified. He threw something on my desk that landed with a thud. Then I heard him hurry across the room toward the exit. The door closed with a soft swoosh behind him.

Shaking all over, I got up from my desk, bumping into

things in the dark, and stumbled over to lock the door. My fingers trembled on the simple lock, but I managed it. I found the light switch, and once more the office was lit.

Then I raced back to my desk.

I barely held back a scream.

On top of the report I'd just typed for Bradley lay a dead rat.

Chapter Twenty-seven

Chilled to the bone and trembling, I put my hands over my face so I couldn't see the rat. Through the cracks in my fingers, I made my way into Bradley's office. I needed him.

No! I was supposed to be a strong, modern woman. I could handle this myself. I started to walk back to my desk, but a noise in the hall made me jump.

Okay, I couldn't handle it myself! But how to reach Bradley? I had his home phone number, but it was on my blotter, tucked into a corner. The blotter where the rat lay. And with my trouble with numbers, I couldn't remember it.

I looked wildly around the office. *Okay, calm down,* I told myself. *It's possible he has his phone number in here.* I went to his Rolodex and flipped through it. Nothing under his name.

Then I looked down at his desk. I cleared some papers away. There was a long list of phone numbers typed by a previous secretary. *Thank God!* I scanned the list: Bernadette, Susannah, Claudia, and it went on all the way down the sheet—all girl's names. *Darn him!*

But at the end of the long list was the blessed word *home.*

I picked up the telephone receiver, my finger shaking in the little round circles of the dial, and prayed he'd answer.

On the third ring, he said, "Hello?"

"Mr. Williams, this is Bebe. I mean, Miss Bennett."

"Miss Bennett. Is there something wrong?"

"Yes! You've got to come help me. There was a man, and it was dark, and he threatened me, and now there's a rat on my desk!" I rushed the words out, trembling.

"Miss Bennett, are you hurt?"

"No, he didn't touch me."

"Is the door to the office locked?"

"Yes."

"Are you in my office?"

"Yes."

"I'll be there right away. Just sit in my chair or lie down on the sofa and take deep breaths."

"Thank you. Please hurry."

I tried to sit down, but couldn't. I paced the office, that menacing voice playing over and over in my head. Who could it have been? One of the guys in the band? Nigel? I didn't recognize it. But then, he had been whispering. Another chill ran down my body.

Finally I heard the office door open. For a moment I was certain the bad man had returned. I looked around for something to defend myself with. Then Bradley came into the room. I forced myself not to run into his arms. He had on a pair of casual slacks and a black turtleneck. He looked sophisticated and sleek. Then I noticed he had a gun in his hand. I was afraid of guns even though Daddy kept an arsenal.

"Come, sit down," Bradley said, leading me to the sofa. "Start from the beginning and tell me what happened."

We sat down. I could hear the ticking of the clock on his desk. I folded my arms together. I couldn't get myself to talk.

"Miss Bennett, would you like a drink?"

I held my hand to my throat. "No, I can't stand the thought of drinking my Coke now that it's been sitting next to the rat."

"I meant something a little stronger." He put the gun in the waistband of his pants, got up, and went to his credenza. From where I sat, I could see bottles of alcohol and glasses. He retrieved a shot glass and poured amber liquid into it. "This is just a little whiskey. Drink it slowly."

I accepted the glass, our fingers touching. Slowly I sipped the contents. Warmth filled me as the liquid went down.

"Better?"

"Yes, thank you."

"All right. Now try again to tell me what happened."

"I had finished typing up a sales report and was working on that last letter you gave me, the one to Patty Gentry's boss."

"I remember."

"All of a sudden the lights in the office went out. Everything was so completely dark, I couldn't see my hand in front of me. Then I realized there was someone in the office."

"Didn't you lock the door like I told you to?"

Ashamed, I remembered that I'd been busy mooning over Bradley's shirts and had completely forgotten about locking the door. "No, I forgot."

Bradley sighed and said, "Then what happened?"

"Someone came right up to the partition beside my desk. He spoke to me—no, he whispered. It was so creepy. I'll never forget it. He had a heavy British accent."

"What did he say?"

"He said, 'You'd better watch yourself, bitch,' and then, 'Stop investigating or you'll be the next one to die.' He threw that rat over the partition, and it landed on my desk. Only I didn't know it was a rat until after I heard the man leave, and I turned on the lights."

"Dammit. He was warning you off snooping around the murders of Philip and Patty. He threatened your life."

"I guess so."

"Will this make you stop, Miss Bennett?"

I straightened my shoulders. "No. These scare tactics won't work with me."

"Excuse me for pointing out the obvious, but you called me for help, and you were quite hysterical."

I thought fast. "That's because it's a man's job to deal with dead animals."

"You were scared, as well you should be."

"Well, anybody would have lost their cool. I'm okay now, though," I lied, my heart skipping and jumping in my chest.

"I think we should call the police. They might be able to get fingerprints off the door to the office."

"No! Don't call the police. The bad man probably had on gloves. No one would carry a dead rat with bare hands. And Detective Finelli would only lecture me again about being involved in the investigation."

"Which would be appropriate," Bradley said firmly. "You're in over your head. That man had you at his mercy."

"Could you just take the rat out of here?"

Bradley stood up. "You're like a puppy with a sock in its mouth and someone is pulling the other end. Come on; I'll grab some newspaper and wrap the rat up. We'll go downstairs together. You've had enough here for one night."

I waited until Bradley had the rat away from view. Holding my nose—the rat had left a stink—I got my purse and gloves from my desk drawer.

Together we went downstairs.

"I'll find a Dumpster and get rid of this. Are you all right to get a cab home alone?" Bradley asked.

"Actually I'm supposed to meet Darlene and Stu over at the Legends," I said. "I'm late."

Bradley shook his head. "Kid, I don't know what more I can say to you."

"Thank you for helping me out tonight, Mr. Williams."

"You're welcome. I just hope the next time you need help, I won't be too late."

He waited until a cab stopped for me and saw me safely inside, then walked away. I turned around in the seat and watched him go.

At the Legends, I headed straight for the lounge. Maria was working. She smiled at me. "Your friends are over there, Bebe. Do you want a drink?"

"A ginger ale sure would taste good about now."

"I'll bring it right over."

"Bebe, you're almost an hour late," Darlene said.

I sat down at the table. "Wait until you hear what kept me." Between sips of ginger ale, I told the story.

Darlene gasped and shuddered. Stu looked at me seriously and said, "If you two are going to continue with this, you're going to have to really be on your guard. Maybe you've gone far enough. Threats from a killer are not to be taken lightly."

Darlene got that militant look on her face, the one that said *Back off, buster.* She said, "We've gotten this far, okay? And just think: If the killer is unnerved enough to threaten Bebe, we must be getting close."

"What if he had decided to eliminate Bebe?" Stu said. "She was all alone, defenseless in that office. Have you thought of that?"

"I won't make that mistake again," I promised.

"Still, this is a dangerous business—"

Darlene interrupted Stu. "Look who's just come in the door."

We all three turned to see Astrid, carrying a full-length fur coat—even though it was in the fifties outside—and wearing a long red dress. She came into the lounge with a tall, well-groomed man of about fifty years old.

Stu said, "I know him."

But before he could tell us who he was, Astrid brought him over to the table. "Hello, everyone. This is Bill Siddons," she announced, running her hand down his arm. "He's the head of Siddons Modeling Agency."

Greetings were exchanged all around. Stu and Bill recognized each other. Stu stood, and some backslapping followed.

Then Astrid cooed, "Bill, darling, would you be a luv and get me a pack of ciggies? The machine is just down that hall."

"Sure, baby," Bill said, and went to do her bidding.

The minute he was away, Astrid turned to us, an ugly look on her face. "Well, you see, you stupid turnips from the South, Bill is my real alibi for the night of Philip's death. Sure, I would have taken Philip back, but the jerk wouldn't have me. And Peter is such a bore with all his anxieties."

Stu said, "How did you hook up with Bill?"

"I met Bill a year ago when he came to London looking for talent. I kept his number and called him the minute we landed in New York. He took me out to dinner—a long, lingering dinner that lasted until the wee hours of the morning, if you get my drift. We've been seeing each other ever since then. Now I've finally persuaded him to let me move in with him. He's signed me on as a model too. I'd been hedging my bets and Bill paid off. So your little murder investigation is over where I'm concerned. I even met with Detective Finelli today, and I'm off the suspect list. You underestimated how clever I am."

"We underestimated what a slut you are," Darlene said.

Astrid ignored her and turned to me. "If you had any sense, you'd be looking at Nigel. He's bitter as hell knowing Philip was going to fire him. Plus he tried to leave the country."

"What about Patty Gentry?" I said.

Astrid shrugged. "Good riddance, if you ask me. Nigel probably did her in for printing that story in the newspaper about his precious boys."

Astrid would have said more, but Bill returned with

her cigarettes. She smiled as if we'd been having the most civil of conversations.

"Good-bye, everyone. Bill and I are here to get my things. I doubt I'll see you again, as we'll hardly be moving in the same circles. Although you might see me in the magazines or on the runway." She blew a tiny kiss in our direction then waltzed off with Bill.

Darlene took a big swig of her drink. "Looks like we're back to square one, boys and girls. I can't believe it."

"Not necessarily," I said slowly. "Maybe we should listen to Astrid. If Nigel's so homesick for England, let's take him out to a British-style pub and get him drunk. Who knows what he might say?"

"Good idea, Bebe. But let me handle Nigel," Darlene said.

Though Darlene didn't see it, I noticed Stu frown.

Chapter Twenty-eight

Tuesday at the office, Bradley maintained his distance. I did my work, feeling bummed, and went home. Darlene was out, I guessed with Stu. I made myself a box of macaroni and cheese, then couldn't eat much. After *The Red Skelton Hour* was over at nine thirty, I went to bed.

The phone rang, waking me out of a deep sleep. Was I late for work? Was something wrong with Darlene? I raced to the phone in the kitchen, tripping over the little daisy area rug I'd found that went with my bedspread.

In the dark kitchen, I grabbed the phone. "Hello?" I said breathlessly.

"Bebe, luv. Keith here."

"Keith?" I stumbled around until I found the light switch. The clock on the wall said quarter to eleven. "What's wrong? Has something happened?"

Keith chuckled. "No, everything's cool. Jean and the baby are asleep, and Reggie, Peter, and I want to have some fun. Things have been too morose here. It's like something out of *The Twilight Zone*."

Geez. "You want to go out at this hour?"

"Oh, come on, Bebe; it's early for New York. You know that. We've been trying to find some slot-car racing, but apparently you Yanks are behind the times and don't have slot cars yet," Keith said with an air of superiority.

"I'm sorry." My brain began to kick into gear. Keith

sounded like he'd been lapping up the vino, if not the bourbon.

"So what do you suggest, Bebe? We don't have any wheels, and we want to go for a ride."

"Have you been on a carriage ride yet over by Central Park?"

"Luv, we've not even been in Central Park, we've been so dull. Are you talking about an old-fashioned carriage?"

"Yes. It's great fun. Darlene took me when I first came to New York."

"Okay," Keith said. "It sounds like a tickle. And it's a beautiful night."

"Well, here's what you do. Get a cab outside the hotel and direct him to Central Park near the Plaza where the carriages are. Be sure to have money with you to pay and tip the carriage driver."

"Bebe! We want you to go with us," Keith said.

"Oh, hey, at any other time I'd love to, but I have to be at work in the morning. You guys go ahead, and have a blast."

"What! That's a ghastly thought, Bebe. It wouldn't be any fun without you. Plus you'll still have plenty of time to sleep. Please, luv," Keith cajoled.

Heck, why not? I thought. "All right. I'll meet you in front of the Legends in thirty to forty minutes."

"That's the spirit, old girl! See you then," Keith said, and hung up.

I went into the living room, lifted the window to the fire escape, and checked the temperature. Mild. I closed the window and dashed to my closet. I selected a pair of slim-cut black pants. Ladies didn't wear pants unless it was for a very casual occasion. Riding in Central Park this late at night seemed to qualify. Plus, I was too lazy to put on a girdle and stockings.

To go with the pants, I chose a pale pink blouse. After making a few swipes at my eyes with liquid liner and black mascara, and sliding my Mary Quant lip gloss on,

I was finished with my face. I threw on some flats and my short black flared jacket, and I was ready to go.

Outside, Harry worked the corner of Lexington and Sixty-fifth.

"Isn't this past your bedtime, Miss Sweet Face?" he greeted me.

My chin rose defiantly. "I have a date with three men."

Harry laughed. "Wish I could see that. Any one of them the one you're in love with?"

"No," I said miserably.

"One day, just you wait, he'll come around."

I noticed Harry's hands shook, and pulled out some quarters from my purse. He took the money and smiled. "You trying to get a cab?"

"I was going to."

"Here, let me." With that Harry moved out into the street. He put two fingers in his mouth and whistled—loudly. A Yellow Cab stopped.

"I'm impressed, Harry," I said, entering the cab.

He blew off the compliment. "You can do it too. Be safe, now."

I waved good-bye. For the hundredth time the question crossed my mind as to why Harry wouldn't try to kick his booze habit and get a job so he could have a decent place to live. I wondered if I'd ever know.

Arriving at the Legends, I told the cab to wait. Running inside, I saw the boys in the lounge drinking and eating cocktail wieners. They spotted me, got up, threw money on the table, and zipped on over.

"Bebe, I dig those pants on you," Keith said, putting an arm around my waist. *Hmmm.* Did he smell funny?

Reggie and Peter joined us, laughing and roughhousing with each other. "Hey, Bebe, you look smashing," Peter said.

"Yeah," Reggie agreed.

"Well, thanks," I replied. "I've got a cab outside with a jump seat. We can all fit in easily."

While we were all piling into the cab, Keith—I know

it was him—pitched my bottom. I turned to scold him, but the guys were laughing, and I didn't want to be a wet rag. Plus, I suspected what they'd been doing earlier.

Once everyone was in the cab, and the order for Central Park had been given, my feeling was confirmed. All the guys smelled like they'd been smoking grass. I knew what it smelled like because a group of guys at Philip Morris used to get high in the men's room.

Oh, well. Nothing I could do about it now. I told myself not to be a fuddy-duddy.

We made it to the park, where we all tumbled out of the cab. Carriages stood in a line waiting for passengers.

Keith threw his hands up in the air. "Isn't it grand? A full moon."

"Why don't you sing a few chords of 'Moon River' for us, Keith," Reggie ribbed.

Not one to back down from a challenge, Keith began singing at the top of his lungs, hands in the air, but he doubled over laughing halfway through the song. The other guys seemed just as amused, as they laughed uproariously. I thought Keith's dramatic rendition of the song was funny too, but felt the hilarity had more to do with the grass they'd been smoking.

As Reggie, Peter, and I stood nearby, Keith went up to one of the carriages and began an animated discussion with the driver, an older man with a blue cap. The driver shrugged and pointed at a carriage two down from his. Money changed hands. Then Keith ran back to the carriage the driver had indicated and began talking with him, a younger, rough sort of man sporting a top hat. Again money changed hands.

The top-hatted driver turned his horses in the direction of the street. They walked up so that the two carriages were aligned.

Keith pulled me by the hand, urging me into the carriage driven by the blue-capped man. Reggie and Peter got into the other carriage.

"Keith," I said, "what are we do—"

The cracking of the whips broke through the sounds of the night. The two carriages bolted ahead. Thrown forward from the seat behind the driver, I landed on my knees at Keith's feet.

"We're cookin' now, Bebe," he said, helping me up and holding me next to him. "We're racing the other carriage!"

As the horses gained speed, I was torn between screaming and laughing. The ride was exhilarating. Who knew the old nags could move so fast! And the carriages were right next to each other.

"A fiver says we beat you!" Reggie yelled from his carriage.

"Clown! No less than a ten!" Keith shouted.

The two drivers bellowed curses at each other. I guessed they'd been rivals.

Peter produced a transistor radio and turned the volume up so high I could hear "Fun Fun Fun" by the Beach Boys over the horses' hooves.

Peter and Reggie began to sing another version of the song: "Fun, fun, fun, till her daddy takes the carriage away."

The guys thought this was a hoot.

Keith yelled, "The joint is jumping."

More bursts of laughter followed. Suddenly the hijinks were cut off as the two carriages came to an abrupt stop. An NYPD car with its lights flashing came to a screeching halt in front of us. The two carriage drivers jumped down and began arguing with the policeman. Peter turned off the radio.

Keith stage-whispered, "This is where we make our exit."

I wasn't about to argue with him. The look on Detective Finelli's face if he found me in jail for drag-racing carriages was not one I wanted to see.

The four of us crept quietly out of the carriages and ran as far as we could around the park.

We were out of breath as we came to a stop opposite the zoo.

Reggie saw it first. "Look, that sign says there are gorillas over there."

"Where?" Keith asked.

"Over there," Peter said.

All three guys immediately started making gorilla noises. I shook my head and chuckled.

"Come on, over the fence we go to see the animals," Keith said.

"Stop!" I cried. "I've had enough for one evening, guys."

"Bebe, you're being a wet blanket," Keith scolded. He came over and kissed me on the lips. A wild thought that Keith had covered up Bradley's kiss crossed my mind. "Come on, baby; you're a cool girl. Let's go down there. Then we can get something to eat. I'm awfully hungry."

"Yeah," Peter said. "I'm sharp-set."

I pulled out of Keith's embrace. "Sorry, I'm cutting out on you. Try not to land in jail." I began walking away.

"All right, be a square," Keith called after me.

I continued walking, refusing to see what they would do if they could make it down to the zoo.

Out on the street, I put my fingers in my mouth the way Harry had done and blew. To my utter surprise, a loud whistle came out of my mouth, and a cab stopped for me.

I felt quite pleased with this accomplishment.

Wednesday morning, when my alarm clock went off, I groaned. I hadn't gotten in until after two. I sleepwalked my way through getting ready for work, putting on a fitted mint-green suit with embroidered sprigs of flowers in a paler shade of green. It was one of my favorite suits, and I figured I'd feel better in something extra pretty.

Darlene was still asleep, so I left the apartment quietly.

At the office, Bradley gave me assignments in a businesslike manner. However, I was cheered considerably when I turned around to adjust my chair and saw him giving me the once-over. Smiling to myself, I began with a letter he'd dictated. I had a lot of work, which made the day go faster.

As I was leaving, Bradley said, "If I haven't told you lately, kid, you're doing a great job."

I cleared my throat. "Thank you, Mr. Williams. I want to do my best for you."

He didn't move. Just stood looking at me. No one was around. I could walk five steps and be in his arms. I felt myself tremble.

Then he broke the spell. "I'd better go. It's the cocktail hour, you know."

"Yes, of course."

A minute later he was gone. I sat at my desk, drawing a deep breath. I told myself I was young and should be dating. That dreaming of a future with Bradley was just that—dreaming. He had different dates all the time. I would only be another conquest. The trouble was, I loved Bradley. Unless that love died, there was no point in seeing other men.

I pulled on my gloves and left the building, stopped by the cleaners for some of my suits, then walked up the steps to my apartment.

Darlene had been asleep when I'd left that morning, but she'd written me a note that she hadn't had any luck getting Nigel to go out with her. She said that Stu was taking her to a Broadway show that night and for me to get some sleep.

No argument from me there. I ate some leftover macaroni and cheese, watched *The Patty Duke Show,* and went to bed.

Thursday morning, I put on a long-sleeved, greenish-blue dress. The dress was simply cut, with a matching narrow belt that had a bow of the same material. The belt showed off my small waist. From the waist down the dress hugged my body. I was pleased when I looked in the mirror. However, I needed help with the back zipper.

"Darlene," I called, walking out of my room.

"In here," she answered from the bathroom. "Come on in; I'm just putting some finishing touches on my makeup."

I stood in the doorway. Darlene had a perfect face of makeup, her red curls lay in sexy disarray, and she wore a formfitting gold-colored dress. She was splashing cologne on her wrists.

"That smells good. What is it?"

"It's Yardley's Bond Street. Stu brought it back from London. According to the ads, it's supposed to give me 'a love letter from Rome, or an invitation to supper at Maxims, or a kitten with a diamond bracelet around its neck.' "

"I'd take the bracelet unless I could have dinner in Paris with Bradley. Can you zip me up?" I asked, turning and holding my dark hair out of the way.

"Sure, honey. Hey, be certain to walk away from Bradley a lot today. This dress gives you a great shape."

"Darlene, you always think the sexiest thoughts," I said, smiling. "That's a good one."

We laughed; then she zipped up the dress and said, "Listen, I've finally gotten Nigel to agree to go out with me tonight, so don't look for me. Stu knows a British-themed pub. I'm taking Nigel there. But first Stu is taking me for lunch and a matinee. I thought I'd get in a bit of shopping before then. Maybe some naughty lingerie."

"Naughty lingerie? Darlene Roland, I don't want to hear about it," I said, adjusting my dress.

Darlene gave me a wicked smile. "Maybe because it makes you think of Bradley."

I pursed my lips.

Darlene chuckled.

I decided to change the subject. "I just don't know what more we can get out of Nigel."

"Don't worry. I intend to get him drunk and—"

We were interrupted by the sound of the downstairs buzzer.

"I'll get it," I said. I walked into the living room, pressed the button, and said, "Good morning. Who's there, please?"

A muffled voice replied over the speaker, "Mrs. Wainwright to see Miss Darlene Roland."

From behind me I heard a loud gasp. Luckily I had my finger off the call button. "Who is she?"

Darlene removed the hand that was stuffed in her mouth. "My supervisor at Skyway! What am I going to do? I'm supposed to be sick in bed with bronchitis, not all dressed up."

"Don't worry; we'll handle this," I said, taking charge. Into the intercom, I addressed Mrs. Wainwright. "Ma'am, let me wake her for you. If you'll be kind enough to wait just one moment." I snapped the intercom off before she could answer.

"Quick, Darlene, come into the bathroom." She hurried after me, fretting the whole way.

In the bathroom I said, "Rip off your false eyelashes."

"That's gonna hurt!" Darlene protested. "I usually use this solution—"

"Get them off! We don't have time." I rummaged in the cupboard under the sink.

"Ouch! Ouch!"

"Good, now turn your face to me." I took a liberal supply of Johnson's baby powder and spread it all over Darlene's face.

Darlene finished smoothing it on. "What do you have baby powder for? Do you want to smell like a baby?"

I took a tissue and told her to clean off her lipstick. I took another tissue and wiped the baby powder that had landed on my dress. "No, I don't want to smell like a baby. It keeps me dry when I would dew. I wear Emeraude."

"That smells good." She turned to the mirror and

looked at herself in horror. "God, I look like the walking dead."

"That's how you're supposed to look. I saw it on TV once."

The buzzer sounded again—urgently.

I grabbed my pink chenille robe and threw it at Darlene. "Put this on up to your neck and get in bed. I'll let her come up. Remember to cough!"

Darlene did as I said. For good measure I grabbed a jar of Vicks VapoRub and put it on Darlene's bedside table.

"Don't put any of that on me," she hissed. "I'll never get the smell off in time to meet Stu."

"Okay, one problem at a time."

When Mrs. Wainwright came into the apartment, I could see why Darlene had looked so scared. The woman was a fading beauty in her forties with unnerving eyes that seemed to see right into your mind. Eyes that said she had heard every excuse from every stewardess and could see through every one of them. She must have been a stewardess at one time herself, as she had all manner of Skyway pins attached to her severe black suit.

"Mrs. Wainwright, I'm Bebe Bennett, Darlene's roommate."

"Pleased to meet you. Where is she?"

"I was able to wake her—her coughing keeps her up at night, you see. Sometimes she sleeps late."

Right on cue from the bedroom came a series of racking coughs.

"She's still in bed. Would you mind seeing her there?"

"Not at all. Lead the way, Miss Bennett."

We went to Darlene's darkened bedroom, which featured a mattress and box spring on the floor. Hung from the ceiling above it was red chiffon that formed a tent over the bed. She had a dresser painted a matching red, and a table holding a phonograph and albums.

Darlene had pulled the covers up to her chin. She still managed to look like she lived in a harem. The only light was what came through the half-closed Venetian blinds. *Good touch, Darlene,* I thought.

Then Mrs. Wainwright snapped on the overhead light, blinding us all, darn her.

Darlene sneezed. For once her nervous habit came in handy.

"Hello, Mrs. Wainwright," Darlene said in a soft, pathetic voice. Sneeze. Sneeze.

"Miss Roland. We at Skyway have been concerned about your lengthy absence. It's been two weeks. When can we expect you to resume your duties?"

Darlene coughed. She reached over and took the jar of Vicks Vaporub, opened it, and waved it under her nose. The mentholated smell filled the room. "Um, I'm not sure."

Mrs. Wainwright did not seem pleased. "We need you, Miss Roland, and would hate to have to keep assigning your flights to other girls. We wouldn't want you transferred to a smaller hub, say, Indianapolis."

Darlene's eyes rounded. "No, I'm sure I'll be well enough to fly by Monday."

My mouth dropped open, but I closed it before anybody could see. How could Darlene make such a rash promise when we didn't have the killer?

Mrs. Wainwright's lips curved slightly, smoothing all the lines around her mouth. "Very good. One of the schedulers will call you Sunday with your flight information."

Darlene nodded.

Mrs. Wainwright turned and waited for me to show her out of the apartment. I led the way. "You know, Darlene has been very, very sick."

"I'm sure she has. But once she's flying again, she'll feel much better. Nothing like work to set a girl straight."

"Yes, ma'am."

Once she was gone, I heaved a sigh of relief. Darlene was still in bed, and I heard her crying. I rushed to her side.

"Oh, Bebe, what am I going to do? They'll fire me for sure if I don't take the flight they assign me on Sunday. Or worse, send me out of New York, which would be just as bad as firing me. I worked hard to have New York as my hub."

"Don't you worry. We'll have gotten you cleared with Detective Finelli by then."

"How?" Darlene wailed.

"I don't know for sure, but we will. Have some faith. And lots of drinks with Nigel tonight. Don't forget Nigel told me that Patty Gentry was a 'terror.' And remember that Philip was going to fire Nigel."

"Okay. Thank you, Bebe. You're the best."

I left her washing her face and headed to the office.

It was a quarter to nine when I arrived at Rip-City.

I made coffee and then poked my nose into Bradley's office. "Would you like a fresh cup of coffee, Mr. Williams?"

"Yes, thank you, Miss Bennett. And some of those delicious cookies you brought in yesterday. I have a busy day lined up."

Heh, heh. I knew the cookies would get to him. "Anything special?"

"No, just more paperwork. And I have to talk to Mr. Purvis. I need his okay to fly to London and look for talent, now that we don't have the Beefeaters."

"So you think Mr. Purvis still wants to jump on the British-Invasion bandwagon?"

"Definitely. It's very hot right now, with no signs of letting up. The Beatles rule the country. The public wants more groups from England."

"Well, I hope Rip-City can sign a British band." If he went to London, I wondered how long he would be gone. And if he liked girls with a British accent.

I also thought about my scheme to help the remaining Beefeaters, and vowed to get on it today.

After I brought Bradley his coffee and cookies, I returned to the reception area to find a stranger standing there.

"May I help you, sir?"

"I'm looking for Bradley Williams's office," he said with a Midwestern twang.

"I'm his secretary, Miss Bennett. Is he expecting you?" I tried to remain poised as he looked me up and down in obvious appreciation. A half smile played about his lips.

"Trust Bradley to have a cute young secretary. Nah, he isn't expecting me. But he'll see me. I'm Drew Pruitt, his cousin."

Chapter Twenty-nine

Drew Pruitt was an average-looking man in his late twenties. I could see no resemblance between him and Bradley. Drew's forehead was square, but then his face angled in sharply. He wore a flashy Italian-cut suit and expensive leather shoes. Mama had taught me to check a man's shoes to tell if he had money. Drew did.

Drew's auburn hair was slicked back on his head. Not a spot of dandruff or lint marred his suit shoulders. I knew from talks with Bradley that Drew ran a large chain of exclusive department stores, the flagship store being in Chicago. What could he be doing here?

"If you'll have a seat," I said, gesturing to the olive-green chairs, "I'll let Mr. Williams know you're here."

"Thanks. Hey, you're not from New York, are you?"

"No, sir. I'm from Richmond, Virginia."

Drew let out a chuckle. "Bradley's been reduced to importing secretaries from other states. How amusing. But I'm charmed by your accent."

"Thank you," I replied stiffly, not liking what he said about Bradley.

He sat down. I went to Bradley's office.

"Yes, what is it, Miss Bennett?"

"Your cousin Drew Pruitt is here to see you."

Bradley looked up from a *Billboard* chart he'd been reading. "What did you say?"

I closed the door behind me. "A man calling himself

Drew Pruitt is here to see you. He talks with a Midwest accent and wears gangster-looking Italian-cut clothes."

Bradley put the chart down. "I can't imagine what would bring him here from Chicago. He's one of the three of us competing for control of Uncle Herman's empire, you know."

I decided then and there that I did not like Drew. "Do you want me to send him in, or tell him you're too busy to see him today?"

"No, no, I'll see the weasel. Give me five minutes. And close the door behind you."

"Yes, Mr. Williams."

Out in the waiting area, Drew had made himself comfortable. He'd lit a cigar and was reading the newspaper.

"Mr. Pruitt, Mr. Williams will see you in about five minutes. May I bring you some coffee while you're waiting?"

He gave me the once-over again, his gaze lingering on my legs. "Sure. I take it with cream and four sugars. I like sweet things." He winked at me.

I ignored this bit of flirtation and went to get his coffee. Behind me I could hear that Vince had come into the room and was greeting Drew. *Darn Vince.* He had antennae when it came to trouble.

When I returned with the coffee, I saw that Vince had a big smile on his face, but that Drew was basically ignoring him. Why would Vince be schmoozing Drew? Unless he thought Herman Shires was about to replace Bradley with Drew? The coffee cup shook in my hand.

"Ah, here she is with my coffee," Drew said, and took a sip. "Just the way I like it."

Vince gave a big cheesy grin. "Yeah, muffin-cup—I mean, Miss Bennett—is something special. She's refused a date with me so far, but I think I can change her mind."

Drew's eyes narrowed at Vince's words. "She looks bright and intelligent to me. Perhaps she'd prefer someone higher up in the company. Like me."

Vince frowned.

Not knowing where to look, I said, "I'd better go back to my desk. Mr. Williams will be buzzing me when he's ready to see you, Mr. Pruitt."

Drew stubbed out his cigar and saluted me with his coffee cup. Vince followed me back to my desk. "So how about it? When are you going to let me show you a good time?"

I straightened papers on my desk, not meeting his gaze. "As I've told you before, Mr. Walsh, I don't date coworkers. Period."

"You need to break that rule. I can show you how to break a lot of rules—"

I was thankful when the buzzer on my phone sounded. I jumped for it. "Yes, Mr. Williams?" I paused to listen to him. "Right away."

"If you'll excuse me, Mr. Walsh." I got up from my chair before he could say anything else.

After I opened the door to Bradley's office, I turned to leave, but to my surprise Drew grabbed my arm. "No need to go anywhere, Miss Bennett."

I looked to Bradley.

Bradley said, "Drew, what brings you to New York? And let go of my secretary."

Drew smirked, but released me. "I have a report to make up. Your cute secretary can take notes."

Bradley kept his cool, but I could tell he was not happy to see Drew. They were rivals, after all. And even though it sounded snobbish, I thought Drew was not in the same class as Bradley.

Bradley said, "All right, we'll play this your way for now. Come in and close the door. Miss Bennett, do you mind staying?"

"No, Mr. Williams."

Bradley held a pencil between his two index fingers and looked at Drew. "What's this all about?"

"What, no small talk, no 'How've you been, cousin'?"

"We aren't exactly on close terms, Drew. So spit it out. Why are you here?"

Drew leaned back in his chair and smiled in a predatory way. "Uncle Herman agreed to my suggestion that I come and find out what the hell you're doing with Rip-City." He turned to me. "Get out a pad and take notes."

I looked to Bradley for approval. He passed me a pad and pencil. "Go ahead, Miss Bennett. I want a record of this meeting as well."

Bradley turned back to Drew. "You say Uncle Herman agreed to *your* suggestion. Then it wasn't his idea that you come here."

Drew took a sip of his coffee and put the cup on Bradley's desk. "He's concerned, Bradley, old boy."

"Funny, he hasn't called me," Bradley said.

"Maybe he wants someone else's opinion."

"Maybe you just wanted to come here and cause trouble," Bradley shot back.

Drew put his hands in the air in a gesture of innocence. "Hey, I'm not the one who parties all the time, not growing up, not meeting my responsibilities."

"And you think I am? You think I've neglected my duties at this company?" Bradley dropped the pencil to the desk, got up, and leaned against his desk, looking down at Drew.

"Face facts," Drew continued. "You went over to London on the company's dime, and spent what? A month? Then you came back to the States after signing this Beefeaters band. No sooner had they landed here than the lead singer was offed."

"It was two weeks, and I signed a talented band that had a lot of stage presence and already had hits in Britain. There was no way for me to know that Philip Royal would die."

Drew raised a brow. "Die? Don't you mean be murdered? And the killer is still on the loose. What a publicity nightmare, Bradley."

"I'm handling it."

"You are? Is that why that woman reporter was murdered after she wrote an unfavorable article about Rip-City dropping the album? Did you have her wiped out? Is that your way of handling things?"

Bradley took a step closer to Drew. Drew stood. The two men held a staring contest. I hadn't written a word, too angry at Drew to record his accusations.

Bradley said, "Maybe that's the way you take care of things in your company in Chicago, but it's not my way. I have no idea who killed Philip Royal or Patty Gentry."

"Is that so? Then how hard can it be to find out? Did you hire a private investigator?"

"The police are handling it. My job is to move the company forward."

"You know what I think, Bradley? I think you're too afraid to have anyone else take a good look at what's going on and how badly you've screwed up."

"I don't like you, and I don't like your accusations," Bradley said.

"Face it, old boy, you're down for the count on this one. Maybe if you didn't spend company time screwing anything in a skirt, tempting as Miss Bennett here is—"

All of a sudden Bradley used his right fist to punch Drew in the face. The move caught Drew off guard. He fell to the floor.

I stood up.

Drew was on the floor holding his bleeding nose. I probably should have gotten him some tissues, but I found I didn't want to. I said to Bradley, "You know, Mr. Williams, I can still smell a rat in here."

Bradley straightened his tie and looked at Drew like he was a roach on his floor. "Get up if you want some more."

Drew didn't move.

"If Uncle Herman wants to know anything at all about Rip-City, he can call me," Bradley said. "Or I will go to him in Palm Beach and report in person. In fact, I think I will call him and tell him about your visit. He didn't send you. You came on your own for your own selfish reasons. And that's how I expect you to leave. On your own. Right now."

Drew pulled a white handkerchief out of his top pocket and wiped his bloody nose. He got up, a cold, hard look in his eye. For a moment, I was worried he would strike Bradley in return. But instead he made his way to the door.

In the doorway, he turned and said, "Uncle will hear about this from me too. You can be sure of that. I've got plenty to tell him. And you can kiss good-bye any chances you have of being left the one in control when Uncle dies. Alfred isn't doing anything to put himself forward. He's too content with his family out in LA, running that movie studio. So it's between you and me, Bradley. And I'm definitely the best man for the job."

With those words, he walked out of the office.

Bradley sat down in his chair. "Miss Bennett, I'm sorry you had to witness that, and I apologize for my cousin's inappropriate remark about you. Drew is obviously being very aggressive in seeking Uncle's favor."

I stood there, chewing my bottom lip. I wanted to comfort him. "Drew Pruitt is a jerk! You're a good man, Mr. Williams. Good men always win out over jerks."

He let out a laugh. "Do you really believe that, Miss Bennett?"

"Yes, I do."

Bradley rubbed a hand over his face. "Go on back to work, kid."

It was hard leaving him, but I did. Ideas swirled in my brain. Darlene needed me. Bradley needed me, whether he would admit it or not.

I wouldn't let either of them down.

Chapter Thirty

After Drew left, Bradley closed his door, telling me he had work to get done. Possibly he would call his uncle now.

I sat at my desk and made a phone call. The secret plan I had for the band—assuming there were no complications in the form of one of them being the killer—advanced. After slipping a copy of the Beefeaters' demo in my purse, I took a trip down to the Village that night to a particular person's studio.

After a long talk, and some skillful negotiation, I came away feeling quite pleased with myself. There was hope for the Beefeaters yet.

I whistled and a cab stopped for me. It didn't smell too good, but I took it anyway. The cab whisked me through traffic to my apartment. The driver was particularly aggressive. I had to close my eyes three times as he veered close to other cabs. The windows were open and he cursed other drivers and used his his horn liberally. I was glad to reach my apartment in one piece.

I turned the key in the lock of our apartment and found Darlene sitting on the pink sectional. She was wearing her purple lounging pajamas with the pant legs rolled up. She squeezed a tube of first-aid cream and spread it thickly over her badly skinned knees.

"What on earth happened to you?" I cried.

"Someone knocked me down and threatened to kill me."

I immediately sat next to her. "Oh, my God! How awful. Are you all right?"

Darlene gently pulled her pant legs down over her knees and rolled up her sleeves. Her elbows were scraped raw too. She applied cream to them. "I'm fine. I had finished with Nigel and went to hail a cab. I couldn't get one in front of the pub and decided to walk down the block to the cross street."

"Oh, is that what you do when you can't get a cab? It makes sense, now that you mention it."

"Bebe, you've lived in New York for over a month now and haven't figured out that you can catch a cab easier on the cross street than in the middle of the block?"

"Hey, tonight I actually whistled and got a cab. Just tell me what happened."

"As I walked along, suddenly someone—a man—came up behind me and shoved me hard to the ground."

"Goodness! Did he take your purse?"

"No. He said, 'Watch your step, bitch. Stop investigating.' And he had a British accent, just like the guy who broke into your office, Bebe."

I sat with my heart beating hard, imagining how Darlene must have felt. "He had to be the same person."

"I agree. Everything happened very fast. But I got up and tried to run after him. I saw him go around the corner. He'd knocked the wind out of me, though. When I ran after him in my heels, I tripped over some broken pavement and went down again. The bastard disappeared."

"Poor Darlene, your elbows and knees. And you must have been so frightened."

"Frightened? I was mad as hell!" Darlene looked at me with her eyes blazing. "I could have caught the bastard. But he escaped."

I touched her arm. "It sounds like you did your very best."

"My best failed. Don't you see, Bebe? I could have had him. I could have had him." Tears welled up in Darlene's eyes, but she dashed them away.

"Let me get us some of that chocolate cake you brought home from the bakery yesterday. Can you make it into the kitchen?"

"I'm okay." She got up and walked stiffly into the tiny kitchen and sat at the table.

I got out the white bakery box and cut us each a generous slice of cake. Putting a plate and fork in front of Darlene, I said, "Detective Finelli, Stu, and Bradley have all said we should stop trying to find the killer. That it's dangerous. Now the killer has managed to catch both of us off guard and threaten us."

Darlene swallowed a mouthful of cake. "You don't think that's going to stop me, do you?"

"No, not any more than it's going to stop me," I said. "It just means we need to keep the men out of this if we can. We don't want them interfering. For some reason they don't think we're capable of taking care of ourselves."

Darlene nodded. "I'll have to tell Stu I fell on the apartment steps."

My brows came together. "How is Stu going to see your arms? It's chilly outside. We're still wearing long sleeves."

Darlene smiled a wicked grin.

I held up my hands in surrender. "Never mind. I don't want to know. Tell me, do you think Nigel could have come out of the pub and pushed you?"

"It's possible," Darlene said. "The man who shoved me had on a trench coat and a hat worn low. Nigel had been wearing a trench coat, but so do a lot of men."

"What did Nigel say in the pub?" I asked, digging into my slice of cake.

"Things have gotten worse with the band cooped up."

"Cooped up? I just went on a wild ride with them after midnight on Tuesday," I reminded her.

Darlene shrugged. "Apparently it wasn't enough. Nigel says Peter is stuffing himself with tranquilizers since Astrid left him.

"Keith went to a supper club last night, got drunk, and was outraged when people there didn't recognize him. The police came, took him away, and threw him in the drunk tank.

"Nigel had to go bail him out. Nigel said Keith always did have a terrible temper," Darlene related.

"Hmmm. That's for sure. What about Reggie?"

"He and Jean are the only ones who have been quiet, biding their time until they can go home. As far as Patty Gentry goes, Nigel said the rock 'n' roll world is better off without her reporting her nasty lies. That she was nothing but a leech."

"He actually said that about Patty?"

"Yes," Darlene confirmed. "Nigel himself is a maudlin drunk. Once he was filled with brown beer and sitting in a place that seemed like home, he started crying. He said he and Philip had fought about coming to America. Nigel said if only Philip had listened to him he would be alive today. That it would be like the good old days and there'd be no talk of getting a fancy American manager. But Philip went so far as to say that Nigel need not come with them to America if he didn't want to."

"You're kidding! I think Nigel is much more hurt about his possible firing than he lets on, and now that we know Philip didn't care if he came to America or not . . ."

"I agree. When Nigel finished talking about getting fired, he laid his head on the bar and wept like a baby."

"What do you think? Could Nigel have killed Philip and Patty?"

Darlene put her fork down. She held her head in her hands and shook it. "It's either him or Keith. Peter doesn't have the guts. Neither Nigel or Keith has a good alibi and both are passionate enough about Philip to have wanted him dead. And that song 'Get out of My Way,' keeps haunting me. Why did the killer write it on the bathroom wall?"

I thought a moment before I spoke. "From the way things have gone, I'd say to throw light on everyone involved with Philip."

"Clever. And neither Nigel nor Keith liked Patty Gentry. Come on, Bebe, it's late. I'm going to bed." She closed the bakery box and rinsed out our plates while I wiped crumbs off the table.

Chapter Thirty-one

Friday, I left Darlene sleeping and went off to work. I tried to concentrate, but I kept thinking about the killer. I pulled out a steno pad and on one side I wrote *Nigel* and on the other side I wrote *Keith*. I then listed in each column each man's motives to see Philip and Patty dead.

The buzzer on my phone sounded. I quickly closed my steno pad. "Yes, Mr. Williams?"

"Come in here please, Miss Bennett."

"Right away."

I hung up and went to Bradley's office. As usual, I couldn't help but admire his sense of style in dress and his truly beautiful face. He was basically a good man, too, if you forgot his blondes.

"Close the door, please, and have a seat."

Uh-oh. Could he have found out about last night?

He leaned back in his chair and looked at me. "I hate to do this, kid, but I figured it's better to tell you now and get it over with."

Alarm raced through me. I wondered if he was going to fire me for my involvement with the murder investigation. "Wh-what is it?"

"I know you like Sal Vitelli."

Whew! This wasn't about me. "I do. He's a great singer. And Mama loves him."

Bradley tapped a piece of paper on his desk with his pencil. "Unfortunately, his sales figures don't measure up, kid. His latest single didn't even make the top forty. The label is dropping him."

"What? Oh, no!"

"I knew you'd be upset. That's why I wanted to tell you before it happens."

"When is it going to happen?"

"He's coming in at four thirty. I timed it that way so that you wouldn't have to be here when he leaves."

"There's nothing you can do to help him, Mr. Williams?"

"No. And you have to learn that this is the way business is. You can't let your personal feelings get in the way. As it is, I've probably kept Sal with us for a year longer than I should have. But this British Invasion has taken over the charts. Sal's time as a star is over. Another, more modest record company might pick him up and put out his albums on a smaller scale."

"You really think so?"

"I do. And that's what I intend to tell him."

I nodded. "Okay. But I want to be here when he leaves, in case he needs someone to talk to."

Bradley looked at me for a long moment. "You're a good person, Miss Bennett. I admire you."

I caught my breath.

Funny how I had just been thinking the same about him. I wanted to tell him that I admired him too— actually, I wanted him to show me how much he admired me by taking me in his arms—but my throat closed.

I smiled and got up out of my chair. My heel caught on the chair leg. I regained my balance before falling. *Darn it!* Why did he cause me to behave like a dimwit? I smoothed my apple-green skirt and held my head high as I walked back to my desk.

At lunchtime I ran downstairs to the street and had a hot dog and a Coke. The chilly day made me scurry back to the office, but not before I thought of my plan for the band. If all went well, tomorrow night would be special.

Unless someone in the band was arrested between now and then.

Bradley called me back into his office around four. He said, "I've gotten approval from Mr. Purvis to go to London for two weeks on a talent search. Even though I know tomorrow's Saturday, could you come in for a few hours and help me catch up on some work? Say from nine to one?"

"Of course."

He smiled.

I'd come in every Saturday for him if he needed me.

At four thirty Sal Vitelli arrived. He wore his expensive, tasteful suit proudly. Smiling at me and greeting me by name, he seemed unaware of what was about to happen. *Oh, no.* I got him a cup of coffee the way he liked it and showed him into Bradley's office.

I sat at my desk, anticipating a loud shouting match.

Vince came up and banged his fist on my desk to get my attention. "Daydreaming, Miss Bennett?"

"Don't do that again! And no, I'm worried about Mr. Vitelli."

"Yeah, he's getting the ax. I talked to him last week and tried to drop a hint in his ear. The old guy doesn't think Rip-City will drop him. He talked about you and your mother, as a matter of fact."

I looked at him, something I tried to avoid doing. It was impossible not to smell him. "What did you say?"

"I was trying to tell him how he wasn't as popular as he thought. That you and your mother only liked him because you're from the South. Southerners don't know better. They even like all that country-western stuff."

Anger welled up in me. "How *dare* you say those things about the South? And how *dare* you ruin the compliment I paid Mr. Vitelli?"

"Hey, Miss Bennett, no need to get all riled up."

"You know, Vince, I'd rather not have to talk to you unless it's about business," I said, I was so angry.

Vince narrowed his eyes at me.

At that moment Bradley's door opened. Sal came out of the office, his face ashen. I shot Vince a look that said I'd scratch his eyes out if he said a word. He turned and went in the direction of his office.

Mr. Vitelli stood like a statue.

"Mr. Vitelli, can I get you anything?" I asked.

He looked at me, his brown eyes focused far away. "No, thank you. I won't need anything anymore."

His choice of words and tone of voice chilled me. What if he was planning on doing something drastic now that he didn't have a contract?

When he left the office, I grabbed my coat and followed him.

Chapter Thirty-two

I caught up with him outside the building. "Mr. Vitelli, it's me, Bebe," I said, gasping for breath.

He looked at me with a beaten expression. "What, did they forget to throw my gold records out with me?"

"No, nothing like that. I thought maybe you could use someone to talk to right now." I had to breathe fast to match his steps.

"I'm going for a drink. I'm going to drink all night."

"May I come with you?"

Sal waved a hand. "It doesn't matter."

He went into the first bar that we came across and ordered a double whiskey. I ordered a ginger ale. When the drinks came, Sal downed his and ordered another. He said nothing.

"Listen, Mr. Vitelli—"

"Call me Sal. I already feel a hundred years old."

"All right, Sal. I can't know precisely how you're feeling now, because I'm not a star like you, but don't you think this is only a small setback? I mean, another record label will scoop you up like you were a tub of chocolate ice cream."

Sal still had that faraway look in his eyes. "This is it for me. I'm finished. Over."

I leaned forward. "That's not true. Think of all your fans. They'll be anxious for your next record. They won't care which label releases it. They just want to hear you sing!"

He looked at me then. "I'm all washed-up. A man my age, trying to get a deal. There's no point. In fact, there's no point in my going on at all."

"Sal! Don't say such a thing! Ever. Didn't you hear what I said? Your fans are still out there, waiting for your new album."

He polished off another double whiskey. "There was a time when I was compared to the big guys, Sinatra even. But those days are long gone. Nobody respects me anymore. The night I came into town—it was the night that young English singer was killed—I went to the Legends, where the label puts up all its talent when they come to town. Vince Walsh was walking through the lobby. He saw me. I know he did. Yet he didn't even bother to acknowledge me. A nothing like Vince Walsh, who couldn't find talent if it was placed in front of him with an audience of a hundred thousand, ignored me. That's how far I've fallen."

"Mama taught me that it doesn't reflect well on the person speaking when they talk bad about someone else," I said. "But I'll say this anyway: Vince Walsh is a moron. You can't let what he does affect you. You *are* a star. There are a lot of people out there who love you. And I'm sure in your personal life there are people who love and care about you too. Am I right?"

He lowered his head. "I've got six grandchildren from my two kids. My wife and I divorced a couple of years ago."

"Your divorce probably made you feel low."

"Yeah."

"But that's in the past. Don't you see the things you have to live for, Sal? There'll be a new record contract. And maybe a special lady will come along for you. Women must be throwing themselves at you!"

His mouth twisted in a half grin. "I can still get my

fair share of attention from the ladies." He heaved a sigh. "I guess I'm just feeling sorry for myself right now. Thanks for talking to me, Bebe."

"You'll call your manager first thing in the morning and have him get you a new contract?"

"Yeah. Yeah, I will."

"Promise?"

"Promise."

"You don't have your fingers crossed behind your back, do you?"

He laughed. "No."

I sat back and stayed to hear some of his stories— stories he'd probably told many times before. He asked me to join him for dinner, but I was bone tired. Plus I needed to check in with Darlene to see if there had been any developments during the day.

I gave Sal a big hug, and he moved into the dining area. A woman spotted him and held out a piece of paper for his autograph.

I smiled. Sal would be okay.

I went outside and started walking down the street to get to the corner. As I walked, I glanced at the stores I passed. A neon sign read, DELI SANDWICHES. NEW YORK SAILORS. REUBENS. PHILLY CHEESESTEAKS."

I stopped.

I stared at the glowing lime green words, PHILLY CHEESESTEAKS. A chill tingled in my blood.

On the night of the murder, Vince was supposed to be in Philadelphia listening to a new folk band. I remembered he even complained to me that he'd missed all the action the night Philip was killed, because he was away in Philadelphia. How could Sal have seen him at the Legends?

Why would Vince lie about being in Philadelphia?

But wait. He didn't lie, I knew, because I saw the report Vince gave Bradley on the band he was supposed to be listening to.

How could Vince be in two places at once?

And why would *Vince* want to kill Philip Royal?

I ran to the end of the street and threw up my hand for a taxi. Several passed that already had passengers until finally one stopped for me.

"Legends Hotel, please. Hurry," I told the driver. He obeyed my order, causing me to flatten against the backseat.

The driver had the radio station tuned to WABC. Scott Muni was praising the Beatles, but I couldn't concentrate on John Lennon just now. All I could think of was Vince.

I tipped the cabdriver heavily when he dropped me at the front door of the Legends Hotel.

I raced across the lobby, past the desk clerk—who luckily was not Mr. Owens—and ran for the elevators. The cars were all on higher floors. I tapped my foot in frustration.

The first one came back down. A young man was operating it. A group of people piled in. "Excuse me! Excuse me!" I cried.

The pimple-faced operator looked at me without interest.

"Is Mr. Duncan working tonight?" I asked him.

The operator shrugged and closed the doors.

I stood next to the bank of elevators. A group of people began milling about waiting with me. I tried to stand in the center of them and not call attention to myself.

Finally the next elevator came down. A crowd of people all talking at once came out. I looked past them and saw Mr. Duncan. *Thank God!* The people around me surged forward. I just made it into the elevator car.

Inching my way across the group, I managed to stand next to the elderly man. "Mr. Duncan," I whispered. "I have to talk to you."

He cupped his ear, looking puzzled. His hearing problem. I'd forgotten.

I rode all the way up to the top floor until the elevator was empty.

"Why didn't you get off at the fifteenth floor?" he asked.

"Because I have to talk to you."

"Okay, but make it fast, because I have to do my job." He pressed the stop button.

"I want to talk about the night the singer was murdered."

"Oh, boy."

"Please! This is very important. I need to know if you took a man up to the fifteenth floor."

"Plenty of them."

"Okay, but this one is about five feet, ten inches tall. He wears his hair greased back. He has a bad dandruff problem."

Mr. Duncan closed his eyes, thinking. "Smell like a polecat?"

"Yes! That's him."

Mr. Duncan opened his eyes. "I remember. I was reading the racing form when he came in. He told me to take him up to the fifteenth floor immediately and to hold the car to wait for him or he'd report me for reading the form on duty. He was really in a hurry."

"Why didn't you tell this to the police?"

"Nobody asked me. I get a lot of rude people. Part of the job. Plus I thought he'd report me for reading the racing form."

"How long was he gone?"

"Now, that I can't remember. I went back to reading the racing form."

Impulsively, I reached over and gave Mr. Duncan a hug. "Go ahead and take me downstairs."

"Sure, miss."

My thoughts were scrambling around in my head like eggs for breakfast. *Vince! Vince!* Nigel was right when he'd said no Englishman would kill Philip. But why Vince? And how could I prove it?

I flew out of the Legends and ran to the nearest phone booth. I put in a dime and dialed the apartment.

Darlene picked up on the third ring. "Hello?"

"What are you doing?" I asked her.

"Stu and I were going out for supper. Why?"

I quickly filled her in.

"But why would this Vince guy want to kill Philip?" she asked. "The band was going to make the record label a lot of money."

"That's what I don't know. We need to go through Vince's office and see what we can find out."

"Can you do that by yourself? I mean, you work there."

I chewed my bottom lip. And I could get fired if anyone saw me pawing through Vince's office, not to mention killed if Vince came in and caught me. "I'm afraid, Darlene. What if Vince is the killer, and he comes in and discovers me? I'd feel much better if you were with me."

"I'm sorry, honey. I should have thought of that. And, hey, is there a phone booth near Rip-City's building?"

"Yes, right across the street. Why?"

"I know we said we weren't going to involve the men anymore if we could help it, but we could use Stu. We could have him stationed out there. He could call up to your phone in the office if anyone comes into the building."

"That's a great plan. When can the two of you be at the building?"

"Say thirty minutes?"

"I'll meet you then," I said, and hung up, shivering.

Chapter Thirty-three

"Oh, you brought a flashlight. Good," I said.

Darlene had dressed all in black. Only her idea of camouflage meant a black strapless cocktail dress. I still had on my apple-green suit, white gloves, and matching green shoes from work.

I opened the door to the office with my key. Darlene trained the light from the flashlight on the floor. "Which one is Vince's office?"

"There." I pointed to a door four down from Bradley's. "Do you think we should search his secretary's— Miss Hawthorne's—desk too?"

"I don't know. You're the one who works with them. Would she cover something up for him?"

I thought of plump Miss Hawthorne and her grandmotherly ways. "No. Let's go straight to his office."

"Why are we whispering?" Darlene asked.

"That's the way they always do it on TV."

"It's probably for the best," Darlene conceded.

We reached Vince's office and I turned the handle. "Damn, it's locked," I said aloud.

Darlene looked at me with mock horror. "Bebe Bennett, did you just say 'damn'?"

Heat rose to my face. "Extenuating circumstances."

"Let me see the lock," Darlene said, nudging me out of the way. "Think, Bebe—what do the locks look like from the other side of the door?"

"What do you mean?"

"Are they keyed like this, or just a button?"

"Oh! Just a button."

"Good. What we need is something slim to insert in the lock that will push that button back."

"You mean like a nail file? That's how they do it on—"

"Yes, I know that's how it is on TV. But this has to be thinner." She looked around and walked to Miss Hawthorne's desk, scrutinizing her pencil holder.

"Wait," I said. "I've got just the thing." I hurried over to my desk, opened the top drawer, and returned with a slim metal instrument. I showed it to Darlene. "One end is to push your cuticles back; the other is to get dirt out from under your fingernails. It's good for your nails, you know. And a lady should always be well-groomed, Mama says."

"Not now, Bebe. Let's see if this works." Darlene took the grooming tool from me and slowly inserted it into the lock. We heard a pop from the other side.

"We did it!" I said, shaking Darlene with enthusiasm.

Darlene turned the knob in her hand, and we were inside the office. "Let's get to work."

The office was spare. No gold records lined the walls. Vince was a football fan, though. He had a signed ball on a stand, a helmet sitting on top of the filing cabinet, and a pile of football trading cards. A grown man with trading cards! The whole office reeked of his cheap cologne.

Darlene took the filing cabinet. I took the desk.

Vince didn't seem to be an overly busy man, I thought as I went through his papers. A mound of solicitations from bands asking him to come hear them play dominated the top of the desk. I read one, and it was full of flattery about Vince's sharp ear for music. That was probably why he kept them on his desk, I thought unkindly—to boost his ego.

I opened one of the wide drawers on the right-hand

side of the desk. A big stack of *Playboy* magazines met my eye. *Ugh!* I had never opened one, but knew what they were like—I thought. Maybe just a peek inside one would confirm my suspicions. Gingerly I picked up the top magazine. I let it open to the centerfold and gasped aloud at what I saw.

"Bebe!"

Darlene's voice made me jump guiltily. I looked up sheepishly to where she stood at the filing cabinet. "I just wanted to see if they were what I thought they were."

"Well, now you know. Put that back and get to the rest of the desk."

I decided to pull each magazine out in case Vince was hiding something in between them. But there was nothing. As I was putting them back, I wondered if Bradley subscribed. The thought made me burn with jealousy.

Vince's other drawer was crammed full of receipts. Poor Miss Hawthorne probably had to make out his expense report from this mess every month.

Just then my phone rang three times—the signal that someone was coming into the building. Darlene and I looked at each other, wide-eyed. I said, "Quick, it might be Vince. Let's go hide in Bradley's office. I have the key."

We slammed Vince's door shut. I grabbed the flashlight from Darlene and led the way to Bradley's office. My fingers were shaking badly, but I managed to unlock the door and then close it behind us.

Darlene sneezed. *Oh, no, not one of her sneezing fits now.* She clamped a hand over her mouth and nose and stared at me with bulging eyes.

We heard someone unlock the door to the main office. Then steps came our way. A key was inserted in Bradley's office lock. Bradley himself was there!

I pulled Darlene around the corner into the executive bathroom.

Bradley switched on his light.

Darlene was trying hard not to sneeze. I put my arm around her for support.

Then we heard the squeak of Bradley's chair as he sat down. I peered around the corner and saw him take a piece of paper from under his desk blotter. He then dialed a number on the phone. We heard him say, "Hello, darling. Sorry to be late. I'm just going to change my shirt, and then I'll grab a cab and be right over." A pause. Then, "I'll see you in ten minutes."

He hung up the phone. Instantly I realized that he would be coming our way, because the shirts were right above where we crouched.

I grabbed Darlene's arm and we tiptoed back to the frosted-glass-walled shower compartment. We stepped inside and closed the door behind us.

Darlene's body jerked as she tried to hold back a sneeze.

Huddled with Darlene in the tiny space, I felt sure we would be discovered. I could just make out Bradley through the frosted glass. If he turned and looked at the shower, he'd see us for sure.

He stripped off his shirt and threw it in a small hamper by the sink.

My mouth dropped open at the sight of him naked to the waist. My breath came faster. His chest was hairless, golden, and very muscular. If I breathed any faster, I'd hyperventilate.

He swiped deodorant under both arms, ran an electric razor over his cheeks, and brushed his teeth.

I was riveted to his every move.

Darlene made a tiny choking sound in the back of her throat. She was trying hard not to sneeze.

I was trying hard not to drool.

Bradley finished buttoning his shirt and then unzipped his pants so he could tuck the shirt in. This was it. I was going to die right now in this shower stall. He was fast, though, and all I caught a glimpse of was white briefs. I tucked that bit of information in the back of my head for further reference.

Bradley then turned out the light, went back to his office, and was soon heard leaving.

Darlene released her breath in one great big whoosh of air. "God, that was close."

"God, he's beautiful," I said, leaning against the shower wall for support.

"Come on, Bebe; you don't have time to moon over him now."

"I wasn't mooning. I was appreciating a work of art by God . . . oh, Darlene, I just realized something."

"What?"

"Bradley took a piece of paper out from under his blotter. I didn't think to look under Vince's blotter."

"Come on then; let's go back."

Darlene worked her magic with the little grooming tool. We were once again in Vince's office.

I hurried to the desk and carefully lifted the blotter. Underneath was a piece of paper. I withdrew it, and Darlene held the flashlight so we could read.

It was a speeding ticket from an officer in East Bergen, New Jersey, with a time of five forty P.M. dated the day of Philip's murder.

I said, "This is it. Plenty of time for Vince to make an appearance in Philadelphia, speed back to New York and kill Philip, write the song lyrics on the wall to place suspicion on the others, then go back to Philadelphia as if he never left."

Darlene grinned. "Bebe, I think we've got our killer."

"But we still don't know why he did it."

"Let him tell the police. Come on; let's get out of here."

I tucked the speeding ticket in my purse, and we left the building.

Darlene flung herself into Stu's arms. Excited, we told him the whole story.

"Doll, it looks like you'll be flying on Monday, no problem. Let's all go out and celebrate."

Darlene smiled. "That's a great idea. Bebe?"

My mind was preoccupied. I wanted to know why Vince had killed Philip. Maybe some time alone would give me the answer. Plus, I was a little down. Hearing Bradley call the woman on the phone *darling* had pricked my heart. "Listen, you two go ahead. I just want to go home and get some sleep. I'm supposed to work a few hours for Bradley tomorrow. That means I need to call Detective Finelli and try to set up a meeting for us with him around eight in the morning."

Both Stu and Darlene groaned. "That early on a Saturday?" Darlene asked.

"You want your name cleared, don't you?"

"You're right," Darlene said. "We won't be out late."

Stu insisted on waiting until I could get a cab before they left.

I leaned my head back on the seat while the cab took me home in short bursts of speed interspersed by stops. I was feeling queasy from all the excitement of the night and the cab ride. At Lexington and Sixty-fifth I told the driver to stop. I paid him and proceeded to walk halfway up the block to my apartment. *Briefs . . . he wore briefs,* I thought, my head in a cloud.

The chilly night air made me shiver as a breeze blew threw the trees lining the sidewalk. I rummaged around in my purse, looking for my key in the dim light thrown down by the streetlight up ahead.

I was so engrossed in my thoughts that I was taken completely off guard when something hard and sharp pressed into my back. A voice said, "Don't move, don't turn around, or I'll shoot you."

Chapter Thirty-four

Fear held me frozen in place. The world shrank down to the gun in my back.

"Give me the ticket. I know you have it."

Vince's voice. And his smell.

The gun pressed harder in my back. "The ticket. Now."

Hands shaking, I reached into my purse, wishing I had some sort of weapon in there. Just as quickly as the thought formed, I dismissed it. I wouldn't have time to do anything with Vince pressing the gun right into my spine.

"Slowly now. Hand it to me over your shoulder, *Miss Bennett*," he said sarcastically. "I know you know it's me."

My hand stilled. "Vince, I don't know what you're talking about."

He laughed. "Don't play dumb. I know you were in my office. I came back to get the phone number of another chick, one easier on a guy than you. From the street I saw the shadow of a light up there. I guessed it was you snooping around where you shouldn't. Tell me, how did you find out it was me who killed Philip?"

His confirmation of the fact made me turn to ice. "I didn't—"

The gun pressed harder in my back. "Don't bullshit me. How did you know?"

"I-I didn't until you just told me. I mean, I figured from the speeding ticket that you were back in the city when you were supposed to be in Philadelphia." No way was I going to involve Sal or Mr. Duncan in this. Let Vince think I had acted alone.

I saw a woman walking a little terrier on the opposite side of the street. I wanted to call out to her. Maybe the dog could be a hero.

Vince must have read my mind, because he moved in closer to me. He put one arm around me, holding my waist, and lowered his head close to mine, making it look like we were lovers.

"You tell anyone else?" he whispered in my ear.

"No! No one else knows." Spotting the light in his office must have been enough for him to come here and lie in wait for me. He had missed seeing Darlene and Stu. "Everyone thinks it's someone with a British accent, because that's who threatened me and Darlene."

"I'm waiting for you to hand over the ticket. Do it now, luv," Vince whispered in a very convincing British accent. "I did try to warn you, but you wouldn't listen, you stupid girl."

I couldn't believe it. The accent. He'd been the one threatening Darlene and me. The way he was holding me made me sick—that and his cologne.

Reluctantly I pulled the ticket from my purse and passed it back to him. My curiosity got the better of me. I said, "Why did you do it, Vince? Philip was going to make money for Rip-City."

Vince squeezed my waist. "That's exactly why I did it. Bradley looks bad, loses his job. I step in and take his place. Drew gave me the idea. It suited both of us. I'd get a promotion, and having Bradley out of the competition makes Drew almost a shoe-in for taking over when the old man finally goes to his grave. And when Drew takes over, he'll remember what I did to help him. I'll be set for life."

Vince chuckled. "Philip made it so easy for me. I

thought I was going to have to shoot him. But when I got to his room, he was getting ready to take a bath while playing his guitar. Fool. Nothing was simpler than putting that plug in the electric socket."

The woman and her dog went inside a building down the block. Not that she had offered much chance for rescue. I had to somehow defend myself. I would not go down without fighting for my life. But how?

"So you and Drew planned to kill Philip just to get rid of Bradley? But it hasn't worked. Bradley still has his job."

"Not once Drew finishes his visit to the old man. That's why Drew came in. He could tell their uncle that he had visited in person and could say that Rip-City was a real mess, that Bradley was screwing his secretary. Again. I admire Drew. He stops at nothing to get what he wants."

Rage rose inside me at Drew's plan, and Vince's statement about Bradley's love life. I turned my head as far away from him as I could. "And you follow his ideals. Even to the point of murder." Another sickening thought occurred to me. "You killed Patty Gentry too. Why?"

"In that article she said that she knew who the killer was. I couldn't take any chances. She let me into her room, because I told her I was from Rip-City. Then, when her back was turned, I picked up that belt and took care of her. She was nothing but a woman anyway."

"You scum! You'll go to jail. Drew won't come to your defense. The police will catch you—"

"Not with you out of the way. You're the only one who knows. Maybe if you'd gone out with me, I could have taken you into my confidence. We could have had some good times. You could have been more than a secretary at Rip-City if we were together. But now I have to say good-bye, Miss Bennett."

Oh, God, he really was going to kill me; he was that cold-blooded. I thought of my mother and father. Of

Darlene. Of me holding Bradley's baby in my arms and him smiling at me.

No! No, he wasn't going to kill me.

The gun pressed into my back.

I remembered something Mama had taught me about unwelcome male attention. I raised my right foot. With the high, pointed heel of my shoe, I unleashed my fury to come down hard on his instep.

He let out a loud yelp of pain.

I twisted in his arms, meaning to poke him in both eyes, but to my surprise I saw a wine bottle come crashing down on his greasy head.

Vince crumpled at my feet, out cold. The gun skittered across the sidewalk.

"Jesus have mercy," Harry said. "I thought it was just his finger in your back. He wasn't bluffing after all."

I threw my arms around him. "Oh, Harry, you saved me!"

"Nah. You were doing pretty darn good on your own. I just helped out."

Picking the speeding ticket up from where it had fallen to the pavement, I said, "Can you watch him while I call the police? Are you all right?"

"I'm okay. Could use a drink. But, yeah, he's out pretty good. You go call the fuzz." He kicked the gun into the bushes.

I ran upstairs to my apartment and called the police. I told them to alert Detective Finelli that I'd caught Philip Royal's murderer.

I searched the cabinets and found a bottle of whiskey Darlene kept. Pouring some into a paper cup, I thought Darlene wouldn't mind my borrowing some. On second thought, I splashed a little in a cup for me too and drank it down.

Downstairs, Harry was sitting on Vince, who was still unconscious. I handed Harry the cup. "Here's a little whiskey against the weather."

"Thanks, Bebe," Harry said, taking the cup and down-ing the contents. Then he shook himself like a dog.

I stood there hugging myself, realizing how close I'd come to death. Realizing how strong I could be when I had to. Everything around me seemed so beautiful. I wanted to kiss the leaves on the trees lining the sidewalk.

Then we heard sirens. Three police cars arrived. I tried to answer a young officer's questions, but the sight of all the flashing lights and the number of uniformed officers unnerved me.

I was never so grateful to see anyone when, a few minutes later, Detective Finelli pulled up in an unmarked Pontiac Tempest.

I threw myself into his arms.

He stepped back. "What have you done now, Miss Bennett?" he said, with a touch of kindness in his voice.

The story came tumbling from my lips. Harry backed me up, though he looked decidedly uncomfortable with all the police around.

Vince came to and was promptly handcuffed. He screamed at me, "You hellcat!"

Detective Finelli and I ignored Vince, though secretly I felt pleased with the name.

The detective said, "I'll need you and, er, Harry here to come down to the station and sign a statement first thing in the morning. Bring Miss Roland and Mr. Daniels."

"We'll do that."

"And Miss Bennett, I told you all along how danger-ous getting involved in a police investigation could be. I hope you see now how right I was." He was back to being the stern detective.

"I know."

"So you won't get involved in any police matters again, will you?"

"Oh, no! Never again," I said.

Gradually everyone left, leaving me standing there with Harry. I pulled a dollar out of my purse. "Here,

Harry, get something to eat. What about a place to stay? Surely there's somewhere you can go?"

Harry accepted the dollar. "I'll be fine; don't worry about me, Miss Sweet Face."

"Thanks for what you did for me tonight. I'll never forget it."

But Harry just waved a careless hand and wandered away.

I went upstairs and changed into my pajamas and robe. My bed looked pretty enticing, but I knew I had to stay up and tell Darlene what had happened. And Bradley . . . But no, I couldn't remember his phone number. Darn my trouble with numbers.

As it turned out, I lay on the sofa for a minute, and when I awoke it was the next morning.

Chapter Thirty-five

I looked at the time: six twenty-five. Darlene wouldn't like it, but I had to wake her.

Coffee would help, so I brewed a pot, then went to her room.

Once she was out of bed, Darlene wandered groggily into the kitchen, where I poured her a cup of coffee. While she drank it, I told her the whole story.

She stared at me. "Bebe, you could have been killed by that nut."

"But I wasn't. We need to get Stu and go to the police station, and Harry has to come too. Don't forget I'm supposed to work a few hours for Bradley this morning, and he doesn't know what happened yet."

"Okay." She got up from her side of the table and came around to hug me. "You're the best friend I've ever had, Bebe. Thank you for everything you did for me."

"Hey, you did just as much snooping as I did. And I couldn't have a better roommate."

Darlene released me and smiled. "We make a good team. Now let's get ready to make our statement for Detective Finelli. I'll bet he's feeling less than a man this morning, having two girls solve his murder case for him."

We collapsed, giggling over that thought.

"And are we agreed that we'll do nothing more about

what we heard those guys in the apartment above us say?" Darlene asked.

"Agreed. I'm not getting involved with any mobsters."

Darlene and I took turns with the persnickety shower, then ran into our rooms to get dressed.

While I waited for Darlene to finish up, I heard the sound of a big truck outside. Curious, I went to the front window and looked out. A moving van was parked outside our building. I could hear footsteps going up to the apartment right above us. The mobsters!

"Darlene, come quick!"

Darlene rushed over and I filled her in. We heard furniture scraping the floor directly above us and waited until footsteps came back downstairs, then peeked out our door.

A slim young man with a goatee spoke to a man dressed in a mover's uniform. The mover was carefully carrying a large wrapped item that could only be a painting.

The young man spoke. "Can you believe that we were actually questioned by the police? Some woman thought we were killers!"

Darlene and I looked at each other, wide-eyed.

The mover laughed. "And all you were doing was talking about repainting your scene?"

"Yeah, they took hearing my partner and me talking about rubbing someone out as . . ."

The voices faded away as the men were on the lower floors.

Darlene closed the door. "They were artists. And we called the police!" She began to laugh.

"Oh, what imaginations we have," I said, and burst out laughing.

"Looks like we'll be getting new neighbors," Darlene said.

"Yes. Hey, we'd better go. We're late," I said.

*   *   *

Later, after we'd been to the police station—where Harry entered and left as fast as he could—I went to my office.

I stood for a moment watching Bradley doing paperwork before he looked up and saw me. If Vince had ended my life, I would never have had a chance to find out if Bradley could grow to love me. As it was, I was alive, and I felt great. I entered his office, sat down in a chair opposite him, and crossed my legs. My pink skirt came up at least four inches above my knee.

"Oh, good morning, kid. How are you?" His gaze dropped to my legs. I was sure sorry to have to divert his thoughts.

I watched the emotions passing over his face as he listened to my account of the night before.

"Thank God you weren't hurt," was the first thing he said. "I warned you not to place yourself in danger." His eyes were intense as they studied me.

He came around the desk and smoothed a piece of my hair back. There went my heart again. His shoulders were so close, I could reach out and pull him down to me. Using his right thumb and hand, he cupped the left side of my face. "You sure you're okay?"

Well, I could be *a lot* better. "I'm fine," I said, and then to change the subject, "I'm outraged by your cousin's tactics to gain your uncle's favor."

Bradley's hand went to my shoulder. "Drew will get away with it, too. From what you described, the murder was an idea planted in Vince's head by Drew. It will be Vince's word against Drew's. There is no hard evidence against Drew. But I had a long talk with my uncle last night after Drew flew down to see him. I'm certain Uncle's okay with how I've handled this situation at the company."

"Thank goodness," I said, looking up at him. "But it's terrible to think about Drew getting away with what he did. You'll have to be careful in the future."

Bradley appeared to become aware that he was touching me. He went back to his desk chair and sat down. Darn it!

He looked at me and said, "I don't think he'll try anything again. But back to your involving yourself in this investigation, I want to say—"

There was a knock on the office door. I went to answer it. A man dressed in a Western Union uniform stood there. "I have a telegram for Bradley Williams."

"I'll take it," I said, signing his book.

I handed the message to Bradley.

"What's this?" Bradley said. At my shrug, he opened it and read aloud: " 'Great job at Rip-City. Stop. Time to move up. Stop. You do like models, don't you? Stop. Report to Ryan Modeling Agency nine A.M. April twenty-seventh. Stop. Herman Shires.' "

Bradley sat back with a big grin on his face. "This is fantastic! It shows Uncle's confidence in me. What a terrific opportunity. Ryan is the biggest modeling agency in the U.S., next to Ford." He let out a short laugh. "Wonder what Drew will do when he finds out I've been given a fabulous new assignment?"

"I hope nothing," I said in a small voice. Bradley was leaving! To reign over a flock of models, no less! I felt like I'd eaten bad egg salad.

He was still staring at the telegram, grinning from ear to ear.

Abruptly he noticed the expression on my face. "Er, Miss Bennett, if I were to give you a five percent increase in your pay, would you consider coming with me to my new job? I know you care about Rip-City, but you're a valuable secretary to me, and I don't want to lose you. Please say yes."

The Rockettes danced in my head. My fairy godmother waved her magic wand over me. A chorus of angels sang in my brain.

"Why, yes, Mr. Williams. I'll come with you. It'll be groovy."

He grinned. "I'm glad to hear it. Now let's get back

to work. There's a lot to get done before we leave. Uncle's given us only a week's notice."

"Yes, Mr. Williams."

I smiled secretly to myself as I settled in to take dictation.

Bradley and I worked until the late afternoon. I enjoyed every minute of it.

But as much as I liked being with him, I had a mission to accomplish that night down in the Village.

At eight o'clock I met Nigel, Keith, Peter, and Reggie at a coffeehouse called Swanky. Inside it was anything but swanky, with scratched wooden tables crowded together in front of a small stage.

Keith said, "What's this all about, Bebe?"

"Yeah," Nigel said. "Your message said it was urgent."

Peter twitched. "You don't think we're going to play here, do you?"

Reggie looked at me. "We haven't fallen this far, have we?"

First I told them all about Vince. There was much grumbling about how they'd like to get their hands on him.

Then I got down to business. "I brought you here to meet Devon Woods. You don't already know him, do you? He's English."

"Never heard of him," Keith replied. "What's the point?"

I could barely contain my excitement. "Darlene brought me down here my first week in New York to hear a singer named Bob Dylan. Before he came on, Devon sang. Devon's been trying to get in with Rip-City for months, but Mr. Williams felt he needed to be part of a band. I thought you could listen to him and see if you like him. If you do, maybe you could join forces."

The guys agreed to this, and we all sat down.

When Devon came on and sang, the guys started whispering among themselves.

After the set was over, I brought Devon over to meet everyone. It was a mutual admiration society from the beginning. Devon turned out to be a big fan of the Beefeaters. He even got along with Keith and shared some of his ideas about the blues.

About an hour later, the guys and Devon got up for an impromptu set. Devon knew the Beefeaters' greatest hits in England. Keith even let Devon take over Philip's place. The guys sounded great together. Keith smiled and gave me the thumbs-up signal from the stage.

I was so excited, I wanted to call Bradley right away. I tried to tell myself Monday morning would be soon enough, but my desire to tell him the Beefeaters lived again overcame me. With my trouble with numbers, I still couldn't remember his phone number.

However, I knew where he lived. There were only a few numbers to remember: 79 West Seventy-fifth Street.

I looked at my watch. It was after nine on a Saturday night. Bradley was probably out. I would go to his apartment and simply leave a note. He just had to know!

Nigel was so into the music, it took me a minute to get his attention. "Nigel, I have to leave. You think everything is okay here?"

"Bebe, you're an angel, that's what you are. I think we've got the band back together again. Maybe Rip-City will want us after all."

"I think there's a good chance of that. The guys can fine-tune what they're doing right now over the rest of the weekend. Then we can get Bradley to listen. With any luck, you'll have a new contract." And Bradley wouldn't have to fly off to London to meet new bands . . . and new girls . . . before tying up loose ends at Rip-City.

I left everyone happy and went outside. New York was even more alive than normal on a Saturday night. There was no chance of getting a taxi. I could take a bus, but . . .

I raised my chin and decided to take the subway. I

marched down the steps and joined the milling crowd. A train came in with a great deal of noise and a gust of wind. People poured out the doors, while others piled in.

I carefully studied the posted map. Once I was pretty sure what to do, I bought a token, confirming my route with the bored-looking man in the booth.

When my train came, I boarded and took a seat. I looked around, determined there weren't any murderers on the train, and got out my little notebook. I wrote Bradley about the new Beefeaters. I folded the square of paper, intending to push it through his mail slot or leave it wedged in the door.

I exited the subway station at Seventy-seventh Street, feeling proud of myself, and walked until I found his apartment. Only it wasn't an apartment. Bradley owned a town house.

The outside of his building was really cool, all black and white marble squares covering the ground leading up to a door painted white with an oval glass circle. The oval circles were repeated on the upstairs windows. Very modern.

Light shone from inside. Should I ring the bell?

I thought of leaving the note and going home, but I did want to see his face when he found out I'd helped put the band back together. Maybe he'd respect me for it. It was important to me to have his respect. I'd grown up a lot in the past two and a half weeks.

Closing my eyes, I rang the bell.

When the door opened, my eyes flew wide. There was Bradley looking like a Hollywood movie star in a white dinner jacket. "Miss Bennett. What a surprise to see you. You look lovely in that rose-colored dress."

"Thank you. I have some news that couldn't wait until Monday morning. I hope you don't mind my coming by this way."

For a moment, he looked confused. "Um, come in."

He held the door open. I stepped into a foyer and followed him into a living room. His apartment struck me as being the epitome of masculinity. Paneled walls, a built-in black velvet sectional, a hi-fi system, a bar built into the wall.

And a sultry redhead sitting at a table set for two.

Uh-oh.

I turned to him, heat infusing my face. "I didn't mean to intrude. I'll just go now. Here's the note that will explain everything." I tried to press it into his hand, but he wouldn't take it.

"Nonsense. Come and meet my friend," he said, going deeper into the town house. I followed, feeling miserable.

Bradley said, "Miss Bennett, this is Donna Moore. Donna, my secretary, Miss Bennett."

"Miss Bennett, I'm pleased to meet you. Bradley, darling, how charming of you to let your little secretary come by."

I felt like a schoolgirl next to Miss Moore's sophisticated white beaded dress, matching white antique handbag, and elaborately high hairdo. And she was a redhead. Had Bradley gone through all of New York's blondes and started on the redheads? When would it be the brunettes' turn?

I tried to keep a smile on my face, but I wished I hadn't come. It was too late now.

Bradley said, "What brings you here?"

The story of Devon and the guys came tumbling out of my mouth. "I'm so excited for the band. They really seemed to hit it off. I think you'll like them."

"I'm impressed, Miss Bennett. First you catch a killer, now you've put talent together, and possibly saved me a trip to London. Is it any wonder I want to keep you as my personal secretary?"

I smiled as if this were everyday work for me.

Miss Moore looked as if she'd like to take the ice pick from a nearby bucket and thrust it into my heart.

Bradley said, "This calls for a celebration. Donna and I were just about to pop open some champagne."

I felt giddy thinking about drinking champagne with the man I adored.

Bradley looked toward his kitchen. "Let me see. Hold on a minute, kid, and I'll get you a . . ."

Oh, no! He wasn't going to get me a soft drink after all I'd done—solving the murder, putting the band back together, and . . . and . . . growing as a woman.

I tilted my head at Bradley and gave him my brightest smile. "Glass of champagne!"

And I didn't even choke on the bubbles.

Look for Bebe Bennett's
next mystery adventure in the
very groovy Murder A-Go-Go series,
coming from Signet
in April 2006.

Secretary Bebe Bennett and her boss, man-about-town Bradley Williams, have a new assignment at the Ryan Modeling Agency. Bebe, who's still in love with Bradley, is more than a bit dismayed by this move, imagining the beautiful women he will meet. Sure enough, he's soon dating top model Suzie Wexford—until one late night when Bebe gets a call from Bradley requesting her help in contacting his lawyer. Not the company's corporate lawyer, but a criminal lawyer, he explains. Suzie Wexford has just been found strangled with the Pucci scarf Bradley recently gave her and now he's in jail for murder!

First in the Yellow Rose Mystery series!

Pick Your Poison
by Leann Sweeney
0-451-21031-X

With a heart the size of Texas—and a bank account
to match—Abby Rose is out of school, out of work,
and out of motivation.

But when she discovers her gardener, Ben, dead in
the greenhouse, and after the sexy detective from the
Houston PD tells her Ben was poisoned, Abby
knows just what she needs to do to pick up
her life's pace—solve a murder, of course.

"A rip-roaring read!" —Carolyn Hart

**"Leann Sweeney is a welcome new voice in
mystery fiction." —Jeff Abbott**

**"A wonderful first novel…and the most likable
sleuth to come along in years." —Rick Riordan**